I0823607

BOOKING FOR TROUBLE

Titles by Jenn McKinlay

Library Lover's Mysteries

BOOKS CAN BE DECEIVING
DUE OR DIE
BOOK, LINE, AND SINKER
READ IT AND WEEP
ON BORROWED TIME
A LIKELY STORY
BETTER LATE THAN NEVER
DEATH IN THE STACKS
HITTING THE BOOKS
WORD TO THE WISE
ONE FOR THE BOOKS
KILLER RESEARCH
THE PLOT AND THE PENDULUM
FATAL FIRST EDITION
A MERRY LITTLE MURDER PLOT
BOOKING FOR TROUBLE

Cupcake Bakery Mysteries

SPRINKLE WITH MURDER
BUTTERCREAM BUMP OFF
DEATH BY THE DOZEN
RED VELVET REVENGE
GOING, GOING, GANACHE
SUGAR AND ICED
DARK CHOCOLATE DEMISE
VANILLA BEANED
CARAMEL CRUSH
WEDDING CAKE CRUMBLE
DYING FOR DEVIL'S FOOD
PUMPKIN SPICE PERIL
FOR BATTER OR WORSE
STRAWBERRIED ALIVE
SUGAR PLUM POISONED
FONDANT FUMBLE

Hat Shop Mysteries

CLOCHE AND DAGGER
DEATH OF A MAD HATTER
AT THE DROP OF A HAT
COPY CAP MURDER
ASSAULT AND BERET
BURIED TO THE BRIM
FATAL FASCINATOR

Bluff Point Romances

ABOUT A DOG
BARKING UP THE WRONG TREE
EVERY DOG HAS HIS DAY

Happily Ever After Romances

THE GOOD ONES
THE CHRISTMAS KEEPER

Stand-alone Novels

PARIS IS ALWAYS A GOOD IDEA
WAIT FOR IT
SUMMER READING
LOVE AT FIRST BOOK
WITCHES OF DUBIOUS ORIGIN

BOOKING FOR TROUBLE

Jenn McKinlay

BERKLEY MYSTERY
New York

BERKLEY MYSTERY
Published by Berkley
An imprint of Penguin Random House LLC
1745 Broadway, New York, NY 10019
penguinrandomhouse.com

Book design by Laura K. Corless

Library of Congress Cataloging-in-Publication Data

Names: McKinlay, Jenn author
Title: Booking for trouble / Jenn McKinlay.
Description: New York: Berkley Mystery, 2026. |
Series: A library lover's mystery; book 16
Identifiers: LCCN 2025037464 (print) | LCCN 2025037465 (ebook) |
ISBN 9780593955505 hardcover | ISBN 9780593955512 ebook
Subjects: LCGFT: Cozy mysteries | Novels | Fiction
Classification: LCC PS3612.A948 B65 2026 (print) |
LCC PS3612.A948 (ebook)
LC record available at https://lccn.loc.gov/2025037464
LC ebook record available at https://lccn.loc.gov/2025037465

Printed in the United States of America
1st Printing

The authorized representative in the EU for product safety and compliance is Penguin Random House Ireland, Morrison Chambers, 32 Nassau Street, Dublin D02 YH68, Ireland, https://eu-contact.penguin.ie.

For all of my librarian supervisors over the years, who shaped both me and my career. I can never thank you enough: Eileen Branciforte, Mary Mitchell, Teresa Landers, Cindy Holt, Mary Lou Goldstein, Elaine Meyers, Beth Van Kirk, Wendy Resnik, Terry Lawler and Rita Hamilton. I am honored to have known you all.

BOOKING FOR TROUBLE

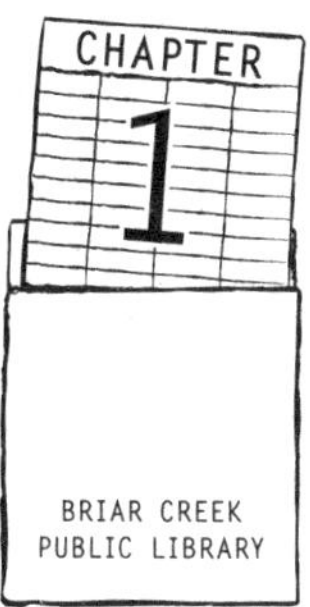

Lindsey Norris Sullivan strode through the front door of the Briar Creek Public Library and immediately felt her anxiety ease. She'd just come from the weekly department head meeting at the town hall and today's subject had been the budget. Mayor Eugenia Cole was a former librarian and Lindsey knew the mayor was doing everything she could to protect the library from budget cuts, but there was only so much she could do when certain town council members believed that libraries were superfluous and no longer necessary.

As the director of the small public library on the Connecticut shoreline, Lindsey felt that it was her duty to save the library. With the drastic cuts the town council was demanding in staffing, hours and materials, she couldn't help but feel that she was failing.

She needed to do something to raise the library's visibility in the community and she needed to do it fast. She glanced around the main room. Patrons were using computers, browsing the new books, having a meeting in one of the study rooms, and several mothers with small children were following a person dressed as a tugboat.

Lindsey smiled. Beth Barker, their indefatigable children's librarian, was wearing a costume that was essentially a cardboard box that had been reconfigured into a boat shape with a pointy bow and square back. It was painted a jaunty shade of yellow with a vibrant red trim, making it hard to miss. Beth was standing in the center of the reformed box, which was held up by a pair of red suspenders, and she topped it off by wearing a captain's hat, naturally.

"Toot toot!" Beth pumped one fist as if pulling an imaginary horn. "All aboard for story time, crew."

The mothers and their offspring marched past Beth toward the designated story time room at the back of the children's area. Spotting Lindsey, Beth held the cardboard boat by both sides and hurried over to her. The cardboard bounced as she jogged but Beth didn't slow down.

"How did it go? Was it as bad as we feared? Are they going to close the library? Are we soon to be unemployed?" Beth's forehead crinkled with worry.

"It went about how we expected." Lindsey sighed. "They want to take a chainsaw to the library budget and nothing I said seemed to sway them in the least. They simply don't care."

"What are we going to do?" Beth clutched her boat more tightly.

"I thought about it on the walk back from the town hall. I have to come up with a way to raise library awareness in the community, something that will give us support from the wealthier residents if I want the vote on the budget to go our way."

"You will," Beth said with a certainty Lindsey wished she felt.

Lindsey glanced into Beth's "boat" and noted that she'd managed to craft a bookshelf in the hull. The picture-book titles were all about boats, which explained her costume.

"A watercraft story time today?" Lindsey asked, knowing the answer was obvious but wanting to pivot the conversation to something else.

"You know it." Beth held up her books. "We have *Lily Leads the Way* by Margi Preus, *Old Wood Boat* by Nikki McClure, and *Sal Boat: A Boat by Sal* by Thyra Heder. And, of course, I'm going to talk about water safety."

"Of course." Lindsey watched Beth tuck her books back into her boat. It was as if Beth had made a bookmobile, but instead of the standard bus, it was a boat. Lindsey felt the zing of an idea hit her like a lightning bolt.

"What's wrong? You have a weird look on your face," Beth said. "Did you forget we have crafternoon today? We're supposed to have been reading *Mrs. Dalloway* by Virginia Woolf before we meet. I still need to finish the last chapter before lunch."

Lindsey nodded distractedly. "I finished it last night. It's not a light read, is it?"

Beth shook her head. "No, but Nancy is providing lunch today, so we know there'll be cookies." She glanced at the story time room to see that all the families had gathered. "Have to motor. We'll talk more later."

"Definitely." Lindsey nodded. "Hey, have I told you lately that you're a genius?"

Beth blinked and then pulled her imaginary air horn. "Toot toot! Yes, but feel free to tell me that anytime you want."

She disappeared into the story time room, leaving Lindsey with a fabulous idea. If Lindsey wanted to create something tangible that the wealthier residents of the community could appreciate, while serving both their needs and the needs of the rest of the village, it had to be something that would cause a splash. She grinned at the thought. A splash was exactly what she planned to make. Lindsey was going to introduce a book boat—like a bookmobile but a boat—to serve the Thumb Islands, an archipelago of over one hundred islands—if large rocks were included—off the coast of their village Briar Creek. It was an underserved community made up of poor, middle- and upper-class residents, who could use a dedicated library service of their own. Also, a book boat would make for some excellent public relations for the library.

You're going to need a boat," Nancy Peyton said. Dressed in her usual ironed jeans paired with a lilac sweatshirt, Nancy's blue eyes twinkled as she patted her short-cropped silver hair into place. She had made stromboli for today's lunch and the aroma of the baked pizza dough turnover, stuffed with mozzarella, provolone, salami and pepperoni made Lindsey's stomach grumble.

"And a captain," Violet La Rue added as she poured glasses of sweet tea. A retired Broadway actress who ran the local community theater, Violet's deep brown complexion and dark eyes were enhanced by the colorful caftans she wore and she moved with an ethereal grace learned from years spent on the stage.

"Good thing I'm married to a captain who has access to boats," Lindsey replied.

Both Violet and Nancy grinned. Mike Sullivan, or Sully as he was known around Briar Creek, ran the local water taxi and boat tour business that serviced the Thumb Islands. Having grown up on the islands, Sully was the perfect person to man the book boat.

When Lindsey had called him to get his take on her idea, he hadn't been able to talk as he'd been in the middle of navigating a double booking by two island residents who refused to share the same water taxi. He'd had to call in his part-time helper, Charlie Peyton, who was Nancy's nephew, to navigate the kerfuffle by picking up one of the ladies.

"Charlie told me that Sully was dealing with the residents of Split Island." Nancy rolled her eyes. "You'd think after living so close to each other all of these years that Gwen Capshaw and Ariel Montgomery would have figured out how to get along by now."

"Bad blood there." Violet shook her head. "Such a waste of energy."

"Maybe when you launch this book boat, you should steer clear of those islands." Nancy looked worried.

"You must be talking about the Montgomery-Capshaw feud." Mary Murphy entered the room with Paula Turner behind her.

Mary was Sully's younger sister and shared his reddish-brown hair and bright blue eyes. She gave Lindsey a quick side hug as she headed for the food.

"Even I've heard of that mess, and I'm still fairly new here," Paula said. She was the head of circulation for the library and was known for her ever-changing hair color—presently, it was blue—and her sleeve of tattoos, which featured a stack of books running up her arm.

"Sully's had to navigate that island for years, I will defer to his experience," Lindsey assured the group. "Besides, Ariel teaches painting at the library. I can't just cut her out of the book boat services because of a feud with her neighbor."

"Book boat? Explain," Mary said.

Beth entered the room still in her boat costume. She dropped it onto the floor and joined them at the table.

"Truthfully, it's all Beth's fault." Lindsey sent her friend a teasing glance.

Beth's eyebrows rose as she took a bite of her stromboli. Once she'd swallowed, she asked, "What did I do?"

"It was your story time costume that inspired me." Lindsey took a sip of her sweet tea. "Remember how I said I needed to raise the visibility of the library?"

Beth nodded.

"Well, after seeing you, it occurred to me that a dedicated book boat, like a bookmobile, would be the way to serve the island community and showcase the library. We've always run books out to the islands, but this would be a way they could count on us every week or every other week, however we can make the schedule work."

"I think that is a very ambitious plan." Mayor Cole entered the crafternoon room. Lindsey met her gaze and the mayor nodded. "I like it. You get the right people on board—pun intended—you just might be able to save your budget with it."

"That's the plan." Lindsey felt a surge of optimism. "I'll talk to Sully tonight and see what he thinks we'll need to do to get it up and running."

"Let us know if we can help," Nancy offered.

"If you can't staff the boat, we could be your volunteers," Violet agreed. She and Nancy leaned their heads together, looking the picture of innocence. Lindsey grinned. She could only imagine what the two septuagenarian besties would get up to if they were put in charge of the book boat.

"On to *Mrs. Dalloway*," Paula said. "Our craft is lavender sachets because it seemed very fitting for a novel set in June of nineteen twenty-three."

"Perfect!" Beth clapped her hands together, looking delighted.

Of course, she would be. Beth and Paula were the crafty members of the group, and while the others were adequate,

Lindsey was hopeless. She simply did not have the crafter gene.

As Paula passed out little canvas drawstring bags and a variety of ink stamps and pads, Lindsey picked up her copy of the book.

"Did you know that *Mrs. Dalloway* was originally called *The Hours*?" Lindsey asked the group.

"Like the movie. I did know that," Nancy said. "True confession, I watched the movie instead of reading the book."

"Nancy Peyton!" Mary gasped.

"What?" Nancy gestured to the table. "I had stromboli to make."

"That's fair." Mayor Cole took a bite of her sandwich.

"Wasn't it originally a short story?" Beth asked.

"It was." Violet put aside her empty plate to make room for her craft supplies. "Actually, it was two short stories, 'Mrs. Dalloway in Bond Street' and 'The Prime Minister.'"

"I liked that Mrs. Dalloway threw a party even when there seemed no reason to do so after a war and the flu epidemic," Beth said. "It was as if she was determined to make the most of things."

"I thought her reflection on the past, loves lost and such, was most relatable," Nancy said.

The twinkle in Nancy's eyes dimmed for a bit and Lindsey knew she was thinking of her late husband. Nancy had been a widow for decades and had never gotten over the loss.

"That is likely the appeal of Mrs. Dalloway," Violet said. "Woolf offers something to everyone who reads it."

"Even me," Paula said. "I thought it was quite shocking that Clarissa Dalloway reflected on a kiss with a woman friend as 'the most exquisite moment of her whole life.' I read it to my partner, Hannah, and she agreed that Woolf was ahead of her time."

Lindsey nodded. "She was brilliant. The critics say she found her voice in this novel and credit her with elevating literature."

"The fact that we all found something of note in the novel speaks to her talent," Mayor Cole agreed.

The conversation continued as they deconstructed the novel or, in Nancy's case, the movie. Lindsey discovered that stamping the small canvas bags was surprisingly fun as she made a border of green leaves around the edges and then stamped purple irises in the center. Stuffing the dried lavender into the bags wasn't a hardship either.

"Look at you," Paula teased her. "Not even asking for help today."

Lindsey laughed. "You might have finally found a craft I can handle."

The group dispersed at the end of their lunch hour. The next book they had agreed to read was a currently popular romantasy that featured dragons and their riders. Paula had chosen it, saying they needed to keep up with what books were hot with their patrons. Lindsey was thrilled. She was a firm believer that great writing could be found in all genres.

When Lindsey returned to her office to create a preliminary budget for her book boat idea, she found her husband waiting for her. As usual, her heart did a flutter at the sight of Sully. Given his windswept hair, chiseled features and the unique scent of the sea and sun that surrounded him, it was small wonder he still made her a little weak in the knees when he was in her orbit.

"Hey, darlin'." He kissed her quickly, mindful that the windows of her office looked out onto the library. "Sorry I couldn't talk earlier, I have a break between runs so thought I'd come over and find out what 'idea' had you so excited."

"You didn't have to do that, but I'm glad you did." Lindsey squeezed his hand in hers and gestured for him to sit in one of the visitor's chairs while she took the other. She didn't want to have her desk between them since she knew he would likely be here for only a few minutes.

"So . . . ?" He raised his eyebrows.

"We had the town budget meeting this morning. It went as badly as I feared." She paused and he nodded. They'd talked about it last night as she'd shared her concerns about the proposed budget cuts with him. "But I think I have an idea to raise our visibility in town and potentially keep the wealthier residents invested in keeping the library at its current budget."

"I'm listening." He rested his chin in his hand and gave her his full attention. That right there was probably why she adored him. On top of being ridiculously handsome, he always listened to her. She never found herself talking to the top of his head while he scrolled through his phone.

"I'm going to need your help," she said, prefacing her explanation.

"You've got it." He reached out and brushed a lock of her long curly blond hair out of her face. She sighed and then shook her head to focus.

"I want to start a book boat, like a bookmobile but on a boat," she said. "I think if we can service all of the islands on a weekly or biweekly basis, the island residents will get used to the service and realize the library is not just for the villagers but for everyone and they'll support the library's current budget and not want it cut."

"That's inspired." He sounded impressed. "Many of the islanders make up the bulk of the wealth in Briar Creek, minus my parents, of course."

Sully and his sister, Mary, had been raised on Bell Island, where his parents had lived for decades and his grandparents before them.

"So, you'll help?" Lindsey leaned forward.

"What do you need?" he asked.

"A boat and a captain."

"The captain part, I have on hand." He grinned. "And I know where we can find a boat."

"Best. Husband. Ever." Lindsey kissed him again, not so quickly this time. "How long will it take to be up and running?"

A knock sounded on the door, and Lindsey called, "Come in!"

Paula popped her head in, but before she could speak, a man's voice sounded from the library, and judging by the tone, he was unhappy. Paula sighed and said, "We have a situation."

Paula stepped aside, leaving room for Lindsey and Sully to walk to the front of the library. Lindsey didn't recognize the voice of the man who sounded to be in full shout mode but then again why would she? Despite having the occasional upset patron, the library was generally a peaceful place where everyone was happy to have materials, resources, programming, and research assistance provided.

Lindsey braced herself to find the man chewing out one of her staff; instead what she found was a man standing in the lobby leaning forward as if trying to be taller than Milton Duffy, who was one of Lindsey's favorite library supporters.

She recognized the shorter man immediately. With his close-cropped silver hair, tanned skin and portly stature, dressed in a bespoke designer suit, town councilman Gideon Trask was easily recognizable.

"You and your library board are no longer needed," Gideon blustered. "The town council has decided to do away with it."

Lindsey sighed. Councilman Trask had muscled his way onto the town council determined to cut library, Parks and Recreation and education services to the community in order to leverage property-tax cuts for himself and the other affluent residents. And now it appeared he was having what amounted to a tantrum in the middle of the library and she was going to have to be nice about it.

"I'll be right back," she told Sully, leaving him with Paula behind the circulation desk.

"The town council doesn't have the authority to abolish the library board," Milton argued. Dressed in his usual tracksuit, Milton looked every bit the yogi he was, except for the faint red tinge to his bald head and his cheeks beneath his perfectly trimmed silver goatee.

"Of course we do." Gideon brushed the sleeve of his blazer as if Milton had contaminated it with his words. "The council can do whatever it wants and not even your lady friend the mayor can stop us."

Milton looked as if he was about to take the bait and yell back. Instead, he put his hands together in front of his chest in the prayer pose and bowed low. "I suppose we'll see, won't we? Namaste."

Milton turned on his heel and strode toward Lindsey. Before she could engage Gideon, Milton took her elbow and turned her around so that they were both walking away from the odious little man.

"Lindsey, just the person I was looking for," Milton said loud enough for Trask to hear him.

He didn't stop walking until they were behind the circulation desk with Sully and Paula. "About the chess club . . ." Milton kept his back to Trask, looked at Sully and said in a low voice, "Tell me when he leaves."

"Is there a scheduling problem?" Lindsey asked, going along with Milton.

"Given the high demand and incredible popularity of the program, I am wondering if we should add another day to the calendar." Milton raised his voice, no doubt to be certain that Trask could hear him.

Before Lindsey could comment, Sully nodded and said, "He's gone."

"Obnoxious little troll," Milton muttered.

"I was going to try and talk to him about the budget," Lindsey said.

"Don't waste your breath," Milton advised. "He sees no value in the library and nothing is going to change his narrow little mind."

"Why is he coming after the library?" Paula asked. "'The maths don't math,' as the kids say. Even if he shuts down the library completely, the savings still wouldn't equal the tax cuts he wants and it'll devalue the town not to have a public library."

"He doesn't care. The budget cuts start with the library and parks, then education," Milton said. "After that, it moves to more vital services like water, roads and other infrastructure. We're going to have to fight."

Sully turned to Lindsey with a considering look. "I think your book boat needs to launch as soon as possible."

"Agreed. How soon can we be ready?" she asked.

"We'll need to find a boat, and even a fixer-upper won't be cheap. Anything we can afford will need some work, which will likely cost more than the library can afford right now." Sully glanced at Lindsey with a regretful look. "Unless of course we could come up with a patron who wants to fund the boat and the necessary maintenance and repairs."

"What's this about the library needing a patron?" Robbie Vine strolled behind the circulation desk as if he were an employee. He carried a tray with a teapot and biscuits as he and Lindsey had developed a habit of enjoying afternoon tea together a couple of times each week. Being British, Robbie was a very big fan of tea and biscuits.

"There are members of the town council who would like to see the library shut down," Milton answered, his tone deeply aggrieved.

"Whatever for?" Robbie asked.

"Because they want to lower property taxes by paying for fewer community services," Lindsey said. "They're starting with the library and will then move on to cut other town services."

"But that's just mental!" Robbie set the tray down on the counter with a bang. "Do they not realize that they benefit from paved roads, trash pickup and firefighters just like everyone else?"

"I don't think they care." Paula sighed. "I guess when you can pay to have your private road paved, you don't care about anyone else's. It appears our town is turning into the have-yachts versus the have-nots."

Robbie plunked his hands on his hips and turned toward Lindsey. "What do you need a patron for?"

"I had the thought that if we started offering a weekly book boat service—like a bookmobile but a boat—that delivered materials to the residents of the islands then we could effectively get those residents on board, so to speak, to fight for the library budget."

"Given that many of the island residents are quite posh and very much enjoy being waited upon, that's an excellent plan." Robbie turned to Sully. "But we need money to make the boat happen, I assume?"

"A bit." Sully narrowed his eyes. "Why? What are you thinking?"

"King's Island," Robbie said.

Sully's eyebrows went up. "I'm listening."

"You know what's on that island." Robbie glanced from side to side and lowered his voice. "The Club."

"No one who isn't a member can get anywhere near that place," Milton protested.

Robbie nodded. "Yes, and I've been invited to join."

"What are they talking about?" Paula asked. Lindsey was grateful as she had no idea. She'd never heard of King's Island or The Club.

"The Club is an ultra-exclusive members-only country club on King's Island," Sully said. "It costs a quarter of a million just to join and members have to be sponsored by an existing member and be approved by the membership committee."

Lindsey gave her husband the side-eye. "How do you know so much about it?"

"When I returned from the Navy, I was asked to be their head of security." He met her gaze. "I declined as it's not really my scene."

"Well, if they wanted you on the island, sailor boy, I don't feel that precious about it," Robbie said, looking chagrined.

"Sorry, old man." Sully patted Robbie's shoulder.

"While this is all very fascinating, what does it have to do with the book boat?" Lindsey asked.

"The Club could sponsor it," Robbie said. "I know that they have pet projects for the community and such as they've given support to the local theater, and The Club members hold a lot of sway with the town council."

"It might be worth it to ask for their support just to stick it to Gideon Trask," Paula said.

"It's a great idea," Lindsey said. "But given that their membership is so exclusive, I wouldn't even know who to approach about such a thing."

"The membership committee," Robbie said. "Those ladies wield their social status and power like a cudgel. Get them on your side and you'll put Trask firmly in his place."

"And I'm supposed to approach them how?" Lindsey asked.

"With me." Robbie pointed to himself as if it were obvious.

Lindsey turned to Sully. "What do you think?"

"Worth a shot." He shrugged. "The worst they can do is say no and then you're no worse off than you are now."

"All right," Lindsey said. "Let's strategize over tea."

Robbie set up the meeting with The Club membership committee for the next day. Because potential members weren't allowed on the island until their membership was approved, the committee asked Robbie to meet them at the Blue Anchor, Briar Creek's only restaurant, for lunch. Robbie agreed, informing them that he would be bringing a friend, which was met with resistance until he insisted. It was clear that the membership committee wanted the famous British actor as a member and Lindsey was happy to use that desire for the library's benefit.

After having Robbie disregard her wardrobe as not posh enough, Lindsey was outfitted in the designer clothes Robbie bought for his girlfriend to wear when attending his red-carpet events.

Since his girlfriend happened to be Emma Plewicki, the chief of police for Briar Creek and the Thumb Islands, she didn't have much use for the wardrobe in her day-to-day uniform-wearing life, meaning most of the clothes had never been worn. When Lindsey asked Emma if it was okay for her to borrow an outfit, Emma had given her an enthusiastic yes, which was how Lindsey found herself walking into the Blue Anchor in Christian Louboutin heels, a Jenny Packham dress, and carrying a Prada handbag.

"I'll do the talking," Robbie instructed as they approached a booth by the window where four ladies of a certain age were all scrolling through their phones.

Lindsey took in the women at a glance. Their hair was long and perfectly styled with the large curls so many women favored, their lips were full, noses thin and eyelashes long. Their clothes were designer labels and their jewelry bold and blingy. Lindsey felt as if she were meeting the Real Housewives of the Thumb Islands and wished Beth were here to appreciate the moment. Despite being a person who generally didn't notice labels, Lindsey knew that Robbie had been right. If she wanted these women to consider her proposal, she needed to look like one of them at least as far as her borrowed wardrobe would allow.

"Ladies, what a pretty picture you make," Robbie greeted them.

Thankfully, their quartet was made up of a blonde, a redhead and two brunettes, one light and one dark, or Lindsey would have had a hard time telling them apart.

"Robbie, darling, how wonderful to see you," the highlighted brunette greeted him. She glanced over Lindsey, pausing on her handbag as if assessing her worth through it, and smiled. "And you must be Robbie's friend."

"Lindsey Sullivan." Robbie gestured to her. "These are my newest friends, Leslie Stone, Tina Baldwin, Mallory Masterson and Harper Winslow."

Lindsey smiled at each of them in turn, committing to memory their name matched to their hair color. Leslie was the brunette with golden highlights, Tina the blonde, Mallory the redhead and Harper the deep brown brunette. Leslie gestured for them to sit and Lindsey took one of the two chairs that had been placed at the end of the booth.

The chairs were lower than the booth by just a couple of inches and Lindsey suspected that the four ladies knew this and did it on purpose. They were establishing dominance by looking down at Robbie and Lindsey.

"Lindsey, Robbie, what are you two doing here?" Mary Murphy asked as she stopped by the booth. Lindsey smiled at Sully's sister, who owned the Blue Anchor with her husband, Ian, relieved to see a friendly face.

"Just meeting up with some friends," Robbie said.

Mary glanced at the women and smiled. "Four of our best customers." Tina, seemingly the friendly one, was the only one who smiled in return. "Can I get anyone anything?"

"A bottle of prosecco for the ladies and a whiskey neat for me," Robbie said. Mallory smiled this time, obviously pleased.

"Iced tea for me," Lindsey said.

"Coming right up." Mary departed and Lindsey turned back to the table.

"Now Robbie, you said your friend had a proposal for us?" Leslie said. "Since our . . . interview with you is to be a private matter, should we start with her request?"

"Of course. Lindsey?" Robbie encouraged her.

Lindsey cleared her throat. She wasn't nervous exactly. It was more that she hated being the center of attention and these women, with their critically assessing gazes, made her feel less than somehow. She closed her eyes and thought about the greater good, saving the library, and centered herself on her purpose.

"Robbie mentioned that his new friends were known for doing great things for the community," Lindsey began.

"We are?" Tina asked, tossing her blond hair over her shoulder. She looked as if she would frown but her eyebrows didn't—or couldn't—move.

"Of course we are," Mallory said. Her long pointy fingernails clicked against the tabletop.

"We did a fund-raiser for the new playground on the town green, didn't we?" Harper asked while examining her red lipstick in the reflection of her phone.

Tina nodded. "That's right."

"And we organized a beach cleanup," Leslie said. "We didn't participate but we did organize it."

"Oh." Tina blinked. "Is that what you're looking to do?"

"Not exactly." Lindsey paused while Mary delivered their drinks.

"I'll pour for the ladies," Robbie offered. Mary handed him the bottle and moved on to her next table.

"What are you looking to do?" Leslie asked. "We have to be very circumspect about how we spend our time and our funds."

"I'm the library director in town," Lindsey said. "And—"

"You don't look like a librarian," Tina interrupted. "Don't they usually wear glasses and they certainly don't dress as well as you."

Lindsey sent Robbie a side-eye. Perhaps she would have been better served to dress more to these ladies' expectations.

He shook his head ever so slightly and she sighed. She met Tina's gaze and said, "Times have changed."

"Clearly." Mallory toyed with the ends of her long red hair. Her eyes were narrowed as she studied Lindsey as if trying to decide whether she trusted her or not. Lindsey wasn't used to being scrutinized in such a blatant way and found it a bit off-putting. She focused on Tina, who smiled at her encouragingly.

"Given that the library building is in the center of town, I feel that we could expand our reach and better serve our entire community." Lindsey gestured to the islands visible through the window.

"Go on." Leslie tapped her chin with her index finger.

"There are twenty-three islands that have houses on them, totaling eighty-one homes, many with young children. I feel that the island residents are underserved by the library, and I would like to change that," Lindsey said.

"Underserved how?" Harper asked.

"Access to materials and programs," Lindsey said. "We have so many resources that the island residents could utilize if there was a way to get those materials and programs out to the islands."

"Are you suggesting building a library out on the islands?" Leslie asked.

"Which one?" Tina looked confused.

"An existing building or a new build?" Mallory's eyes widened in alarm.

"Oh, no, I wasn't thinking on as grand a scale as that, although I do love the idea," Lindsey said. "I was thinking more along the lines of a traveling library—a book boat, in fact."

Leslie cupped her chin and glanced at her friends. The foursome seemed to be having a silent conversation, which Lindsey found to be a bit unnerving. Robbie must have sensed it, because he reached over and patted her hand.

"I, for one, think it's brilliant," he said. "I would definitely join . . . a club . . . that supported the local library in such a way."

"Would you?" Leslie challenged him.

"Definitely." Robbie toasted her with his whiskey.

"Do you have a proposal for us?" Mallory asked.

"I do." Lindsey opened her handbag and pulled out four copies of the price breakdown that she and Sully had worked out. It wasn't an exorbitant sum but it was more than she had available in her budget. She handed a copy to each of the women and watched as they scanned over the numbers. Their faces were blank and she had no idea what they were thinking. Maddening.

"We will discuss this after our interview with Robbie,"

Leslie declared. She set the paper aside and met Lindsey's gaze. "And we'll let you know."

Lindsey knew when she was being dismissed. She supposed the fact that they were considering it was the best she could have hoped for. She stood and pushed in her seat, smiling at each of the women in turn. "Thank you for your time."

"It was really nice to meet you," Tina said. Her large blue eyes were steady and her smile warm. Lindsey's instincts told her that Tina was being sincere.

"You, too." Lindsey turned to Robbie and said, "See you later."

"Of course you know how much I love the library." He winked at her and Lindsey smiled. She knew he'd do his best to sell the ladies on the idea of supporting the book boat. It wasn't just the money that was important. It was having the wealthy residents of the islands supporting the library in a showy, impossible-to-ignore way that would make it more difficult for the town council to cut the library's budget.

Lindsey waved to Mary and Ian and left the Anchor to head back to the library. As she walked back across the street, she felt oddly powerful in her red-soled heels, but she also just wanted to get back to her low-heeled comfortable pumps. High fashion was clearly not for the weak.

Standing across the street from the library, she watched as John Felton carried Naomi Rockwood's books as she made her way up the ramp. Naomi was in her eighties and used a walker. While Lindsey was sure the feisty Naomi could have managed on her own, it warmed her heart that John stepped up to help. This was one of the many things she loved about the library—the sense of community it gave to the village—and she would fight for this library with every bit of her soul.

When she entered the building, the crafternooners who had championed the book boat as their project were waiting for her in the main room. Violet and Nancy were seated in two of the comfortable armchairs, each reading a copy of the novel selected for their next crafternoon while they waited.

"How did it go?" Beth hurried over from the children's department. She was dressed in an oversize black hooded sweatshirt that she had crafted into a penguin using large pieces of felt adhered with hot glue to form a white belly on the front and an orange and black beak and eyes on the hood. Obviously, Beth's afternoon story time had just ended, and Lindsey smiled despite her anxiety.

"Did they agree to fund it?" Nancy put aside her book and clasped her hands in her lap.

"What did Robbie think?" Violet bit her lip.

"If it's a go, I can start selecting books for the boat," Paula offered.

Lindsey held up her hands in a *slow down* gesture. "They're thinking about it." There was a collective groan. "But I'm feeling oddly optimistic." That visibly perked up the crafternooners, and Lindsey desperately hoped she wasn't wrong.

Gideon Trask was going to steamroll those budget cuts

right over the library unless she had some very powerful people on her side. Lindsey left the crafternooners and headed to her office. She told herself that all she could do was hope for the best but prepare for the worst.

Lindsey had just changed into her comfortable shoes when there was a knock on her office door. "Come in."

"Really sorry to bother you," Paula said. "But our nemesis is back."

Nemesis?" Lindsey asked.

"Trask." Paula frowned.

Lindsey stood up and came around her desk, glancing out the window that looked out over the library. "Is he yelling at anyone?"

"No, but he's carrying around a little black notebook and watching everyone. It's creepy and I don't trust him," Paula said.

Lindsey sighed. She didn't enjoy conflict but she suspected that Gideon Trask thrived on it. "I'll take care of it."

She left her office and strode into the main part of the library. She didn't see Gideon right away, so she toured the building, looking for him. On her way, she helped two customers, checked in with her adult services librarian and straightened some of the items on the new-book display.

Just when she was about to give up and assume Gideon had left, she found him seated at a table in the corner, staring at Paula, who was working behind the circulation desk. Although she wasn't working at the moment. Instead, she had her arms crossed over her chest and was locked in a staring contest with Trask.

Lindsey didn't need Paula to spell it out for her. Trask was staring at her, watching her work, and Paula had stopped working to stare him down. Lindsey didn't fault her one bit. Having someone stare at you while you tried to do your job was unnerving and Paula didn't have to put up with that sort of microaggression.

"Mr. Trask." Lindsey approached his table, intentionally standing in front of him and blocking his view of Paula. "How are you?"

"You're in my way." Trask leaned over to one side and then the other, trying to see around her but Lindsey moved with him, effectively blocking his view.

"Did you need something? Because I can't let you just sit here and stare at my employees, it makes for a hostile work environment, and I know you don't want that." Lindsey tried to sound agreeable and not like she wanted to toss him out on his ear.

Trask slammed his notebook shut and tapped the cover. "I don't need anything from you. I'm getting it all noted right here." He paused to laugh and it sounded remarkably like a villain's laugh in a superhero movie.

"Getting what?" Lindsey asked in confusion.

"The overspending at the library," he said. "We don't

need all of this. How many staff persons do you have? All we need is one old, cat lady spinster to spend her days here and the library could cut all of the other workers."

"I'm sorry, did you just say 'cat lady spinster'?" Lindsey gaped.

"Yes. Just like the good old days when spinsters were teachers and they taught all the kids in town. They didn't need all these extras at school like the music, art and sports we have now. Parents can pay for that stuff out of their own pocket if little Johnny wants to play the clarinet so bad. It's just so wasteful." He pulled back his sleeve and checked the time. The diamonds on his Rolex sparkled in the overhead lighting.

"You don't say." Lindsey didn't know much about watches but she suspected his cost about the same as a first-year teacher's salary.

"I do say." He wagged his little black notebook at her. "I'm watching you; I'm watching all of you and I'm noting every bit of wasted taxpayer money. Why do we have more than one copy of the latest bestsellers? And story time, why? Can't parents read to their own children or hire someone to do it? And why should my money pay for someone else's book club? Or for a cooking class? I won't have it. Enjoy this place while you can, Lindsey, because I will have it shut down by summer, mark my words." With that, Trask pushed back his chair and strode out of the building.

Lindsey tried to do the calming breathwork Milton had taught her but she found she really just wanted to punch something.

"Here." Milton approached her, carrying one of the cushions from the children's story time room. "You can either scream into it or throw it onto the ground as hard as you can."

"What about breathing?" she asked.

"Sometimes you need something a little more . . ."

"Violent?" Lindsey asked.

Milton shrugged.

Lindsey took the pillow and heaved it onto the floor as if it were Trask. Then she kicked it.

She turned to Milton and he smiled. "And now we breathe," he said.

It was late afternoon when Robbie stopped by the library. He swaggered into her office looking a bit tipsy and Lindsey raised her eyebrows as he plopped into the chair across from her desk. She was almost afraid to ask, but curiosity got the better of her.

"How did it go?" She turned away from her computer and gave him her full attention.

"Swimmingly." Robbie pantomimed the breaststroke.

Lindsey rolled her eyes. "How many whiskeys did you have?"

"Too many. My sponsor for membership in The Club is George Carraway, and he joined us after my initial interview." Robbie shook his head. His strawberry-blond hair was cut short but his bangs flopped over his forehead in charming disarray.

"George Carraway, the movie star?" Lindsey asked. "I didn't even know he had a place on the islands."

"He keeps it very hush-hush." Robbie hiccupped.

"Do I need to call Emma to come get you?"

"No, I'm going to walk over to the police department as soon as I hand this off to you." He reached into his pants pocket and pulled out a folded piece of paper. "You'll be happy to know that George was the one who convinced the ladies that supporting the library was a noble endeavor."

Lindsey took it from his extended hand. She unfolded it and found that it was a check made out to the library for the exact amount of money they would need to get the book boat ready. Her jaw dropped.

"You did it!" she gasped.

Robbie shook his head. "You did it. They adored you."

Lindsey narrowed her eyes at him. She knew very well that his celebrity star power and George's had been what sealed the deal. "Are you officially a member of The Club now?"

"I have probationary status as a member. So long as I don't do anything untoward for the next ninety days, I'll be accepted," he said.

"I hope you didn't have to join for this, because there are other ways for the library's book boat to get funded and membership to The Club is insanely expensive. I'd be ill if I thought you'd paid for that for us to have this." Lindsey frowned and held up the check. "I mean, for a tenth of the cost of The Club membership, you could be the book boat sponsor."

"But that wouldn't achieve your goal of getting the wealthy residents of the islands to be invested in the book boat and tangentially the library, correct?"

"Fair point. Still . . ." Lindsey winced. "The cost."

"Not to worry, I'm quite certain I will do something egregious and be tossed to the curb before my first payment is due." His grin was full of mischief and Lindsey shook her head. She didn't want to know what chicanery he had planned.

"Well, on behalf of the library, I appreciate you taking one for the team."

"Happy to help." Robbie pushed up out of his chair. "And now I'm off to see my darling chief of police and hope that she has brewed some of her battery acid–strength coffee."

Robbie departed with a wobbly salute and Lindsey reached for her phone to call her husband and share the news.

"Congratulations, darling, that's fantastic," Sully said when she finished sharing. "But we have one problem."

"What's that?" Lindsey frowned, trying to think of what she'd missed.

"We're going to need a name for the boat."

Lindsey and Sully toured the boats for sale at the Briar Creek marina. It was slim pickings, but then she saw it. Hidden under a tarp was a fishing boat with a canopy that seemed like it would function nicely with a few modifications.

"What about this one?" Lindsey asked Sully.

He left the boat he'd been examining and joined her. He tugged the rest of the tarp off and let out a low whistle. "You have fancy taste in boats, darling."

Lindsey watched as he ran his hands over the hull and then climbed the step stool beside it to peer into the body of the boat.

"How many books do you think you'll be taking out to the islands?" he asked.

"I thought I'd start with two hundred and adjust as needed."

Sully climbed into the boat. "Are you thinking built-in shelves? Say, twenty-five books per shelf?"

Lindsey shrugged. "I hadn't thought about it, but if we did that, we'd need eight shelves with each one being thirty-two or thirty-six inches long and twelve inches deep," she said. "Is there room for that?"

Sully pulled a measuring tape out of his pocket and worked his way around the back of the boat. He made some markings on the floor and the interior walls before he moved to the open space of the bow, where he did some more measuring.

"If we do six shelves in the back and two in the front, it'll work," he said.

Lindsey considered this. "We could make the shelves in front the children's area."

"Easy enough and there's room for a small play area," Sully said.

Lindsey felt a thrill flutter inside of her. A book boat. How cool was this going to be? Then she frowned.

"We can't have open shelves though. The books would fall out and get wet," she said.

"That's no problem," he said. "We'll use dry box technology and modify the shelves so that there's a waterproof door that latches over each shelf."

"That would be amazing," Lindsey said. "But I don't have a lot of time if I want to get this thing going as soon as possible."

"Let me ask around and see if any of the boat repair outfits in the area have time for a custom job, although it'll cost you," he said.

"Worth it," Lindsey assured him. "And I know the crafternooners and the Friends of the Library are all eager to help so we have plenty of people on hand to get the boat in shape."

"She's a beauty," Sully said. "But she needs a lot of TLC before she's seaworthy."

"Let's just start with step one and buy the boat," Lindsey said.

By the end of the day, the library was the proud owner of the village's very first book boat. In order to get it ready as fast as possible, Lindsey sent a call for help far and wide. To her delight, people answered and two weeks were spent cleaning, painting, and installing the custom dry shelves.

There were a few hiccups, such as the inboard motor needed to be overhauled and the heavy cloth canopy replaced, also the marine paint they'd ordered came in a particularly vivid shade of blue.

"Is that cerulean?" Nancy asked as she and Violet helped Lindsey paint the hull. They'd spent the past several days cleaning, sanding and applying primer. Today was painting day and Lindsey found herself weirdly nervous.

"I pictured it darker." Violet stared at the section she'd just painted with a roller.

"Maybe it dries a darker shade." Nancy offered, pausing to examine her own work.

The commentary wasn't helping Lindsey's nerves. "However it dries, it is what it is, since we're almost out of the money the ladies of The Club gave us to launch the book boat."

Violet and Nancy exchanged a considering look. "I'm sure it will be lovely," Nancy said.

"Absolutely," Violet agreed.

As they resumed painting, Lindsey had the feeling they'd been humoring her. She turned back to the boat and sighed, reminding herself that launch day was in three days and it didn't matter if this paint dried a shade of gangrene. They'd make it work.

I christen thee, *The Jolly Reader*!" Mayor Cole stood beside the newly refurbished book boat—painted a cheerful shade of blue—brandishing a bottle of sparkling cider that she tapped against the bow, not breaking it because she didn't want to have any broken glass polluting the bay.

The crowd, made up of library staff, friends of the library and library board members, all applauded. Milton came forward with a tray of small paper cups, which the mayor poured the cider into. Once the cups had been distributed amid the crowd, Mayor Cole raised her cup and toasted Lindsey for the creation of the library's book boat.

"To our fabulous library director, Lindsey, and our captain, Sully, safe travels." The crowd shouted, "Hear! Hear!" before they raised their glasses and drank.

Lindsey smiled and waved from her spot on the boat beside Sully. She had double-checked the built-in shelves to make sure the books would stay dry and in place on their shelves. She hoped her husband was right and that the dry box covers would work. She'd also brought a tablet to register any residents of the islands who asked for library cards, which she kept in a portable dry box by her seat. She and Sully had spent the previous evening mapping out their course, determined to reach as many of the inhabited islands as they could.

"Well, well, well, if it isn't the mayor wasting more of the taxpayers' money." Gideon Trask strolled through the crowd, wearing a straw sun hat and looking—at least to Lindsey—like any villain in a low-budget Hollywood movie. "I hope you don't think this is going to stop the town council from cutting the library from the budget."

"Now is not the time, Gideon," Mayor Cole chastised him.

"I think it's the perfect time," Gideon countered. "I want to know how this was paid for. Did it come out of the library budget? Who approved this boat thing? Was it you, Mayor?" He actually sneered when he addressed her by her title as if he couldn't bear it. "It seems to me, the town council should be the body to approve this sort of expenditure."

Mayor Cole ignored him. Instead, she turned to Sully and Lindsey and said, "Bon voyage!"

"Not so fast!" Gideon stepped forward and put his foot on the side of their boat as if he could physically stop them.

"Oh, for pity's sake, Gideon, you're making an ass of yourself." Leslie Stone stepped out of the crowd, flanked by Tina, Harper and Mallory. All four of them wore sundresses and wide-brimmed straw hats, chunky jewelry and stylish sandals. The perfect ensembles to wear when celebrating their good works for the community.

"Leslie!" Gideon started, causing the untied boat to shift away from the dock. "What are you doing here?"

"Um . . . Mr. Trask," Lindsey tried to get his attention. He ignored her.

"I'm here because we"—Leslie gestured between herself and the other three women—"as the membership committee of The Club, are the ones who sponsored this book boat. Now move so they can go about their business."

Gideon Trask made a face as if he'd just swallowed a bug.

"Bye, Lindsey!" Tina stood on her tiptoes and waved enthusiastically at them.

Lindsey returned it, studying the women whom she was weirdly beginning to think of as the library's fairy godmothers. They weren't an overly likable bunch but that didn't matter when the library's future swung in the balance.

"Stop! You can't leave until I know for certain that none of the town's money has gone into this venture," Gideon insisted, keeping one foot on the boat and one foot on the dock.

Mallory, who didn't look happy to be there—at all—glared at him and strode forward. Keeping eye contact with Gideon, she lifted her leg and pushed the boat with one kitten heel sandal–wearing foot. The boat drifted farther out, causing Gideon's legs to spread.

"We should grab him before—" Whatever Sully had been about to say was cut off by the enormous splash Gideon made when he plunged into the water. "Oops, too late."

"That's a shame." Lindsey shook her head as Gideon surfaced, spluttering curse words and slapping the top of the water.

"Yup, a real pity. Ready?" Sully gestured to the seat beside the captain's.

"More than." Lindsey sank into it then turned and waved to their friends, some of whom were helping Gideon out of the water because they were bighearted like that.

Sully increased the speed while still maintaining no wake, as they headed away from Briar Creek and out into the bay.

Lindsey loved the Thumb Islands. There was something so magical about the homes scattered out on their own chunks of land. Some of the land masses had several homes on them, separated by hills, forests and fields while others amounted to little more than a rock with a house perched on it.

She knew that Sully had loved growing up out here and that he hoped to retire on the islands one day. She had to admit the idea had appeal. Given that their dog, Heathcliff, loved boats, she knew he'd love island life. Zelda, their cat, however, was going to be a tougher sell as she was resistant to most everything.

"What are you thinking about?" Sully asked her.

"That the idea of living out here seems very romantic," she said.

Sully smiled. "There have been some legendary romances out here."

"Really? Do tell." Lindsey leaned in.

"Spinster Island, for starters." Sully pointed to one of the islands in the distance. "Everyone believed it was a home for spinsters as the six women who lived out there in the nineteen twenties were all unmarried and of a certain age."

"It wasn't?"

"Turns out they weren't six single women but rather three couples," he said. "Shocked the town to its core when the last of them passed away, leaving behind a very scandalous journal."

"I'd like to read that," Lindsey said. "For purely historical reasons, naturally."

Sully winked at her. "Naturally." He pointed to another island, closer than the last, and said, "And that is Split Island, the most recent of the islands embroiled in a romance."

"Split Island?" Lindsey frowned. "Isn't that where our artist friend Ariel lives with her husband, Dane Montgomery?"

"That's the one." Sully steered the boat toward the island.

"And isn't that where you recently had an incident between the residents?"

"It is." Sully frowned.

"Mary said something about the Capshaw-Montgomery feud? Is that why it's called Split Island?"

"It's an appropriate name, for sure, but the island is actually named after the natural split that runs down the middle of the land mass, dividing it in two. There used to be a bridge that connected the two sides but no more."

"And the other half of the island is owned by the Capshaws?" Lindsey asked.

"Yes, Gwen and Perry Capshaw live on the other side of the island," Sully said.

"Wait." Lindsey held up her hand. "I know that name. Perry Capshaw is a famous ornithologist. He's authored several bird books that we have in the library."

"Perry is a brilliant scientist," Sully agreed. "When I was a kid, he'd invite all the island kids to go with him on birding expeditions. I learned so much not just about birds but the entire local ecosystem from him." Sully steered *The Jolly Reader* up to the first dock, which was attached to the smaller of the two islands.

"And the two families are feuding?" Lindsey asked. "How long has that been going on?"

"Well over a decade now," he said.

"What happened?"

"Ariel and Dane had a son—" Sully began but he was interrupted by a cheerful shout.

"Sully, is that you?" A woman in a pair of paint-spattered overalls appeared on the dock.

Lindsey recognized Ariel immediately. She waved in return and called out, "Hi, Ariel."

"And Lindsey, too?" Ariel hurried toward them. She was wearing a blue scarf over her long red hair, protecting it from her painting, no doubt. She knelt beside their boat and tied the rope Sully tossed her with expert hands.

"What brings you here?" Ariel's brown eyes were bright with welcome. "You have to come up and see my studio. Do you have time? I'm working on a piece and I'd love to get your input."

Lindsey blinked. Ariel was talking a mile a minute, which was what she always did, but it was jarring against the serenity of the boat ride they'd just enjoyed.

"I'm talking too much, aren't I?" Ariel asked. "I can't help it. I haven't been off the island for days and I've worn Dane out with all my jabbering."

"I doubt that." Sully stepped onto the dock. "Your husband adores you, always has, always will."

Ariel waved a dismissive hand but she looked pleased. "Are you here to talk about my next painting session at the library?"

"No, but we could if you have some ideas," Lindsey said. "Your classes are always so popular."

"I do have some ideas," Ariel said. "I thought we could start in July. I won't be teaching any private lessons, last summer ruined that for me, so this summer my schedule will be wide-open."

"July is perfect." Lindsey loved Ariel's painting classes primarily because she loved to watch Ariel work. She was a gifted artist who was just beginning to come into her own and be recognized for her skill. "But I'm really here because we are launching a book boat."

Ariel tipped her head to the side in confusion.

"It's essentially a bookmobile on a boat to reach the library patrons out on the islands." Lindsey removed the covers to the built-in shelves, pleased to see that the books were in place and perfectly dry.

"Look at that!" Ariel cried. "How clever. Is this a plan to push back against the budget cuts that odious troll Gideon is trying to implement?"

"You know about that?"

Ariel nodded. "Dane heard it from someone who heard it from somebody."

"The usual way news travels in the Thumb Islands," Sully said.

"I don't know how the villagers are feeling but the islanders are not happy," Ariel said. "What can I do to show support?"

"Check out some books?" Lindsey gestured to the books she'd brought.

"I'd be delighted." Ariel clapped her hands together. "You know I love the library but between my work and Dane having the boat most days to go ashore to take out his fishing charter, I just can't get into town as much as I'd like."

Lindsey felt a little thrill inside as she realized that the book boat might be exactly what the island residents needed.

Sully assisted Ariel onto the boat and she began to browse, immediately snagging *The Book That Wouldn't Burn* by Mark Lawrence. "Oh, I've been looking for this one." Ariel continued browsing and Lindsey exchanged a pleased smile with Sully. He nodded, letting her know that he thought this plan of hers might just work.

"Excuse me!" A shout interrupted the ambient sound of the waves gently lapping against the boat's hull.

Sully glanced over at the dock belonging to the larger part of Split Island, and Lindsey followed the line of his gaze. Standing twenty feet away on the adjacent wooden platform was a woman with her hands on her hips, about the same age as Ariel, but dressed in designer clothes, looking very Ralph Lauren spring collection, which complemented her pale blond bob and oversize sunglasses. She had her hand in the air as if she were calling for a waiter.

Sully blew out a breath. "Oh, this isn't going to go well."

Excuse me!" the woman repeated, her voice as shrill and insistent as a seagull scouting for food. Lindsey frowned. She had never seen this woman before in her life.

"Is that . . . ?" Lindsey began but Ariel interrupted.

"Gwen Capshaw, the one and only, thank goodness." Ariel hugged the book she'd selected to her chest as if she feared the other woman would try to take it. "I'll just check this one out and be on my way. I do not have the patience for that woman today or any day, for that matter. I absolutely loathe her."

"Sully, a word?" Gwen called out across the water.

"Be right there, Gwen." He smiled and waved as if impervious to her glare.

Lindsey used the tablet she'd brought to check out the book Ariel had chosen. "Thanks for the support."

"Of course." Ariel grinned. "Libraries are the cornerstones of their communities. Speaking of which, when I offer my painting workshop this summer, you should sign up. We paint on small canvases and use acrylic paint so it dries quickly. If you make a mistake, you just paint over it."

Lindsey lifted her eyebrows. "Oh, I'm not the artsy type."

"Which is precisely why you should take the class," Ariel retorted as she stepped out of the boat and back onto her dock. "You and Sully could take it together as a couple's evening out."

Sully glanced at Lindsey with a small smile. "Might be fun."

Lindsey considered her husband. She knew he was a talented artist, but her not so much. Still, it would be fun to do something together. "Maybe we should."

"Excuse me!" Gwen waved again. Her voice was piercing as she was clearly at the end of her patience.

"You'd better go, before it gets unpleasant. Of course with Gwen, it's always unpleasant." Ariel began to walk up the dock. "See you in two weeks if not before."

Lindsey waved, watching as Ariel hurried from the dock to the stairs that led up to her island and disappeared among the trees that surrounded the perimeter of her home.

Sully untied the boat while Lindsey secured the bookshelf covers, before they motored the short distance to Gwen's dock. She was standing with her arms crossed over her chest, the picture of displeasure.

Sully coasted the boat right up against her dock, making

it gently rock. Lindsey hopped out and tied the boat, leaving Sully to greet the woman who was now glowering at both of them.

"Morning, Gwen," Sully greeted her. "How are you today?"

"Wondering what this is." She paused to gesture at the book boat. "It's not your usual water taxi."

"That's because it's not a water taxi," Sully said. "It's *The Jolly Reader*, a book boat like a bookmobile but a boat. It's a new service the library is offering to island residents."

"In that case, I'd like to know why you stopped at the Montgomery dock before mine." Gwen's tone was so frosty Lindsey was surprised her breath didn't plume in the air.

"We came from the west, so their dock appeared first," Sully said. His tone was very reasonable and Lindsey knew he managed his testier water taxi clients by remaining unflappable. "Also, Ariel saw us and waved us in."

Gwen's jaw was tight. "My husband and I are much more prominent residents of the Thumb Islands than *them*. I would think your first stop would be here."

"We don't have a hierarchy of residents in the islands," Sully replied. "Everyone is treated equally."

Lindsey watched in silence. Sully's words were uncharacteristically clipped, which she knew meant her husband wasn't pleased.

"Humph." Gwen let out a huff of disapproval. She turned to Lindsey and asked, "And you are?"

"My wife," Sully answered before Lindsey could. His

tone made it clear that no disrespect would be tolerated. He stepped out of the boat and gestured between them. "Lindsey, this is Gwen Capshaw."

"Nice to meet you." Lindsey held out her hand, which Gwen ignored. Lindsey decided not to take it personally and stepped back into the boat and started removing the covers on the bookshelves.

"I've heard about you. This pet project of yours was engineered to save the library." Gwen looked at the shelves of books with disdain. "Gideon Trask happens to be a friend of mine, and I think he's right. We need to cut all the waste in the town budget. I mean, what do we even need the library for? The internet can do anything the library can do much more efficiently. And I've heard that you sponsor art classes provided by talentless hacks. Why should I have to pay for that?" Gwen waved in the direction of Ariel's studio just visible through the trees.

Anger surged so hard through Lindsey's body that she thought she could feel her pupils dilate. She closed her eyes and took a deep breath just as Milton had coached her when dealing with Trask. She exhaled, feeling a teeny bit less annoyed.

"So, no books for you?" Lindsey asked.

Gwen shook her blond bob. "Of course not. If I need a book, I *buy* it. If people can't afford books, I really don't see why my tax dollars should be spent buying books for them. It's not my fault they're poor."

Lindsey slowly turned away from Gwen and knelt down to put the dry box covers back on the bookshelves. She might have snapped them in a bit more forcefully than was needed but it was all in the name of keeping the books safe. "Okay, then. I guess we can go on to our next island, honey." She kept her voice light and breezy. She might have overdone it as Sully's eyes went wide. He knew her well enough to know when she was peeved. He swiftly untied the boat and hopped in.

"Since Mrs. Capshaw sees no need for libraries, she clearly doesn't want to have us delivering the latest bestsellers right to her door, or sign up for any of our book clubs, cooking classes or our summer concert series. I'm sure she'll be just fine on her little island all alone with no community. Thankfully, the ladies of The Club feel differently and were so generous about donating the boat to our cause."

"What did you say?" Gwen snapped. "The ladies of The Club? As in Leslie Stone?"

"Yes, and Tina Baldwin, Mallory Masterson and Harper Winslow," Lindsey said. "They're the ones who funded *The Jolly Reader* for all the island residents. Speaking of which, we really need to stay on schedule."

Lindsey used her foot to shove the boat away from the dock with more force than was necessary. Sully steadied himself against the captain's chair and fired up the engine.

"Bye now!" Lindsey waved at Gwen, who stood with her mouth agape as if she had no idea why Lindsey would be so dismissive of her.

"And now I understand precisely why Ariel said she had no time for Gwen. What a horrible woman," Lindsey fumed as Sully piloted them to the next island. "I mean, she could have just said 'No thank you' when she discovered why we were there. Instead, she berated us for not making her the first stop when she had no intention of using the service and then went on and on about how she supported shutting down the library. The audacity!"

Sully reached out and took her hand in his, giving her fingers a squeeze. "Breathe."

Lindsey blew out a breath, closed her eyes and inhaled slowly through her nose. The salty scent of the sea air calmed her and she exhaled, feeling her annoyance with Gwen Capshaw diminish.

"Better?" Sully asked.

"A little." Lindsey shook her head. "I can't imagine living next door to such a rude person. Poor Ariel."

"Oh, there's more to it than rudeness," Sully said.

"You started to say that Ariel and Dane had a son before we landed . . . now you can spill the rest of it." Lindsey slid onto her seat and turned to face her husband.

"I should probably give some backstory," Sully said. "Dane Montgomery, Ariel's husband, grew up on Split Island. His parents worked for Perry Capshaw's parents, who owned the entire island. Dane's father was the caretaker of the island and his wife was the Capshaw's housekeeper. When Perry's mother passed away shortly after his father, she bequeathed the house and the smaller island to the Montgomerys for all their years of service."

"That was incredibly generous," Lindsey acknowledged.

"Yes and no," Sully said. "Perry's father was in poor

health his entire life and there was no way the Capshaws could have lived out on the island without the Montgomerys, who were on call all day, every day to take care of Mr. Capshaw. That's why there used to be a bridge between the two islands. It made for easy access for the Montgomerys to reach Mr. Capshaw."

"All day, every day is a lot," Lindsey said.

"Agreed, which is why leaving the other half of the island to them was generous but they definitely earned it," Sully said. "When Dane's parents decided to leave the cold and retire to Florida, they signed over the island to their only son, Dane, who already had his fishing charter business up and running and had no desire to move. Eventually, he met Ariel, married her, and she joined him on the island."

Lindsey nodded. "Were Dane and Perry friends?"

"My parents say they were the best of friends growing up, almost like brothers," Sully said. "Until Perry married Gwen and brought her to live on the island and then things changed."

"How so?"

"According to my mom, who knows everything about everyone in the islands . . ." Sully paused and Lindsey smiled because her mother-in-law was the information superhighway of the Thumb Islands. "Gwen wanted Perry to buy the smaller island back from Dane, but Dane refused."

"Oh." Lindsey had already figured out that Gwen was the sort who would not handle the word "no" very well.

"Exactly. Then Dane brought his bride, Ariel, to his island and the tension got worse. It peaked when Gwen and

Perry had their daughter, Jordan, just after Dane and Ariel had their son, Ryan."

"You would think they'd enjoy raising their children together," Lindsey said. "You know that it-takes-a-village thing."

"Gwen wasn't having any of that." Sully steered the boat toward the dock of their next island. "Gwen forbade Jordan from having anything to do with Ryan, so you can imagine how that turned out."

"They fell in love and ran away together," Lindsey guessed, although she was mostly teasing.

"That's exactly what they did," Sully confirmed. "Gwen blamed Dane and Ariel, naturally, and in her fury, she blew up the bridge between the two islands."

"When you say blew up—" Lindsey began but Sully interrupted her.

"Kaboom."

Lindsey's jaw dropped and she barely had the wherewithal to hop out of the boat and tie it to the dock. Once the ropes were secure, she stood and faced Sully. "But how?"

"Apparently, she got the directions on how to build a bomb from a YouTube video." Sully shrugged.

"I'm speechless," Lindsey said. "I am without speech. No wonder she's such a fan of the internet."

"It will come as no surprise to you that Ryan and Jordan left shortly after that episode and never looked back," Sully said. "No one has seen them in years." He glanced out over the water. "They were younger than me, more Mary's age group than mine, but they both seemed nice enough. I hope they made it."

Lindsey nodded. It was a story almost as tragic as *Romeo and Juliet*, except Ryan and Jordan had gotten away. Potentially.

"Lindsey! Sully! What brings you out here?" Mr. Parsons, the lone resident on Harborview Island, greeted them as he strode down the dock, carrying his fishing pole.

He was wearing shorts and a T-shirt with a red windbreaker. His thinning gray hair and pale complexion were protected from the sun by a wide-brimmed straw hat that had a variety of lures hooked into the crown. Mr. Parsons had been born and raised in this house on Harborview Island and he told anyone who listened that he planned to die here.

Lindsey wondered how much he'd seen with his view of Split Island. The two teens sneaking around? The bridge blowing up? Given the way his eyes lit up when Sully told him about the book boat, Lindsey knew she had another customer and supporter of the library, so at least there was that.

While Sully showed Mr. Parsons the books, Lindsey glanced back at Split Island. So much unnecessary pain over what? Property? Status? Control? It didn't seem worth it. Like Sully, she, too, hoped that Ryan and Jordan had made it.

Two weeks after her first journey out to the islands, Lindsey was ready for her second run. She packed the boat with a wide selection of titles, including plenty of books for the kids who spent their summer out on the islands. She'd managed to fill all the requests she'd taken on her previous trip and she now had her tablet enabled to check out and take new requests in real time so she didn't have to wait until she returned to the library to process holds and loans.

Before departure, she emailed Leslie to keep her in the loop as to the book boat's progress. She was gratified to get an enthusiastic response from the woman she found more than a little intimidating.

Sully was again her captain on *The Jolly Reader* and they stopped at Bell Island first, where Sully's parents resided. The Sullivans owned one of the four houses on the island and they, along with their neighbors, met Sully and Lindsey on the main dock.

"How is the book boat business?" Mike, Sully's father, asked. "Keeping afloat?"

He laughed at his own dad joke and Joan, Sully's mother, rolled her eyes. "He's been waiting all morning to say that."

Lindsey grinned. In the in-law department, she had hit the jackpot, even factoring in Mike's horrible dad jokes.

"I invited the neighbors down to meet you because I heard Gideon Trask is claiming that this book boat is being paid for with our taxes," Joan said. She glanced over her shoulder at one man in particular. "Is that true, Lindsey?"

"No." Lindsey shook her head. "The membership ladies of The Club were actually the ones to sponsor the book boat."

"Isn't that interesting, Damon?" Joan asked the man, standing off to the side.

Damon stepped forward and shook his head. "All right, Joan, you've made your point. The book boat isn't being funded by our taxes. Still, there is a lot of waste in our town and Gideon isn't wrong that it needs to be rooted out."

He sounded very passionate and Lindsey knew there was nothing she could say that would change his mind, so she decided to offer him something to think about instead. "If you were to cut waste in your own household budget, how would you do it?"

Damon frowned. "I'd go over the budget and eliminate what was wasteful."

"And if you had a very complicated budget?" Lindsey tapped her chin with her finger in a thoughtful pose.

"I'd hire an accountant," Damon said.

"Not a town councilman with a vested interest in lowering his property tax?" Lindsey asked.

Damon blinked at her then he nodded. "I see what you did there."

Mike clapped Damon on the shoulder and said, "Why don't you see what books she's brought? I bet she has some of those thrillers by Jack Carr that you like so well."

"Jack Carr? Why didn't you say so?" Damon asked Lindsey with a grin.

Lindsey watched Damon climb aboard the boat, feeling as if she was winning over the islanders one reader at a time.

"Looks like you acquired another supporter for the book boat," Joan whispered behind her hand. "Leave me some flyers with its schedule and I'll make sure they make their way through the islands."

"Thanks, Joan, you're the best." Lindsey handed her the bright colored flyers Paula had made up with the schedule and all of the events happening at the library this summer. Gideon Trask might win in the end but Lindsey wasn't going to make it easy for him.

The stop quickly became a flurry of checking out and Lindsey was thrilled with the enthusiasm of the residents. Sully's parents invited them for Sunday dinner and Lindsey and Sully eagerly agreed. Sully's dad was an amazing cook and it was always a treat to enjoy whatever he conjured out of his kitchen.

Now that Lindsey was visiting the islands every two weeks, she wanted to get to know the island residents as well as she did the villagers. As Sully had said, his mother was the information superhighway of the islands and Lindsey wanted to tap that knowledge to know what to bring on her next visit. Bestsellers were easy to supply but she wanted to know who the gardeners were, who liked cooking, which residents wanted to borrow puzzles or board games, and that sort of thing. Sunday dinner would be an opportunity to tailor the boat's inventory to the islanders specifically.

"Did they clean us out?" Sully asked as they shoved off Bell Island and made their way to their next stop, Split Island.

"No, but they put a nice dent in the collection." Lindsey smiled. The breeze was cool and the sun was warm. June was one of her favorite months in Briar Creek as the weather was gorgeous but the summer residents hadn't arrived yet so it was still quiet in the village. She suspected the book boat would only get busier as many of the part-time summer residents returned.

"I assume we're stopping at Ariel's dock and avoiding Gwen's?" she asked.

"You did make it clear that you didn't think Gwen needed library services of any kind," Sully said.

Lindsey frowned. She wasn't the type to flounce by nature and she knew she'd had a bit of a fit when Gwen had said she didn't want her tax dollars spent on the library. Gwen's support of Gideon Trask's agenda had peeved Lindsey to no end. Her reaction to Gwen hadn't sat right with Lindsey for the past two weeks.

"I suppose I should try again," Lindsey said. "Maybe I can win her over if we stop by her dock first."

"Are you sure?" Sully asked. "Because I've known Gwen a long time and she has never been what I would call pleasant to deal with. I think she's only polite to me because she uses the taxi when her husband takes the boat and she needs to go somewhere."

"So what you're saying is that her relationships with people are transactional?" Lindsey asked. "She's only nice if she wants something?"

"That sounds about right."

"Then I have to try and make her want something from the library." Lindsey glanced at the island with the two docks. "I don't know how much sway she has with Trask but maybe if I change her mind, she'll encourage him to stop trying to cut funding for the library."

"I suppose it's worth a shot." He maneuvered the boat toward the Capshaw side of Split Island. Lindsey shielded her eyes with her hand as she searched the dock, hoping Gwen would have a change of heart and make an appearance. Judging by Sully's dubious expression, she doubted it.

Lindsey scanned the titles of the books she had left. She knew that if someone were trying to win her over all they'd have to do was offer her a good book. Which one of these would appeal to Gwen? She had a mystery by Deanna Raybourn, a romantic comedy by Jen DeLuca, and a fantasy from Kevin Hearne. Surely, one of those would appeal to her. Then again, maybe she was a nonfiction reader. Lindsey sifted through the titles until she found the latest positive-lifestyle book by Tabitha Brown and added it to the pile. There had to be something here that spoke to Gwen.

Sully pulled up alongside the dock. No one appeared to greet them. Lindsey glanced at Sully and asked, "Do you think they're away?"

He frowned. "Their boat is here. I suppose they could have been picked up by someone else, but . . ."

He scanned the island and Lindsey did, too. This was such a new venture there was no protocol. Should she take the stairs from the dock up to the island and knock on their door? Would that be too intrusive? She didn't know.

From their vantage point below the island, they could just make out the upper story and roof of the house. She didn't see anyone, so she decided to make an executive decision.

"I'm going to just pop up the stairs and wave from the upper deck to see if anyone is home."

"Do you want me to come with you?" Sully hopped out of the boat and tied it next to the Capshaws' motorboat.

"No, if no one is there, we can just go to Ariel's." Lindsey gestured to the neighboring dock.

"Give me a shout if you need me." Sully took the book selections from her arms and held out his hand to help her step onto the dock. Lindsey retrieved the books from him and hurried up the steps to the small deck above.

The Capshaws' upper deck was built on top of the rocky cliffs that made up the sides of the island. Lindsey supposed they'd put the stairs and deck here because the shallow cove gave their dock some protection from storms. The Montgomerys had the same setup on the other side of the cove—the two docks, stairs and upper platforms were almost mirror images of each other.

The Capshaw upper deck had two Adirondack chairs and several pots of petunias in full bloom, giving the space a homey feel. It was cheerful, which didn't jibe with the taciturn Gwen that Lindsey had met two weeks before but maybe that was because Gwen's feelings had been hurt. Lindsey tried to see it from that angle even though it had felt like a manufactured affront on Gwen's part at the time.

Lindsey cradled the books in her arms, hoping that Gwen could be swayed to see the importance of the library. If she felt Lindsey was trying, maybe Gwen would meet her halfway and become an advocate for library services. Gwen had been surprised that the ladies of The Club were sponsoring the book boat; perhaps that would encourage her to rethink her position on libraries. It was a long shot but Lindsey had to give it her all. She was fighting for the library, after all, and personal feelings had to be put aside for the greater good.

Lindsey glanced across the manicured lawn to the two-story modern building perched on the far side of the small island. Flowers circled the perimeter of the house and the yard. Fountains and bird feeders were abundant and tucked into the foliage. The sound of the birds singing was loud and joyous and Lindsey watched in fascination as a variety of songbirds flitted from feeder to feeder. Darn it, she should have brought some books on birds or backyard gardens or even a mystery with a birder as the amateur sleuth.

"Hello?" she called across the yard. Other than startling the birds into flight, there was no response. She waited and then tried again, cradling her books in one arm and offering a big wave with her other. "Hello? Is anyone home?"

No one answered. There was no sign of Gwen or her husband. Lindsey debated crossing the lawn to knock on the door but given how poorly her last conversation with Gwen had gone, she felt that might be considered pushy. She would just have to try again in two weeks.

She turned to go when she caught sight of something blue tucked in behind the pink rose bushes. This was not the sort of hydrangea blue one found in nature in Connecticut. This was a tropical aqua color and had no business being tucked in among the pink summer roses.

Lindsey put the books down on the table between the two chairs and crossed the corner of the yard until she was in front of the rose bushes. Pops of bright blue were visible through the leaves and she crouched down trying to get a better look. The foliage was thick and when she reached forward to push a branch aside the thorns snagged her palm and she jerked her hand back.

Spots of blood appeared on her palm and she hissed. She didn't have anything to clean up with so she pressed her palms together and raised her hands over her head to try to stop the bleeding. She sighed, feeling annoyed with herself. Most likely whatever was back there was some sort of watering system or fertilizer mechanism and here she was being nosy and now she had a bloody hand. She pushed up to her feet. Sully had a first aid kit in the boat. She could clean her hand and bandage it with that.

She stepped away from the roses when her eye was caught by what appeared to be a shoe, poking out from beneath the lowest branch of leaves. Lindsey felt her heart thump in her chest. She swallowed and sank back down to the ground, hoping that it was something else, anything else.

A second glance and she noted it was an off-white espadrille with a smear of mud across the toe and along the side. Had someone dropped their shoe back there? Kicked it beneath the bushes somehow? The rose bushes were dangerously close to the rocky edge of the island and Lindsey couldn't imagine how a shoe had gotten left there.

Forgetting about her punctured palm, Lindsey pressed herself close to the ground, trying to peer beneath the thick foliage. Bees were buzzing all over the pungent blooms and Lindsey remembered how she had come to dislike the smell of roses a few years ago, having had to run for her life in a massive rose garden maze. She pushed away the memory and carefully crept closer. Wondering if there was a person who belonged to the shoe and the bright blue patches of color she could see, she whispered, "Hello?"

There was no response. She reached into her pocket for

her phone but remembered she'd left it on the boat. She wanted to call Sully to come up here but she didn't want to leave in case there was a person in some sort of distress lying behind the bushes.

Lindsey crawled to the end of the line of roses, hoping to see behind them. Their fragrance was thick under the warm sun. She took a deep breath through her mouth and moved closer to the edge. She glanced at the rocky ground behind the bushes and immediately recognized the short blond bob. Gwen Capshaw! She was lying ten feet away on her side on the narrow rock ledge that gave way to a sheer thirty-foot drop into the cove below. There was no room for Lindsey to crawl along the edge to reach Gwen. The rock ledge was too narrow and the bushes would be impossible to get past with their thorny branches.

"Gwen!" Lindsey cried. "Can you hear me?"

Gwen didn't respond. How the heck had she gotten behind the roses? Did she stumble, hit her head and black out?

Lindsey scurried back around the bushes, hoping to find an opening to get through. There was none. The bushes were thick with thorny branches and when she reached under one to try to shake Gwen, she couldn't reach her and her arm was punctured and scratched and started bleeding just like her hand.

Lindsey ignored the pain and lay flat on her stomach. She reached farther until her fingers closed on Gwen's bare arm. Her skin was cold to the touch, and Lindsey felt her stomach lurch. How long had Gwen been on that ledge? Overnight?

"Lindsey!" Sully came jogging toward her. "Is everything all right?"

Lindsey scuttled back from the bushes and pushed up to her feet. She shook her head and reached out to him. When he grabbed her hand, she pulled him down to the ground with her.

"I found Gwen." Her voice was shaky but she pressed on. "Sully, I think she's dead."

"What?" Sully hunkered low and reached under the bushes just as Lindsey had until he grasped Gwen's wrist in his hand. He pressed his fingers to the inside of her wrist, searching for her pulse. Then he shoved his way deeper into the roses, ignoring the thorns that tore his clothing and scratched his skin. He moved his hand to place his fingers on the base of her throat, but an object protruding out of her chest stopped him.

Sully took his phone out of his pocket and turned on the flashlight feature. The shade under the bushes made it impossible to see clearly. He swept the light over Gwen's body, pausing on the wooden handle that stuck out from her body. A puddle of red soaked the fabric around the wooden handle.

"She's been stabbed." Sully moved the light over her

face. Gwen's eyes were shut and she appeared in peaceful repose. "Fatally, I'm afraid."

"Oh, no." Lindsey shook her head as if she could reject what they had found and make it not true.

Sully pushed his way deeper into the rose bush and gently placed a hand on Gwen's chest to see if she was breathing. After a moment, his head drooped and Lindsey knew Gwen was dead.

With his arm caught by the rose's thorns, Sully had to work his way out. With his free hand, he held out his phone to Lindsey. "Call Emma, please."

Lindsey took the phone and with shaky fingers she opened the contacts list and pressed the name of the chief of police—Emma Plewicki. Emma picked up on the second ring.

"Sully, how are—" Emma answered but Lindsey interrupted.

"It's not Sully, it's me, Lindsey." Something in her voice must have given away her distress because Emma immediately started firing questions at her.

"What's wrong? Where are you? Is Sully okay?"

"Sully's fine, but we're out on the book boat on Split Island and Gwen Capshaw is not okay," Lindsey said.

"Explain."

"We found her on the ground behind some rose bushes in her yard. She has no pulse and she's not breathing and there's a knife lodged in her chest." Lindsey inhaled, trying to keep it together. "Emma, she's dead."

"I'm on my way," Emma said. "Hold tight. Do not move the body or touch anything in the surrounding area."

"We won't."

"Call me immediately if anything should come up. Is her husband there?" Emma asked.

Lindsey glanced at the house. "I don't think so. I only went to the upper deck when I saw the color of her clothes, which didn't fit with the bushes. When I went closer, I found her. Their boat is here. Do you want me to check the house or the yard to see if he's here?"

"Just knock on the front door and see if he answers." Emma's breath was rapid and Lindsey knew she was running for the police boat in the marina. "Unless you have a reason to go in the house, don't. If her husband is there, don't let him near Gwen. In fact, have Sully check the house just in case Perry answers."

"All right."

"I'll be there in fifteen minutes, twenty tops."

The call ended and Lindsey pocketed the phone. She glanced at Sully. His arm was bleeding from multiple scratches and his shirt sported a few small tears. One particularly nasty branch wasn't letting go of him, so Lindsey reached forward and carefully removed the thorns from the back of his shirt.

"Thanks." Sully grabbed her hand and squeezed. "Are you all right?"

Lindsey nodded. She wasn't but this wasn't about her. "Emma is on her way. She suggested you check the house for Mr. Capshaw."

Sully glanced past her and nodded. "I doubt he's home or he would have come out, but I'll knock to make sure."

"Emma said not to go inside unless you had a reason to and to try not to disturb anything. I'll wait here with Gwen." Lindsey couldn't make herself say *the body.*

Sully patted her shoulder and strode to the house. Lindsey watched him rap on the wooden door. He stepped to the side and peered through the window. He knocked again. In moments he was back.

"Perry isn't home." He glanced at the rose bushes and his brow furrowed. He took Lindsey's hand and said, "I think we should stand back. We've undoubtedly contaminated the scene already but we should at least try not to make it worse."

Lindsey followed him to the upper deck, where she'd left her stack of books. She scanned the water looking for the Briar Creek police boat. Where was Emma? How much time had passed? Who had stabbed Gwen? How long had she been there? The questions ricocheted through Lindsey's brain like pinballs.

Sully pulled her into a half hug and kissed the top of her head. "Hey, it's going to be all right."

"I just feel awful," Lindsey said. "The last time I saw her I was not nice. She struck a nerve about the library's funding and I lashed back. It was not my finest moment."

"You were extremely professional. The truth is Gwen could be prickly," Sully said. There was no judgment in his voice, just truth. "You're not the only one who's had words with her and it appears someone had more than words."

Lindsey sighed and leaned against him. "I still feel terrible."

Sully held her close and rubbed her back, offering comfort. They stood like that until the sound of a boat motor broke through the chatter of the seagulls riding on the ocean breeze. Lindsey spotted the police boat as it rounded the western side of the island. Emma was here.

"Should we go down?" she asked.

Sully shook his head. "I think we should stay with Gwen. Emma has Officer Kirkland with her. She won't be long."

The sound of another boat interrupted the quiet and Lindsey felt her heart jump. Could it be Gwen's husband? It wasn't. She recognized the crime scene personnel immediately.

"How did Emma get the crime scene techs here so fast?" Lindsey asked.

"I'm guessing they were at a meeting together," he said. "Usually, it takes them hours to get out to the islands."

Emma hopped off the boat and hit the dock at a run, leaving Officer Kirkland to tie up their boat. Officer Wilcox, who'd been driving the second boat, waved his passengers on as he tied up their boat.

The two crime scene investigators, Dr. Rogers and his assistant, Callie Bristow, followed Emma at a brisk pace, carrying their equipment with them. Lindsey had met the overly serious Dr. Rogers with his bushy brown beard going gray and his dark framed glasses and found him to be exceedingly serious about his profession, which was a good thing, she supposed. But his assistant, the twenty-something Callie with the dragonfly tattoo on her neck and her thick dark hair, perpetually styled into a ball on the top of her head, was much easier for Lindsey to relate to. Callie had the ability to say the most inappropriate thing at the worst possible moments and Lindsey rather liked her for it. Also, Callie had become a regular library patron over the past couple of years and her love of manga and graphic novels had informed Beth as to what to buy for the collection.

"Emma, she's over here." Sully gestured to the rose bushes as Emma stepped onto the upper deck.

"Show me." Emma squeezed Lindsey's arm in greeting as she walked by, and Lindsey nodded in return. Emma had been the Briar Creek chief of police for years and had become one of Lindsey's closest friends. With her heart-shaped face and thick dark hair, Emma was an attractive woman, which led many criminals to underestimate her fierce intelligence. Lindsey knew better.

"Lindsey, how are you?" Dr. Rogers wheezed as he reached the top step. His brow was sweaty and his face red.

"You need to work out more, Doc," Callie said as she elbowed him aside. "Lindsey, how are you? Isn't it a beautiful day? I was psyched we got to come out to the islands."

Dr. Rogers pinched the bridge of his nose beneath his glasses and said, "Callie, we're here to examine a body. Adjust your enthusiasm for the weather to an appropriate appreciation, please."

Callie grimaced. "Sorry." She glanced at Lindsey. "I mean that the weather is nice despite the horrible circumstances that bring us here." She glanced at Dr. Rogers in question and he nodded.

He turned and left the deck to join Sully and Emma beside Gwen's body.

Callie leaned close to Lindsey and whispered, "Can you imagine living out here? I mean, look at this view. It's stunning and you'd have no pesky neighbors, no traffic, just the sound of nature to soothe your soul." She heaved a deep sigh. "Of course, if a murderer comes for you there's no one to save you, so there's that."

"There's that," Lindsey echoed as Callie stepped off the deck to join the others.

Lindsey glanced around the island. It was ringed with trees, as many of the islands were, to protect the house from inclement weather. The lawn was small but lushly green and the flower beds surrounding the lawn were in a riot of color. It really was picturesque with the modern two-story house perched behind it as if it were added as an afterthought.

Lindsey wondered what it would have been like to grow up out here. She knew from Sully's stories what his childhood on the islands had been like and truthfully it sounded magical. But from what he'd told her about Split Island, she wasn't so sure that the Capshaws and the Montgomerys had enjoyed the same experience.

She glanced at the smaller neighboring island. How would Ariel and Dane feel when they learned what had happened over here? Lindsey thought that the sight of the police boat would have brought someone out to the dock to find out what was happening, but it remained empty.

"What are you thinking?" Sully rejoined her on the deck.

"That it feels weird that no one from the other side of the island has noticed that the police boat came out here," Lindsey said.

Sully glanced at the Montgomerys' half of Split Island. "Maybe they didn't hear the boat."

"Ariel heard our boat when we arrived the other day." Lindsey met his gaze.

"Maybe, like Perry, they're not home," Sully said. His tone was reasonable and Lindsey nodded. He was probably right.

Officers Kirkland and Wilcox stepped onto the platform from the stairs. Kirkland was a robust redhead, who'd been on the force for years, but not as long as Officer Wilcox. They both nodded to Lindsey and Sully as they joined the chief and the crime scene techs.

"Should we stay?" Lindsey asked Sully. "I feel as if we're in the way and we need to get going if we're going to visit any more islands."

"You can leave as soon as we take your statements," Emma answered for Sully as she joined them. "Officer Kirkland will take them. We'll try to be as quick as we can so you can get back out there."

"I don't want to rush you," Lindsey said. It felt heartless to worry about her book boat when a woman was lying murdered just yards away. But in truth, it wasn't so much about the book boat as it was her desire to get out of there. She'd dealt with enough dead bodies to last a lifetime. She had no interest in dealing with any more, especially if it was a murder.

"I appreciate that, but I also know that The Club is funding the book boat so you need to be consistent and show up." Emma's expression was grim. "With Trask trying to cut the budget to all of our departments, we need to keep our alternative resources coming in."

It was a grim reminder of the current precarious position of the library as well as the other town departments.

"Um, Emma, looks like Perry Capshaw is here." Sully gestured to a boat motoring toward the island.

Emma took a bracing breath. "I hate this part."

She straightened her broad-brimmed hat and started down the stairs to meet Perry on the dock. Lindsey watched from above, partly to be ready to assist if Emma needed help but also because, and Lindsey had to be honest with herself about this, she was curious to see how Perry Capshaw would respond to the news of his wife's death.

"I don't envy her that task." Sully's voice was low as if he couldn't imagine being the recipient of such horrible news. Lindsey squeezed his hand with hers.

"Emma has had a lot of practice with this sort of thing," Lindsey said. "But the Capshaws were married for a long time, yes?"

"Has to be about forty years," Sully said. "Their daughter, Jordan, is in her midthirties like my sister, Mary."

"Jordan's been gone a long time then?" Lindsey asked.

"Over fifteen years."

"Do you think she's maintained contact with her father?"

Sully shrugged. "I don't know, but I imagine he'll have to reach out to her to tell her."

They both glanced down at the incoming boat. Perry Capshaw was tall and lanky as he sat in the passenger seat of the small motorboat. He was wearing a ball cap and sunglasses and sported a neatly trimmed beard. His clothing was loose, a pair of khakis with a white T-shirt and an unbuttoned blue plaid flannel over it. The person piloting the boat was slighter in stature, also wearing a hat and sunglasses, and when they turned the boat, Lindsey noted it was a woman.

As the boat drew closer to the dock, Perry greeted Emma with a smile of welcome that shifted into a frown of concern. He hopped onto the dock and Emma spoke to the pilot of the small watercraft. The woman waved as Emma gave the boat a push and the woman steered the boat back out of the cove.

Lindsey and Sully watched Emma reach up and put her hand on Perry's shoulder in a gesture of comfort while she spoke to him. Perry glanced from Emma up to the deck where Lindsey and Sully stood. In a blink, he was running for the stairs with Emma calling after him.

"Mr. Capshaw, Perry, wait!" Emma spread her hands wide and then gestured for Sully to block the stairs. Sully moved into position and Lindsey stood behind him, feeling terrible. She'd never met Mr. Capshaw and she had no idea what to say to him so she said nothing.

"Move aside, Sully," Mr. Capshaw ordered. He stared past Sully to where Dr. Rogers and Callie were taking photos and collecting anything that might be considered evidence as to what had happened here.

Sully didn't budge. "I can't, Perry. The investigators are

examining the scene . . . er . . . situation and we can't interrupt them."

"The hell I can't!" Perry spluttered. "That's my wife!" His voice broke on the last word and he lurched forward.

Sully caught him by the shoulders and guided him to one of the deck chairs. Emma popped up onto the deck as Sully assisted Perry into a seat. The poor man sat hunched over his knees as if he was trying to catch his breath.

After a moment, Perry pulled his hat off, revealing a thick head of white hair. Against his deeply tanned skin, it was quite striking and Lindsey realized that the Capshaws had made quite a complementary pair.

"I'm sorry," Emma said. "The team will be done shortly and you can see Gwen."

Perry glanced up at her with a bewildered expression. His dark eyes were full of questions. But when he spoke, he only had one word. "How?"

Emma sat in the chair beside his and leaned in. Her eyes were full of compassion when she said, "It appears she was stabbed."

Perry swallowed. "Who?"

"We don't know." Emma gestured to Sully and Lindsey. "They found her body but didn't see anyone else on the island. Do you know of anyone else who may have been here this morning?"

Perry shook his head. "Andrea picked me up at dawn to go set up osprey perches in the marsh with our team. No one was here besides Gwen, and she was sleeping when I left." He glanced at Sully. "Why did you come here?"

"My wife, Lindsey, is running a book boat, a lending library, to the islands. We stopped by to see if Gwen was interested in borrowing any books."

Perry's eyebrows lifted in surprise. "I'm surprised you came back after your last visit."

"She told you about that?" Lindsey asked.

"Oh, yeah." Mr. Capshaw nodded his head. "She had a lot to say about your venture, particularly about how you were being sponsored by The Club."

Lindsey wasn't sure what to make of that. Did he mean Gwen had a lot to say as in she was angry that Lindsey had been so rude or was it more?

He gazed at the rose bushes, trying to get a glimpse of his wife. His right leg jogged up and down as if he had to release some energy or he'd fly apart. Lindsey wondered how long he'd have to wait until he could see his wife.

"Perry, do you have any gardeners, household staff or anyone who might have been here today?" Emma asked.

"Thursdays." He nodded. "The landscaper and a cleaning woman come on Thursdays. They're a married couple who've worked for us for years, ever since . . ."

His voice trailed off and he rose to his feet. He moved across the deck until he was standing on the side that faced the Montgomerys' island.

"Ever since when?" Emma followed him.

"Since the Montgomerys stopped working for my parents, which was right when *they* inherited the house over there."

Emma nodded in understanding. Clearly, she knew

about the feud. "Did you see either of the Montgomerys today before you left?"

Perry shot her a questioning glance. "You're not saying . . . ?"

"I'm not saying anything." Emma held her hands out in a calming gesture. "I am merely trying to ascertain the whereabouts of anyone in the vicinity during the time when Gwen was stabbed."

A shudder rippled through Perry from head to toe. "Can I see her now?" His tone was pleading and Emma considered him for a moment.

"All right, but let's not disturb the investigators."

"Of course not," Perry agreed. They crossed the lawn and Lindsey and Sully followed them.

Dr. Rogers and Callie had moved Gwen's body from behind the bushes. She was tucked into a body bag with just her face visible.

Perry dropped to his knees beside his wife and sobbed. "Oh, my dearest girl." His hand shook as he reached out and brushed a lock of her blond hair off her forehead in a gesture so tender, it made Lindsey's throat draw tight. Sully shifted on his feet beside her and she knew he was responding to the same raw emotion coming from Perry. It was devastating.

Dr. Rogers and Emma moved out of earshot while Callie stood with Perry as he sobbed over his wife. Instead of her usual lack of tact, Callie knelt beside Perry, offering him her support.

"We'll have to take the body to the lab to run more

tests," Dr. Rogers said. "But we did remove the implement that caused her death."

"Really?" Emma asked. "What was it?"

"A palette knife." Dr. Rogers held up an evidence bag. "You know the sort of knife an artist uses to mix paint."

"Can't imagine where such a thing would have come from unless one of the Capshaws is a painter," Dr. Rogers said. "In all my years as a medical examiner, I've never seen anyone stabbed with a palette knife."

Lindsey felt her stomach bottom out. Ariel. Ariel was an artist. Her studio was on the next island. She'd said she had no use for Gwen. Lindsey glanced at Sully and found him studying the neighboring island and she knew he was thinking the same thing.

"I'll talk to Perry and see if he recognizes it," Emma said. "We'll need to check it for fingerprints or any other DNA."

"Of course," Dr. Rogers said.

"Was there anything else?" Emma asked.

"Nothing as significant. The rest of our findings will have to be studied at the lab."

"I have a question," Lindsey said. Both Emma and Dr. Rogers turned to her and she realized that she wasn't in a position to ask questions, but she had found the body and that felt as if it should count for something. "How or why was she behind the rose bushes? I mean, did she crawl there herself to hide or did the killer put her there on purpose?"

Emma turned to Dr. Rogers. "It's a good question."

Dr. Rogers stroked his beard and pushed his glasses up

on his nose. "It *is*. Unfortunately, I don't have an answer as yet. Callie is examining the area surrounding the body, seeking evidence of another person, but, again, we won't know until we go over what we've gathered."

Lindsey felt Sully squeeze her shoulder and she knew he was trying to comfort her. It helped a little but she knew it would be a long time before she forgot how distraught Perry had been to find his wife dead.

"Come on, I'll walk you guys down to your boat." Emma led the way down the stairs. "I know you have other islands to visit and it appears we'll be here for a while."

"I can cancel . . ." Lindsey offered.

"No need," Emma said. She stepped onto the dock and waited for them to join her. "If you can drop by the station later, we'll take your official statements then."

"Will do," Sully agreed.

"Hi, Lindsey! Sully!" A voice called to them and Lindsey turned to see Ariel standing on her dock, waving at them.

Lindsey glanced at Emma, who frowned as she took in Ariel's paint-splattered overalls and the paintbrush in her hand.

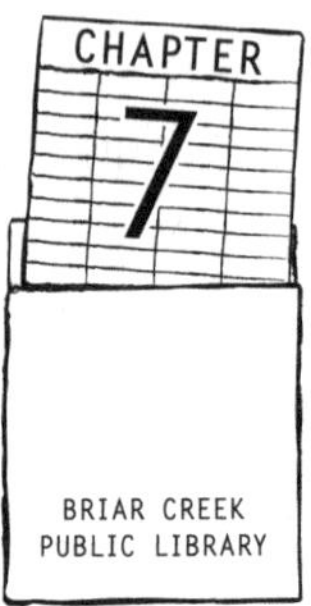

Hi, Ariel," Emma called back. "Mind if I come on over and talk to you for a minute?" Without waiting for Ariel to answer, Emma turned to Sully. "Give me a lift."

"Okay." Sully glanced at Lindsey and she suspected she looked as uneasy as he did.

Ariel's career as an artist had blossomed over the past couple of years. With galleries in Greenwich and New York demanding her work, she was finally getting recognized for her talent. The fact that the weapon used to kill Gwen had been a palette knife didn't look good for Ariel, especially given the long-running animosity between the two women.

Did Lindsey believe that Ariel had anything to do with Gwen's death? Absolutely not.

But it was extremely awkward that she had heard Ariel mention how much she loathed Gwen and that there was bad blood between the two families and everyone knew about it.

Emma hopped into *The Jolly Reader* while Lindsey untied the boat. Sully held out his hand to assist Lindsey aboard and they motored gently to the neighboring dock. Ariel caught the craft as it sidled up to her dock and Lindsey tossed her the rope. If Ariel found it odd that the chief of police was with them, she didn't say anything.

"I can't believe it's been two weeks since you were here," Ariel said. "I haven't finished the book I borrowed last time." She waved her paintbrush in the air. "I've been inspired."

"That's all right," Lindsey said. "Loan time is four weeks, so take your time."

"Hey, Emma," Ariel greeted the chief as Emma stepped onto the dock. "Are you joining the book boat to do community outreach? It must be nice to get out of the station for a bit."

"Actually, no." Emma crossed her arms over her chest. "I'm out here on official business."

"Oh." Ariel grimaced. "Sorry. That can't be good. Anything I can do to help?"

Emma nodded. "I have a few questions for you."

Ariel glanced at Lindsey and Sully as they stepped onto the dock before she returned her attention to the chief. "Okay."

"Have you been home all morning?"

"Yes, I've been painting in my studio since Dane left to take out a fishing charter." Ariel tipped her head to the side. "Why?"

"Did you see anyone arrive or depart from the Capshaws'?" Emma asked.

"No." Ariel shook her head. "But that's not surprising as my studio is on the far side of our island facing away from the split." She studied Emma and then Sully and Lindsey. "What's going on? I'm getting a really weird vibe off all of you."

Emma considered her for a moment and then said, "Gwen Capshaw is dead."

Ariel's mouth dropped open and she blinked. "What?"

"I'm sorry. I know she was your neighbor and it must be a shock." Emma studied Ariel's face, observing her reaction.

"How?" Ariel asked. "How did she die? Does Jordan know? Does Perry?"

"Yes, Perry knows and I'm sure he'll contact their daughter." Emma took a card out of her pocket and handed it to Ariel. "I'm not at liberty to say anything else, but if you think of anything you heard or saw today that was out of the ordinary, please give me a call."

Ariel nodded. Her eyes were wide and her face pale as if she couldn't comprehend what Emma had told her. She glanced at the Capshaws' side of the island and her brow furrowed in what could have been confusion or possibly regret.

"Why don't you take Emma back and I'll wait here with Ariel?" Lindsey asked Sully.

"Sure. I'll be right back," he agreed.

Emma glanced at Lindsey, giving her a stern look that

indicated Lindsey should not say anything about the particulars of finding Gwen—particularly the palette knife in Gwen's chest—to Ariel. Lindsey nodded in understanding.

Lindsey untied the boat and gave it a shove in the direction of the neighboring dock. Lindsey turned back to Ariel to find her staring after Emma. She turned to Lindsey with a frown and said, "It's bad, isn't it?"

Lindsey nodded. Knowing that she couldn't talk about Gwen's death, she gestured to Ariel's island and asked, "Is the offer of a tour of your studio still available? It looks like I have a few minutes."

"Yeah, of course, sure," Ariel said. "Standing here isn't going to do much good, is it?"

She turned and walked up the dock toward the stairs that led up to the Montgomery side of Split Island. Much like Gwen and Perry's, the perimeter of the island was surrounded by trees, but where the Capshaws had a lawn and flower beds, the Montgomerys had a thriving garden consisting of raised beds that filled the yard.

Tomato plants that were just beginning to grow were supported by round trellises in the first one. A variety of lettuces and greens filled the next section, and a profusion of other vegetables that were just beginning to sprout filled the remaining rectangular bed.

Closer to the house was an herb garden and Lindsey noted the mint and lavender were already thriving, as well as a patch of basil and a myriad of other pungent herbs. She took a deep breath and let the scent of the sun-warmed plants calm her frazzled nerves.

Two cushioned swinging chairs hung from chains on the sheltered porch, overlooking the garden, and Lindsey thought it was about as perfect a reading space as she had ever seen. Ariel led her down a cobblestone pathway around the side of the gray-shingled cottage to a smaller replica of the house. It had sliding doors that were open and Lindsey wondered if it was an old shed they had converted into a studio.

"This used to be a storage shed," Ariel confirmed. "But Dane said I needed a space to work that was separate from the house so that I could separate work life and personal life. The lines are blurry as I'm always thinking about work, but it does help to keep the two separated."

The studio was one open room with large windows that looked out at the sea. Stacks and stacks of canvases were propped against one wall while the other was composed of a large shelving unit full of paints, brushes, palettes and other assorted materials. On an easel in front of the windows was a large canvas and Lindsey crossed the room to stand in front of it.

"It's not finished yet," Ariel said. "I use oil paint, which takes a long time to dry, which means I have plenty of time to overthink my work." There was a note of anxiety in her voice as if she was worried about what Lindsey thought of the piece.

It was a dramatic painting full of swirls of blue in a variety of shades. Lindsey stared at it for a long time and then she turned to Ariel and said, "I feel as if I'm drowning in it but it's not scary or sad. It's a welcome feeling."

A small sad smile curved Ariel's lips. "That's exactly how you're supposed to feel when you look at it. Sometimes I just feel as if life is too much and it's too hard and I just can't do another day and I want to disappear but not in a horrible way, rather I want to be embraced back into the flow and surrender to the beauty that is life."

They stood silently, taking in the piece until Ariel broke the silence. "I can't believe she's gone."

Lindsey didn't know what to say. *I'm sorry* felt wrong given that Ariel had said she loathed Gwen. But still, it had to be a shock to have her neighbor of so many years die so suddenly.

"Do you want to call Dane?" Lindsey asked.

Ariel shook her head. "I don't want to bother him when he's working and there's nothing he can do."

Lindsey knew she'd feel the same way. When Sully was out on the water, she didn't like to bother him, knowing he'd spend the day fretting and be unable to do anything to help her.

"It wasn't natural causes, was it?" Ariel asked.

Lindsey knew Emma wouldn't want her to confirm or deny so she shrugged. "I suppose we'll know soon enough."

Ariel studied her expression and then began to pace. "Don't take this the wrong way, Lindsey, but you're terrible at evasion, truly just the worst."

"I know." Lindsey shrugged. "Most of the time, it's not a bad thing. But I really can't share any information."

"I understand, I do," Ariel said. "I just . . . Gwen never liked me. When Dane and I got married and I arrived on our island, I had this crazy idea that my husband's best friend, Perry, would have a wife I could become dear friends with and that it would be the four of us against the world, growing old together. I was so wrong. That woman hated me from the day I moved in and there was nothing I could do to get her to like me. Then it all just became too complicated and now it can never be fixed."

Ariel looked at the painting on the easel and Lindsey wondered if it had been inspired by Ariel's own desire to escape the strained relationships between the residents of Split Island. Was that what had been on her mind when she painted this piece? When her son ran away with the girl next door, Ariel had essentially lost her son—surely that had to bother her.

"Ready to go, Lindsey?" Sully appeared in the doorway.

"Yes. Will you be all right on your own, Ariel?" Lindsey asked. "I don't like leaving you here."

"I'll be fine." Ariel gestured to the studio around her. "I can get busy and keep my mind off things until Dane comes home. And if not, I can always call Emma. I have her number."

Lindsey squeezed her arm and said, "You can call us, too. We'll be delivering books to the islands for the next couple of hours and can come back if you need us."

"Thank you. I appreciate that." Ariel patted her hand.

"Will Dane be back soon?" Sully led the way out of the studio.

"A couple of hours," Ariel said. "They left before sunrise this morning but it wasn't a full-day charter."

Ariel led the way around the house to the garden. She glanced at the plants and Lindsey had the feeling she wasn't really seeing them. Ariel rubbed her arms as the sun passed behind the clouds and the temperature immediately dropped.

"Ariel." Sully's voice was somber. "I think you should stay in the house until Dane comes home and I would recommend keeping the doors locked and your phone near you."

Ariel's eyes went wide. "What are you saying?"

"Just that a little bit of caution until we know what happened to Gwen wouldn't be out of order." Sully's blue gaze was kind but steady.

Ariel stepped back toward her house. "I think I have some cleaning that needs to be done or I can bake some bread. Dane always enjoys his carbs after a day on the water."

"There you go." Sully's voice was full of encouragement.

They watched as Ariel let herself in the front door and waved to them. Lindsey heard the lock click and she turned to Sully. "Do you think she's in danger here?"

"No, but Emma and I agreed it's better safe than sorry." He took her hand in his and led her through the garden and down the steps to the boat waiting at the dock. "That being said, if it makes you feel better to stay with Ariel, I can do the library run on my own."

Lindsey looked at her husband in surprise. "You would do that?"

"Of course." He shrugged. "We're a team."

Lindsey hugged him. "I appreciate that more than I can

say, but I think I'd better come with you. The tablet is janky and needs to be handled with care. One more reason why the library can't afford any more budget cuts."

"Understood." Sully handed her into the boat. He untied the ropes and climbed aboard.

As Sully fired up the engine, Lindsey glanced up at the Capshaw side of the island. Perry was standing alone on the upper deck. His hands were gripping the railing as he glared down at the Montgomery house on the smaller half of the island.

A feeling of unease skittered over Lindsey's skin. Perhaps Emma and Sully had been right to have Ariel stay inside until Dane returned home. As *The Jolly Reader* skirted the island Perry Capshaw disappeared from view, but Lindsey knew she would never forget the image of him or the feeling that crawled over her skin as he loomed over the smaller island.

Lindsey and Sully finished their visits to the islands. They didn't speak of Gwen or what had happened, especially when visiting with other islanders, but Lindsey felt the weight of it pressing down on both of them as they forced smiles and made small talk with the other island residents who had no idea what had occurred. Lindsey was relieved when they finished their last stop and finally headed back to Briar Creek. She couldn't wait to find solace in her library.

Together they packed the remaining books into boxes and loaded them into the bed of Sully's pickup truck. It was a new swanky truck compared to the vintage one he used to drive. An unfortunate incident with a fence while Lindsey had been trying to flee a murderer had regrettably sent the old beater to the scrapyard.

"When do you think Emma will be back from Split Island?" Lindsey asked when Sully parked at the back of the library, giving them access to the staff entrance.

"Hard to say," he said. "Given that it's a murder investigation and all."

Lindsey nodded as she stepped out of the truck and joined him by the bed. She knew what he said was accurate but it was the first time either of them had acknowledged it so plainly.

"It's a problem for Ariel that the weapon appears to be a palette knife, isn't it?" Lindsey hefted one of the plastic tubs out of the back and set it on the ground beside the one Sully unloaded.

"It certainly looks bad, especially given the ongoing feud between the two women since Ryan and Jordan left home." Sully grabbed the remaining tubs and stacked them on top of the others.

"How long until the news leaks?" Lindsey asked. Sully had grown up in this village and he knew the gossip vine better than anyone.

"I'd say right about—"

The back door to the library banged open and Paula appeared. Her eyes were wide and she looked shocked. "Have you heard? Gwen Capshaw was found murdered on Split Island!"

"Now," Sully said.

Paula pushed a book cart out to the truck to help load up the containers of books that hadn't been borrowed as well as the ones that were being returned.

"I just can't believe it," Paula continued. "I mean, I didn't know her, but a murder on one of the islands? That's just . . . how?"

"Emma is out there investigating," Lindsey said. "If anyone can figure it out, she can."

Paula glanced from Lindsey to Sully and her eyes went even wider. She nodded, understanding immediately that they had been there when Gwen was found.

Sully hefted the boxes onto the cart. He pulled Lindsey into a half hug and kissed her head. "Call me if you need me. I'll be in my office."

"I will." Lindsey hesitated and then said, "Be careful."

Sully gave her a small smile, as if he knew that finding Gwen had rattled her, reminding her of how fragile life was. "You, too."

Lindsey and Paula unloaded the boxes onto separate book trucks in the workroom. The returns Paula would check in and the books that no one had checked out were put on another cart to be shelved by the teen workers. As Paula took her truck to the circulation desk, Lindsey disappeared into her office with a fresh cup of coffee, hoping to put the events of the day behind her as best she could.

She had entered the statistics for the book boat and was opening her email to send the numbers to the mayor when Ann Marie, her adult services librarian, appeared at her door. Ann Marie had been part-time when Lindsey became the director but Ann Marie had gotten her degree and become the adult services librarian, preparing for the day when her two sons headed off to college. Ann Marie refused to say she was going to be an *empty nester* preferring the term *free bird*.

"Sorry to interrupt you, but Leslie Stone is here to see you." Ann Marie's expression gave away nothing, giving Lindsey the impression that Leslie was right behind her.

"Oh, okay," Lindsey said. "Show her in, please."

Ann Marie stepped aside and Leslie strode into the office, leaving Ann Marie to shut the door behind her. Leslie was wearing a pretty pink floral dress with matching low-heeled mules. Her light brown hair was pinned up with a few artfully arranged curls framing her face. Her expression was serene but Lindsey sensed that all was not well, given that Leslie didn't return her smile.

"Leslie, good to see you." Lindsey stood and gestured for Leslie to take one of the chairs across from her desk. "Can I offer you water, coffee, soda?"

"No thank you." Leslie took a moment to assess the small space, the slight curl to her lip making it obvious that she clearly found it lacking.

Lindsey glanced around her office, trying to see it through Leslie's eyes. The art pieces on the walls were all done by local artists. One of the pieces, a swirl of blues and greens with flecks of bright yellow, was Ariel's. Lindsey had fallen in love with the piece at first sight. It had made her feel the same euphoria she experienced when she spotted the first crocus breaking through the ground in spring.

Her bookcase was a mix of leadership and supervisor manuals, as well as a few favorite novels. Scattered amid the books were treasured gifts from her favorite patrons, including a cheerfully painted birdhouse and a collection of seashells. She'd also put some of the crafts she'd done during her crafternoons on the shelf. Most were not display-worthy but a few had made the cut. In the middle of it all was a picture of her and Sully taken on their wedding, a snowy day in December. There were also photos of Heathcliff being goofy and Zelda eternally unimpressed.

The surface of Lindsey's desk was neat and tidy, the only tchotchke in sight was the pencil holder crafted from her niece Josie's chubby toddler hands. It tipped to one side and was painted an eye-searing shade of orange. Lindsey treasured it.

Lindsey waited while Leslie gingerly sat on the edge of her seat. Leslie's scrutiny was not just for the office; she also examined Lindsey, who had chosen to wear linen pants, comfortable shoes and a pink and blue plaid blouse for her excursion to the islands—not exactly the couture clothing she had been wearing when Leslie met her—and it was clear that Leslie found her outfit wanting as well.

Lindsey resumed her seat and folded her hands on her desk. "What can I help you with?"

"I'll get right to it," Leslie said. "The Club has some concerns."

"About?" Lindsey encouraged her to continue.

"Apparently, our book boat was at the island when Gwen Capshaw's body was found," Leslie said.

Lindsey took a deep breath. She knew Emma wouldn't want her to discuss the situation, but it appeared as if everyone in Briar Creek and the Thumb Islands already knew.

"I'm not in a position to discuss anything involving Gwen Capshaw's passing," Lindsey said. "At least, not until the police chief gives me the okay."

Leslie waved her hand. "It doesn't matter what happened."

Lindsey's eyebrows shot up.

"That came out wrong," Leslie conceded. "Of course, it matters for that poor unfortunate woman and her family, but the greater concern for me is that our sponsorship of the book boat might be tainted by being associated with the death of an islander."

"I can assure you that the book boat and its crew had nothing to do with what happened on the island," Lindsey said.

"Of course not." Leslie put her hand on her chest and the diamonds on her fingers flashed in the overhead lighting. "I didn't mean to insinuate anything."

"Then what did you mean?" Lindsey forced a smile, trying to soften the question.

"Our library sponsorship was to be a reflection of our commitment to our community. Having *The Jolly Reader* at the scene of a murder—"

"Who said it was a murder?" Lindsey interrupted.

Leslie picked a fleck of lint off her skirt and dropped it on the floor. "My husband, Arthur, is a well-known defense attorney."

Lindsey tipped her head to the side, waiting for Leslie to continue.

"People call him when they're in trouble." Leslie gave

Lindsey a pointed look. Did she think Lindsey needed her husband to represent her? Why? She didn't even know Gwen Capshaw. "People whose spouses are found unalived." Leslie waved her hand in a circular motion as if beckoning Lindsey to put it all together.

"Oh." Lindsey concluded that Perry must have called Leslie's husband. She flashed on the image of Perry staring down at the Montgomery house. Now she had a million questions for Leslie but she knew Leslie wouldn't be able to answer them as it would be privileged information.

"Exactly." Leslie stood to leave. "I'm not saying that we're going to pull our funding for the book boat but if we find that the publicity negatively impacts our relationship then we'll have to cease funding the project immediately. I'm sure you understand."

"I don't actually." Lindsey tipped her chin up. "I don't think being in a certain place at a certain time should cause any sort of negative publicity."

Leslie pursed her full lips. They were painted a deep red and she tapped her chin with her fingernail painted in a matching shade.

"Ordinarily, I would agree with you, however, the persons who discovered poor Gwen Capshaw have a reputation for stumbling across dead bodies." Lindsey found herself on the receiving end of a very uncomfortable stare. "This is something that the board of directors of The Club is simply not willing to be connected to. I'm sure you understand."

"Of course," Lindsey muttered. What else could she

say? She had run into an inordinate number of bodies over the years and, truthfully, she wasn't sure she'd want to be connected to a person like her either.

"I'm glad you understand. Let's hope they catch whoever committed this hideous crime swiftly and then we can put the entire matter behind us. I'll be in touch when I hear what the board says." Leslie sent Lindsey a little finger wave as she left the office.

Lindsey sat staring blankly at her desktop. She couldn't shake the feeling that Leslie had in a very roundabout way accused her of having something to do with Gwen Capshaw's murder just because she had been the one to find the body, which was absolutely bonkers. No. Lindsey shook her head. She was just being oversensitive because it had been a brutal day. And to think it had started with such an enthusiastic email from Leslie about the book boat's second tour. How swiftly it had all changed.

Opening her desk drawer, Lindsey took out a legal pad and a pencil from the vibrant holder on the corner of her desk. She needed to jot down what Leslie had said so that she didn't forget the important points.

She started with the most critical item, which was the library's loss of funding for the book boat. That was simply unacceptable. She then added that her own reputation for finding bodies had put the book boat at risk. That hurt her feelings, which was ridiculous; it wasn't as if she went looking for crimes or bodies or bad guys. The library was the hub of the community and she cared about the residents of Briar Creek. If someone needed help, she believed it was her job to help them, especially if they were accused of a crime they didn't commit. And her final point was that Leslie seemed to feel the sooner the case on Gwen Capshaw was closed, the better for the library and its funding from The Club. But why?

Was there a reason the murder had to be solved quickly? Wasn't it just important that it be solved? Did Leslie or the board of directors think that The Club would be dragged into the investigation just because they sponsored the book boat and Lindsey and Sully were the ones who found Gwen?

Why did it matter who found her? Why did The Club care if their project was associated with finding a body? Did Leslie's warning mean that Lindsey needed to find out what happened to Gwen Capshaw?

The image of Gwen beneath the rose bushes was seared into Lindsey's brain. She still didn't understand how Gwen had gotten there. She wondered if Emma or the crime scene investigators had had a breakthrough. Maybe it had just been a crazy accident. Perhaps Gwen had fallen on the palette knife while doing some gardening. It didn't seem likely at all, but Lindsey was willing to consider all possibilities.

Not knowing how the investigation had gone was maddening. Lindsey needed more information. Without overthinking it, she picked up her cell phone and called Emma.

The chief's personal line went right to voice mail. Lindsey debated calling the station but knew she'd get put on hold, given that everyone was undoubtedly busy dealing with the case. Was Emma still on the island? Had they determined what had happened? Why wasn't she answering her phone?

Lindsey glanced at the clock. It was four-thirty and she knew if she wanted answers, her best bet was to walk next door to the police department and ask. Grabbing her handbag out of the bottom drawer of her desk, she shut off her computer and headed out the door.

Lindsey stopped by the adult services desk, which was a large service station nestled between the adult fiction and nonfiction. She stood to the side and waited while Ann Marie assisted an elderly male patron who was doing some genealogical research. He had a long paper made of several sheets of legal paper that were taped together laid out on the reference desk. A spidery scrawl across the pages filled in the names and dates of his family tree. "I've traced my family back to the Vikings in the seventh century. I'm descended from a man named Trygve," he told her.

Ann Marie smiled. "That's an impressive amount of research you've done, Mr. Anderson."

"Do you know what that means? Trygve?"

"I don't," Ann Marie said. "Would you like me to look it up for you?"

"No need." Mr. Anderson puffed up his bony chest with pride. "I looked it up myself. It means 'trustworthy.'"

"Look at you." Ann Marie winked at him and said, "Keep up the brilliant research and I'll think you're after my job."

Mr. Anderson grinned, clearly pleased, but he waved his

hand at her and made a "pfft" noise. Ann Marie glanced up and noticed Lindsey. She gave her a slight nod.

"Excuse me," Ann Marie said. "I'll be right back."

She rose from her seat and joined Lindsey at the side of the desk where a curated collection of the most requested reference items were kept on a small bookcase.

"Everything all right?" Ann Marie asked. She wore ballet flats, a slim denim skirt and a floral top. Her dark hair was styled in a high ponytail; she looked the picture of springtime.

"Yes, I just need to step out for a few minutes and wanted to let you know you're in charge," Lindsey said.

"Oh, goody." Ann Marie clapped. "I love it when I get to pretend to know what I'm doing . . . not. How long will you be gone?"

"Half hour tops," Lindsey promised.

"All right, I will attempt to maintain order in your absence," Ann Marie teased.

"Thank you." Lindsey started to go but then turned back and said, "If you need me . . ."

"I'll call you right away."

"Thanks." Lindsey knew the library would be fine in Ann Marie's care. On the weekends and evenings that Lindsey was off, Ann Marie was in charge and nothing bad had ever happened. But today had been unexpectedly awful and Lindsey couldn't shake the feeling of impending doom, especially now that Leslie Stone had tied the Split Island tragedy to the funding for the book boat.

A sharp breeze was blowing in off the water and Lindsey lifted her face to it, inhaling the briny smell of the incoming high tide. It calmed her and she was grateful for the moment of peace. She had no idea what she would learn from Emma, if anything, and she needed to find her zen before asking the chief of police for information she likely wouldn't or couldn't share.

She walked down the sidewalk, contemplating the different ways she could approach Emma. By the time she reached the door to the station, she had an inkling of a plan. She would simply explain that the library's funding was in jeopardy and hope that Emma had some good news, as in, they knew what had happened to Gwen. Then Leslie and the board would be appeased and the book boat safe.

The automatic door opened as soon as Lindsey stepped on the mat. She entered the station to find Molly, the administrative assistant, behind the main desk. Molly was wearing a wireless headset with a mic and she glanced up at Lindsey and held up one finger, indicating that she needed a minute.

"I'm sorry, but I'm not at liberty to give out any information as yet." Molly was gently rounded and always smelled like freshly baked cookies. She brought a calming empathy to the police station that balanced Emma's brusque no-nonsense demeanor. "Of course, you can call back later to see if there are any updates."

Molly tapped the button on the headpiece, ending the call. She glanced up at Lindsey and said, "If you're here for information about Gwen Capshaw, I have nothing."

"Is that because you actually have nothing or because Emma told you to keep it on the down-low?" Lindsey asked.

"Doesn't matter which, either way, I have nothing," Molly said. "However, if you must see her, the chief is in her office and I suspect she could use a friendly face."

"Did something happen?" Lindsey asked.

"Mr. Capshaw couldn't inform his daughter, Jordan, of the tragedy—he was too overwrought—so Emma had to do it over the phone as the daughter lives in Massachusetts."

"Oh, that had to be rough." Lindsey winced.

"It was bad," Molly agreed. "I was out here and I could hear the wailing on the phone."

"I'll go check on her," Lindsey said.

"May I offer a suggestion?"

"Of course."

"Bring her a cup of coffee," Molly said. "Emma never turns away coffee."

Lindsey grinned. "Done." She left the main room and headed toward the back. She stopped in the break room and made Emma a fresh cup of coffee. Then she brought it to her office and knocked on the closed door.

"Emma, it's Lindsey."

"Go away, I'm busy," Emma said.

"I have coffee."

There was a beat of silence and then the door was yanked open. "Molly told you to do that, didn't she?"

"What? I can't bring a friend a cup of coffee when she's

had a bad day?" Lindsey tried to look innocent. Emma's eyebrow ticked up. "Okay, fine, she suggested that you might need it."

Lindsey held out the mug and Emma took it in both of her hands, breathing in the scent of the bitter brew. "Thank you. My morning caffeine rush ended a few hours ago and I need the boost."

Emma gestured for Lindsey to join her in the office and Lindsey stepped inside, closing the door behind her. The room was warm and welcoming, reflecting Emma's love of their community. Crayon drawings from the local schoolkids covered her bulletin board, while local artists' works graced the walls. A leather couch and two armchairs took up one side of the office while her desk and a wall of books, mostly law and criminal justice books, filled the other side.

Emma sat in one of the chairs and Lindsey noted that the coffee table in front of her had a legal notepad on it, much like the one Lindsey had used in her office, and it was full of notes. When Lindsey took the chair beside Emma's, Emma flipped the notebook facedown.

"What brings you by?" Emma asked.

"What have you learned about Gwen's death?" Lindsey asked.

"You didn't even try to soft-sell it." Emma blew across the surface of her coffee, trying to cool it. "Just jumped right in with both feet." Lindsey shrugged. "You know I can't tell you anything about an ongoing investigation."

"So, you suspect someone," Lindsey said.

"Didn't say that," Emma said. "I'm doing my job and

following every lead so that we can determine what happened to Gwen Capshaw." She leveled a scrutinizing look at Lindsey. "Why are you so invested? I didn't think you knew Gwen."

"Because I found her," Lindsey said. It was a half-truth and it sounded like one.

"And?" Emma asked. It was brutal having the chief of police know her so well.

"Leslie Stone came to see me about an hour ago," Lindsey said. "She and the board of directors are concerned that the book boat being on-site when a body was found will reflect poorly on The Club as sponsors of the boat."

Emma sipped her coffee. "That feels odd. It's not your fault that you happened to be the one to find Gwen."

"I thought so, too." Lindsey agreed. "But Leslie didn't seem to care. The reputation of The Club is taken very seriously."

Emma put her coffee down and picked up her notebook. She flipped until she reached a blank page and made a small note. "What do you know about The Club?"

"Honestly, until Robbie introduced me to the committee, I had never heard of it," Lindsey said. "Sorry about that, by the way, it appears he'll have to be a member or at least be considered for membership. It was the unspoken condition of The Club's support of the book boat, which at the time seemed like no big deal but now it feels like we made a bad bargain."

"No worries," Emma said. "I don't like having exclusive groups in my town. This way, as his partner, I get to attend their events and meet these secretive people. Whenever there's that much money involved, you know there are bad characters in the mix."

There was an abrupt knock on the door just before it burst open. Standing on the threshold was a thirty-something woman who looked vaguely familiar, and a man about the same age. The woman was pale and had red-rimmed eyes. It was clear she'd been crying. The man looked uncomfortable as if he wasn't certain of his purpose at the moment.

"Can I help you?" Emma frowned at the intrusion, her hand instinctively going to the Taser in the utility belt on her waist.

Molly bustled in, carrying a box of tissues. She handed the box to the young woman and then turned to Emma, sending her a meaningful glance. "Jordan and Ryan Montgomery here to see you, Chief Plewicki."

Emma's eyes flashed with understanding. "Come on in, Mr. and Mrs. Montgomery."

"What happened to my mother?" Jordan demanded, not moving from the doorway. "You said on the phone that she passed away. How? Where's my father? Why doesn't he answer his phone? What's going on?" She dug her fingers into her long blond hair—so like her mother's—and tugged as if she'd pull it out. Her husband put his hand on her shoulder, but she shrugged him off.

"Come in and sit." Emma's voice was firm. "Can Molly get you anything?"

"No. Thank you." Jordan sat on the couch.

Emma glanced at Ryan.

"Coffee would be great." He sounded exhausted. Jordan

shot him a chastising look but Ryan ran a hand over his face and said, "Sorry, but I was on shift all night. I'm beat."

"On shift?" Emma asked.

"I'm a PA, a physician's assistant, at a hospital emergency room." He sat beside his wife, leaving a few inches of space between them.

"Ah, I'll be right back with your coffee." Molly glanced at Jordan and asked, "Are you sure you don't want some water, dear?"

Jordan looked like she was about to refuse but Molly had a way about her that invited second chances. "Yes, please."

Molly nodded and left the room. Lindsey expected Emma to dismiss her, but she didn't. Instead, she turned to face the Montgomerys.

"I want to see my mother." Jordan's voice was strained. "And I want to go to the island and see my father."

Emma glanced at Lindsey and said, "We'll call the water taxi for you. But it'll take a few minutes for Sully to get here. I'll try to answer your questions as best as I can while we wait."

Lindsey took that as her cue to reach out to Sully and have him bring the taxi. She texted him the situation and in moments he responded that he was en route.

"Sully is on his way," she said.

"Sully?" Ryan blinked. "I haven't seen him or his sister, Mary, in years."

"You've been gone a long time," Emma observed.

Jordan squirmed in her seat and Lindsey suspected that the haunted look in her eyes was one of guilt. Being estranged from her mother and then having her mother pass away unexpectedly without the opportunity to mend the hurt had to be a brutal weight to carry.

"It's been fifteen years since we left," Jordan said.

"Had you spoken to your mother recently?" Emma asked.

Jordan shook her head. She had the same fine features as her mother, the small nose, high cheekbones and arching brows. But where those features had been sharp on Gwen they were softer on Jordan, giving her a gamine appeal.

"We talked once a year," Jordan said. "I would call her on her birthday, but that usually ended in either yelling or tears."

"Did she ever call you?" Emma asked.

"No." Jordan shook her head. A single tear slid down her cheek and she blotted it with a tissue. "My dad and I talked every few weeks and he relayed information between us. It was just easier that way."

"And how about you, Ryan? Are you in touch with your parents?" Emma asked.

Ryan frowned as if he wasn't sure why the conversation had switched to him, but he answered, "Yes. I talk to them every week and they come to visit us in Boston every other month."

"So, you're close?" Emma pressed.

"As close as we can be, I suppose," Ryan said.

Jordan's head was lowered and she was hunkered in on herself as if she wanted to curl up into a ball and disappear.

Molly bustled into the room, bringing a mug of coffee

for Ryan and a bottle of water for Jordan. They expressed their thanks and Molly left.

"What does any of this have to do with my mother?" Jordan asked. She held the bottle but didn't drink.

Emma drew a deep breath as if stealing herself. "Jordan, there is something about your mother's death that I didn't tell you over the phone."

Jordan's eyes went wide and she reached out for her husband, who clasped her hand in his. "What is it? She didn't . . . it wasn't . . ." She paused and closed her eyes for a moment. When she opened them, she met Emma's gaze and asked, "She didn't take her own life, did she?"

Emma's lips parted in surprise. "The medical examiner didn't make that determination. Why do you ask?"

"Because she threatened to do it often enough." Jordan's tears began to fall in earnest and she turned into her husband's waiting arms and sobbed into his shoulder.

Ryan glanced at them over his wife's head. He stroked her back, gently offering her comfort, but his voice was firm when he said, "If you could give us a couple of minutes."

"Of course." Emma led the way out of the office and Lindsey followed.

Her mind was reeling. Gwen had been stabbed with a palette knife. There was no way that was self-inflicted. Was it? She closed the door behind them and turned to face Emma.

"What do you make of that?"

Emma shook her head. "I have no idea."

Lindsey lowered her voice. "There's no way it could have been self-inflicted, right?"

"It seems unlikely." Emma frowned. "They're doing an autopsy. We'll know more then. In the meantime, I know you know this but do not discuss what you saw on the island, or in here, with anyone."

"Understood." Lindsey nodded. "What are you going to tell Jordan about her mother's death that you didn't tell her over the phone?"

"I was going to let her know that the circumstances were suspicious and that we're doing an investigation," Emma said.

"Are you still going to tell her that?" Lindsey studied Emma's face. She looked conflicted but then nodded.

"Yes, her father knows that Gwen was stabbed but not with what so there's no point in not telling Jordan at least that much. She has given us a new angle to look at the case from, as unlikely as it seems."

The door to her office opened and Ryan appeared. "Jordan can continue now."

"Thanks, I'll be right there." Emma waited for Ryan to go back inside and then she turned to Lindsey. "If you happen to talk to Sully's parents today and the subject of Split Island comes up, please make a note of any information Joan has to share. I know she's plugged into the island residents like no one's business."

"Maybe I could take the water taxi out with Sully and the Montgomerys and we can pop in on his parents on the way back?" Lindsey suggested.

Emma pursed her lips while she pondered the suggestion. "Just be mindful about what you say."

"Of course," Lindsey promised. "Loose lips sink ships and all that."

"No talk of sinking ships when a sailor is present, please." Sully came around the corner. His hair was windblown and his cheeks ruddy. Lindsey knew if she hugged him, he'd smell like the sea.

"Sorry," she said. "Of course that could never happen on your watch."

He inclined his head and Emma glanced between them. "Wait here. I'll finish up with Ryan and Jordan and send them out."

She disappeared into the office and Sully pulled Lindsey into a hug. She leaned her head on his shoulder and said, "Thanks."

"You looked like you needed it." He gave her one last squeeze then released her. He nodded toward Emma's office and asked, "How's it going in there?"

"Rough. Lots of unresolved stuff, from what I heard."

"Mary said it was quite a scene when Ryan and Jordan left. I was stationed overseas at the time and missed it." Sully put his hand on the back of his neck as if the thought of so much conflict made him uncomfortable.

"A bigger scene than Gwen blowing up the bridge between the two islands?" Lindsey asked.

"That was one and done," Sully said. "The bigger scene came when Gwen discovered that Ryan and Jordan had gotten married. She disowned her daughter and told her to never return."

"Harsh." Lindsey glanced at the closed office door. "No wonder Jordan looks so hurt. Any chance at repairing the rift between them died with Gwen."

Sully nodded and his eyes were sad as if he couldn't imagine an estrangement in his family. Lindsey felt the same. Her parents lived in New Hampshire and her brother, Jack, in Boston but they texted constantly in their family group chat and got together as often as possible. She'd be lost without them.

The door to the office opened and Emma stepped outside with Ryan and Jordan right behind her. Jordan's face was tear streaked but she was no longer crying.

"You know Sully," Emma said, and gestured to where Sully stood.

Ryan's eyes lit with recognition and he stepped forward with his hand out. The two men clasped hands and pulled each other in and slapped each other's shoulder in the standard guy greeting.

"It's been a long time." Ryan gazed at Sully, taking in the differences the years had made in him.

"Well over a decade." Sully released his hand and turned to Jordan. He opened his arms and she stepped in for a hug. "I'm sorry about your mom, Jordie."

Jordan burrowed her face against his shirt and made a snuffling nose. "No one calls me Jordie except you and Mary and the other island kids."

"Sorry, but you'll always be Jordie to me." Sully released her and gently tapped Ryan on the shoulder and said, "Just like he'll always be Ry-boy."

Ryan rolled his eyes but there was a smile parting his lips. "I haven't heard that nickname in years." He glanced at his wife and they exchanged knowing smiles as if coming back had triggered happy memories that they'd forgotten.

"Sully is going to take you out to Split Island," Emma said. "I have your contact information, so if I hear anything or have more questions, I'll be in touch."

"Thank you," Jordan and Ryan said together.

"My wife, Lindsey, is coming with us." Sully grabbed Lindsey's hand and pulled her forward.

"Emma told us that you two found my mom," Jordan said. Her face crumpled and she took a shaky breath. "Was she . . . did she . . . was she at peace?"

Lindsey thought about how Gwen's eyes had been closed and that Lindsey had first thought she'd fallen asleep back behind the bushes. She hadn't suspected Gwen to be murdered at all.

"She was in her garden," Lindsey said. "By the roses."

"She loved her garden," Jordan said, her voice heavy with sadness. Ryan pulled her in for a hug and Jordan clutched him close.

"Should we head out?" Sully asked, his voice gentle.

Both Jordan and Ryan nodded. Ryan held out his hand and Jordan laced her fingers with his as if it were as natural as breathing. After so many years together, it was obvious that they still found comfort in each other.

They left the police station and stopped by the vehicle Ryan and Jordan had used to come down from Boston. Ryan opened the hatch and they retrieved two hard-case carry-on bags on wheels.

"I wasn't sure what to pack," Jordan admitted. "I went for layers remembering the Thumb Island mercurial weather system. Sometimes we dressed for winter, spring and summer all in the same day."

"What was it Mr. Parsons used to say?" Ryan mused. "If you don't like the weather, wait ten minutes, it'll change."

Lindsey noticed that the three of them had a camaraderie built on years of a shared history of growing up on the islands. As they talked about the people they knew, the landmarks of significance and their shared memories, she could see both Ryan and Jordan start to relax.

The water taxi was tied up at the town pier and ready to go. Sully assisted Jordan and Ryan into the boat while Lindsey untied the ropes. As soon as all four of them were seated, Sully started the engine and headed back out into the bay.

The late afternoon was cooler than the morning had been and Lindsey noted how right Jordan had been about the weather and wished she'd brought a jacket. She wrapped her arms about her middle and kept her gaze on thc islands ahead. Ryan and Jordan were sharing a bench seat at the back of the boat and he had his arm around her as they both stared at the home they hadn't seen in years.

Sully dropped his windbreaker around Lindsey's shoulders and she glanced at him in surprise. She would have refused but it was warm from his body and she was shivering. Besides, one look at her husband's determined face and she knew arguing would be a waste of breath.

"Thank you," she said over the sound of the boat motor and the roar of the wind.

When they arrived at Split Island, Ariel and Dane were waiting on the dock. Dane was in jeans and a T-shirt with an unbuttoned faded flannel over it. Ariel was in a pretty, pale green maxi dress with white flowers embroidered along its hem and neckline layered with a warm cream-colored cardigan. She started to wave as soon as they drew close.

Both Ryan and Jordan stood up as if they couldn't wait to be home. Sully brought the boat up against the dock and tossed the line to Dane, who tied it up. Ariel hopped from foot to foot as she waited for Ryan and Jordan to exit the boat.

Ryan stepped onto the dock first and turned to offer Jordan his hand. She used his support to step onto the dock, where she was engulfed in a hug by Ariel.

"Oh, sweet girl, I am so sorry, so very sorry," Ariel said as she hugged Jordan.

Jordan tried to speak but a sob was the only sound she made. She hugged Ariel tight and sobbed, leaving Ryan to hug his father and wait patiently for the crying to ease. When Ariel released her, Jordan turned to Dane and hugged him while Ryan embraced his mother. Ryan had been telling the truth. They were close to his parents. Lindsey wondered if that contributed to Gwen's hatred of Ariel.

"Jordan!" Jordan started and stepped away from Dane, who Lindsey realized looked like a middle-aged version of his son. As one, they all followed the sound of the shout to the neighboring dock where Perry stood, looking furious.

"Dad!" Jordan waved but her father didn't return it. He simply glared at the lot of them.

"I should go over there," Jordan said.

"I'll come with you," Ryan insisted. Jordan looked doubtful but nodded.

"We'll be right back," Ryan told his parents. Ariel bit her lip, clearly anxious, but she didn't say anything.

Ryan and Jordan stepped back into the boat with Lindsey and Sully. Dane tossed the rope to Sully. They eased their way to the other dock and Sully had barely stopped it before Jordan was jumping out and running to her father.

He grabbed her close and held her tight. Lindsey could see that they were both crying. Ryan stepped out of the boat and waited, holding the line to keep the boat from drifting. When the father and daughter broke apart, Perry Capshaw glared at Ryan.

"Get off my dock, Ryan Montgomery, you're not welcome here."

"Dad!" Jordan protested.

Perry glared at his daughter; his brows were lowered

and his mouth a thin angry line. "His parents are responsible for your mother's death. I won't have him here."

Jordan recoiled but Ryan stepped forward. "That's a lie. My parents have nothing to do with whatever happened to Gwen."

"Get off my dock!" Perry yelled.

Lindsey glanced over at the Montgomerys. Both Ariel and Dane looked stricken as if they couldn't believe Perry would say such things about them.

"Dad, stop it!" Jordan cried. "Ryan is my husband and I won't—"

"You don't know!" Perry bellowed. "Your mother was murdered by his mother. I'd bet my life on it."

"Hey, now, that's not—" Ryan sputtered.

"Go! Now!" Perry bellowed. His face was red, his hair mussed, and as Lindsey studied him, she noted he was listing to the side ever so slightly. Perry Capshaw was drunk.

Sully must have registered the same thing. He stepped out of the boat, placing himself beside Jordan and between the two men. Lindsey knew he would intervene if the confrontation got physical, but she really hoped it didn't.

With Sully at her side, Jordan straightened her spine and stood more confidently between her husband and her father. "Ryan, go ahead and go to your parents' side of the island. My dad needs me right now."

"But—" Ryan protested but Jordan cut him off.

"It's all right," she said. "I'll call you later."

Ryan cupped her cheek but Jordan pulled away as if not wanting to upset her father by a show of affection between her and her husband. A look of hurt flashed in Ryan's eyes, but Jordan turned away, taking her father's arm and guiding him along the dock to the stairs.

Ryan stared after them with a worried look. His brow was furrowed and his lips pressed into a straight line as if he was afraid that the person he loved most in the world was about to be taken from him.

She'll be back, Ryan." Ariel put an arm around her son, consoling him when Sully and Lindsey returned him to his family's side of the island. "Just give them some time to process."

He nodded his head and then looked at his parents. "What happened? Why is Mr. Capshaw so angry with you? He said some unforgivable things, Mom."

Dane shook his head and Ariel shrugged. They both seemed completely at a loss.

"We don't really know," Ariel said. "We only know what we've been told by the police chief and that's that Gwen died unexpectedly. Do you know what happened?"

"Sort of, the police chief told us that her death was suspicious, that she'd been stabbed," Ryan said. He glanced at Sully and Lindsey, who nodded.

Ariel gasped and put her hand over her mouth. "But who? How? Why?"

"That's what the chief is trying to figure out," Ryan said. He glanced at the other island; his brow furrowed with worry.

"I called Perry a few hours ago, but he didn't answer," Dane said. He was tall and broad like his son with the same dark hair and eyes. Lindsey didn't know him well, but whenever he came into the library with Ariel, he was friendly. "How did Jordan take it?"

"Not well." Ryan shook his head. "It was hard enough that her mother disowned her but now . . . she'll have to live with her mother's rejection for the rest of her life."

"Poor Jordan." Ariel sighed. "I wish we could help."

Ryan glanced at his parents. "I don't like that she's over there on her own."

"Perry's with her," Dane said.

"But I'm not." Ryan countered. "And if Gwen was murdered, isn't the spouse usually the main suspect? Doesn't that put her at risk, being alone with Mr. Capshaw? What if he's having some sort of nervous breakdown and he killed his wife and his daughter is next? I hate this."

Sully reached out and put his hand on Ryan's shoulder. "I wouldn't like it either if I was you, but I can tell you that Lindsey and I were there when Perry was told about his wife and his shock and grief seemed genuine." He glanced at Lindsey and she nodded.

"It's true," she said. "He was distraught." She didn't mention seeing him glower at their side of the island. Now that she'd heard him blame the Montgomerys for his wife's death, she suspected that was why he'd been glaring at their home. In his mind, they had killed his wife. She thought about how drunk he'd appeared when they dropped Jordan off.

"He isn't a violent drunk or anything, is he?" she asked.

"No." Dane shook his head. "Perry never drinks. Why?"

"It was clear he'd had a few when we were over there," Sully said. "Hopefully, he'll sleep it off and his anger toward you will burn out with it."

"I hope so." Ariel's voice was soft and her eyes sad.

Ryan and Dane followed her gaze to the neighboring island; instinctively they both stepped closer to her as if to protect her from Perry's anger.

Lindsey and Sully left the Montgomery family on the smaller island and headed to his parents' house on Bell Island. Lindsey was eager to be in a place that was warm and friendly with no one yelling at anyone and no bodies to be found.

The sun was setting and the wind coming off the water was fierce. Lindsey burrowed into Sully's windbreaker. It smelled like him and that calmed her. She swiveled her seat to face him and studied his profile. His eyes were narrowed, the wind tousled his hair and his cheeks were ruddy from the cold. He seemed pensive and she wondered if he was thinking about Gwen's death, too.

"What did you think about Perry refusing to let Ryan join him and Jordan on their island?" Lindsey asked.

"Weird." Sully didn't hesitate. "Even if Perry and Gwen

weren't happy about the marriage, Jordan and Ryan have been together for years. Time to get over it."

"I thought it was strange, too. Maybe his grief made him just want to have some alone time with his daughter," Lindsey suggested.

"Then he should have said that," Sully said. "Don't get drunk and ban him from the island as if he's a criminal."

"Do you think Perry knows about the palette knife?" Lindsey asked.

"I doubt it," Sully said. "He wasn't there when it was bagged and I'd be willing to bet Emma is keeping the murder weapon quiet to see if anyone slips during their interview because the only person who would know that it was a palette knife, aside from the people on the island when Gwen was found, would be the killer."

Lindsey shivered but not from the cold.

"Who do you suppose stood to benefit the most from Gwen's murder?" Lindsey raised her voice to be heard over the sound of the engine.

"As Ryan said, it's usually the spouse, especially if there is a hefty life insurance payout involved," Sully said. "Perry wasn't there when we arrived but that doesn't mean he wasn't there earlier. It'll be interesting to see if the woman who dropped him off is also the one who picked him up if he was really gone as long as he said he was and if Gwen was murdered in that same time frame. Hopefully, Dr. Rogers and Callie can narrow it down."

"You told me Perry was the one who taught you so much about the islands and their ecosystem," Lindsey said as Sully navigated his boat to his parents' dock. "Does he strike you as a person who could become a killer?"

Sully shrugged. "I wish I could say no, but we've been here before. We've met people we never would have suspected of murder and then we discover the worst about them."

Lindsey knew he was right. She couldn't shake the image of Perry watching the smaller island earlier that day. Had he been guilty and trying to see if they suspected him? Or did he really think Ariel murdered his wife, given the hostility between the two women? What about what Leslie had told her that Perry had reached out to her husband as a defense attorney? Why would he do that if he was innocent? Maybe Perry's relationship with Gwen had become strained over the estrangement with their daughter? Maybe he'd gotten drunk because he regretted what he did.

There were so many possibilities and somehow Lindsey had to keep *The Jolly Reader* from being implicated in any of it or risk losing the funding for the project. She wished she could just give Leslie Stone and The Club the money back and walk away from the whole thing but the money had already been spent and she couldn't ask the town to cover for her—it would be exactly the excuse Gideon Trask needed to close the library for good.

"Come on, let's go see if my mom has any insight for us," Sully said. "She said Dad made a pot roast—everything is better with pot roast."

"You're not wrong." Lindsey smiled. Sully pulled her

close against his side and together, they made their way to the house.

Joan and Mike Sullivan were bustling around the kitchen together like the cogs in a well-oiled machine. Mike carved the meat, Joan tossed the salad, and dinner was served right on time.

The day had been exhausting and Lindsey let Sully tell his parents about Gwen Capshaw. Neither Joan nor Mike looked surprised, leading Lindsey to suspect that they already knew.

"She was stabbed, wasn't she?" Joan asked.

"Mom, how did you know?"

"Our neighbor Linda's niece works for the medical examiner's office," Joan said. "The niece told her mother who naturally called Linda, who told us."

Sully glanced at Lindsey across the table and shook his head.

"What's that look for?" Joan asked.

"I'm just amazed at how plugged in you are to everything that happens on the islands," Sully said.

"Well, I've lived here most of my life," Joan said. "And it's not just idle gossip; we all look out for each other out here as you well know."

"I do." Sully raised his hands in surrender.

"Speaking of the islands and the community," Lindsey said. "What do you know about The Club on King's Island?"

Mike and Joan both went still. Mike put his fork down and leaned back in his chair. "That'd be the one island that is not a part of the looking-out-for-each-other that the rest of us adhere to."

"Do you think The Club has something to do with Gwen's death?" Joan asked.

"No, nothing like that," Lindsey said. "They sponsored the book boat and Leslie Stone let me know that the board of The Club would be reviewing their support because the book boat was on-site when a body was found. It was very . . . unsettling."

"Do you need me to find out anything in particular?" Joan asked.

"Now, Joanie . . ." Mike began but Joan interrupted him.

"I'll be subtle."

Lindsey exchanged a smile with Sully before she said, "There's no need to ask about it, but if you hear anything in passing that you think would be of interest, that'd be great."

Joan sat up straighter. "I have mah-jongg with my lady friends tomorrow. I'll invite them to share with me what they know about The Club. Anything else?"

"Who are the artists who live out on the islands?" Lindsey asked. "I know Ariel Montgomery since she volunteers to teach painting at the library, but are there a lot of artists residing on the islands?"

"Does this have something to do with Gwen's death?" Joan asked.

Sully and Lindsey exchanged a look and Sully said, "We don't know."

Joan nodded in acceptance. She looked across the table

at her husband and said, "There's Bernie Mueller, the wood-carver, and Mary Sheldrick, the potter. Who else?"

"We were thinking more about the painters," Sully said.

"Oh, then Stan Leavitt, for sure," Mike said. "And Harper Winslow was doing really well before . . ."

"Before what?" Lindsey asked.

"She had a gallery showing in New York but it was cut short," Joan said. "No one knows why but she pulled all of her pieces and then Ariel Montgomery took her place."

"Seems like there might be some bad blood there," Sully said.

"You'd think, but Harper insisted that leaving the gallery was her choice." Joan shrugged. "Does any of that help?"

"It does, thank you," Lindsey said. She glanced at Sully to see if he was okay with putting his parents on the spot and he shot her a quick wink. The conversation changed to Mike and Joan's latest visit with their granddaughter, Josie, Mary and Ian's daughter, and Lindsey was relieved. Listening to the stories of Josie's antics was a welcome balm after such an emotionally wrenching day.

Given how things had been going lately, Lindsey contemplated the day ahead. She fully expected another visit from Leslie or Gideon or some other library hater and decided to prepare accordingly. She dressed for success that morning in a navy blue tailored jacket over an ecru linen chemise. When she joined Sully in the kitchen he gave a low whistle.

"Wearing the power outfit today?" He toasted her with his coffee mug.

"I'm trying to be ready in the event that I have to stand up for the library in the face of Gideon Trask or Leslie Stone," she said. "I don't enjoy feeling as if the library has a bull's-eye on it."

"That's wise, but don't forget the community supports you." Sully handed her a mug with her coffee prepared exactly as she liked it. "You're the best director we've ever had and everyone knows it. Plus, Mayor Cole is on your side."

Lindsey knew he was right. She had allies. It was going to be okay. She felt something press against her ankle and reached down to scratch their cat Zelda's chin just the way she preferred. In moments, Zelda was thrust aside by Heathcliff, their dog, as he muscled his way in and demanded love.

"Someone is feeling jealous," Sully observed as he picked up Zelda and finished the chin scratches Lindsey had started.

"Are you taking him to work with you today?" Lindsey asked.

"Yes, I think our boy needs some time on the boat, and besides, the tourists love him."

Lindsey looked down at her sweet dog and asked, "Are you going on the boat, Heathcliff?"

He hopped up on his hind legs and hugged Lindsey about the knees, his tail wagging furiously as if he were trying to make enough air to achieve liftoff. Lindsey laughed and hugged him close. "That's my good boy."

Sully and Heathcliff dropped Lindsey off at the staff entrance and Lindsey entered the library, enjoying the comforting quiet that greeted her. It was an hour before they opened for the day and Lindsey loved having the place just for the library workers for a little while.

She stopped by the break room to make some coffee and found Beth sitting at the lunch table. "I just made a pot. Help yourself."

"Excellent. You're now my favorite children's librarian," Lindsey said.

"I'm the only children's librarian." Beth sipped from her mug while pushing aside a stack of craft paper, glue sticks and scissors.

"Doesn't make it not true." Lindsey poured a mug and sat at the table.

"I heard about Gwen Capshaw," Beth said. "Paula said you went to the police station but then ended up taking Jordan and Ryan Montgomery out to Split Island?"

"I did." Lindsey took a bracing sip. "It was very emotional for everyone, especially Jordan. Sully told me about the rift between her and her mom."

"Yeah." Beth sighed. "I remember when all of that went down."

"You knew about it?"

"Jordan was one of my teen workers the very first year I worked here." Beth fiddled with a glue stick, checking the cap. She set it down and glanced up at Lindsey. "They were ridiculously in love. Ryan would hang out waiting for Jordan to take a break and then they'd just sit together, quietly reading graphic novels while holding hands. They were sweet."

"Was there a reason that Gwen disliked Ryan so much?" Lindsey sipped her coffee, feeling its warmth in her chest.

"Gwen had bigger aspirations for Jordan."

"Meaning?"

"Gwen was obsessed with The Club," Beth said. "Ironic, since they're now funding our book boat."

Lindsey remembered the expression on Gwen's face when she found out The Club was sponsoring the boat. She realized now that it had been a mix of surprise and consternation.

"Why was Gwen so obsessed?" Lindsey asked.

"Because membership is very exclusive," Beth said. "And according to Jordan, it ate at Gwen that she didn't make the cut."

"Why wouldn't she?" Lindsey asked. "I mean, they live on the islands, Perry's family has been there for generations and he's a renowned ornithologist—they seem like a perfect fit."

"They would be, however, Perry blocked a very important real estate venture from being developed when it would destroy the local osprey habitats. He fought to keep the development away from the nesting areas and he won. The real estate mogul who lost his deal made certain that Perry and by extension Gwen were blackballed from The Club."

"Seems to me, Perry did the right thing," Lindsey muttered. "And I'm surprised The Club didn't feel the same way."

"The Club is all about conspicuous consumption," Beth said. "They'd only care about preserving wildlife if there was a hefty remuneration to be made from it."

Lindsey shook her head. As a public servant, she'd never understood consumption as a status symbol. "What does any of that have to do with Jordan?"

"Gwen wanted Jordan to get a job at The Club, because she thought Jordan was wasting her time at the library." Beth rolled her eyes, letting Lindsey know what she thought of that. "Gwen believed if Jordan worked at The Club, Jordan would meet and date one of the young men whose family belonged to The Club and Jordan would be Gwen's way into becoming a member."

"That's . . . wow." Lindsey didn't know what to call that.

"'Wrong' is the word I think you're looking for. It's just all around wrong," Beth said. "Obviously, when Jordan refused to leave the library and Gwen found out about her romance with Ryan, she went ballistic."

"Oh, I heard about the bridge so I imagine that can't have gone well," Lindsey said. She remembered her teen years and how her brother, Jack, also a teen, had taken any sort of parental limit as a personal challenge.

"Understatement." Beth took a sip of her coffee before

continuing. "They were caught in the 'altogether,' if you know what I mean."

"Got it." Lindsey held up her hand to indicate she didn't need more descriptors.

"It was after hours in the high school football stadium," Beth said. "One of the town cops was doing a security check and found them. They'd fallen asleep in the announcer's booth. They were both seventeen so their parents were called to pick them up at the station. That was it for Gwen. She forbade Jordan from having anything to do with Ryan."

Lindsey felt for the two teens. Young love was so all-consuming. They must have felt desperate.

"Of course, that was the worst thing she could do," Beth said. "They just became sneakier."

Lindsey studied her friend. "Why do I feel as if you had a hand in this sneakiness?"

"Me?" Beth batted her long dark lashes. "Whatever do you mean?"

"Oh, please, you forget I've known you for decades. You cry over puppy memes on social media," Lindsey said. "You're a total pushover. If you saw young love being thwarted you would absolutely facilitate it."

"I might have let them meet in my office a time or two," Beth admitted. "But in my defense, Jordan was a really good worker and seeing her cry all day, every day was just heartbreaking. Even the lemon couldn't take it."

Lindsey smiled at Mayor Cole's former nickname from the days when she worked at the library and was their chief fine enforcer and shusher. Mayor Cole had certainly changed since those early days.

"I thought it was just a matter of time," Beth said. "I assumed when everyone calmed down all would be forgiven and the kids would be allowed to see each other again. I was so wrong. Gwen was not going to change her mind. Shocking everyone, Jordan and Ryan didn't show up for graduation and the entire town was buzzing."

"I'll bet." Lindsey could only imagine. Even her brother hadn't been that bold.

"Long story short, they eloped," Beth said. "And they never came back."

"Never?"

"Not until yesterday," Beth confirmed. "Gwen disowned Jordan, although I heard that she started to accept one call from her every year."

"Yes, on Gwen's birthday. Jordan told us," Lindsey said. "How sad. So much time wasted. If Gwen just could have accepted Ryan, it all would have been so different."

"Hanging on to anger is exhausting," Beth said. "I tried it when Rick plagiarized my children's book, but it turned me into someone I didn't like so I stopped. Plus, he was murdered so that seemed like punishment enough."

"Was Rick a member of The Club?" Lindsey asked. She hadn't liked Beth's former boyfriend at all and was delighted that her friend had started writing again and found love with a fellow children's librarian, Aidan Barker.

"Yes. Why do you ask?" Beth got a suspicious look in her eye.

"No reason, just curious," Lindsey answered. "You know, I think I want to see The Club."

"Really?" Beth looked perplexed. "They're not a friendly bunch. I would think you'd want to stay as far away from that place as possible."

"On any other day, I would," Lindsey said. "But I have questions that can only be answered by a visit."

"What sorts of questions?" Beth frowned, looking concerned.

"I saw Gwen's expression when I told her that The Club was sponsoring the book boat. I didn't know about her relationship with The Club at the time and now I'm wondering if Gwen let go of belonging to The Club or did it fester? I find it hard to believe that she would disown her daughter over a relationship of which she didn't approve and give up on her desire to belong to The Club. If she could hold on to her grudge with her own child, I doubt she'd give up on wanting to belong. And if she didn't give up, what lengths would she go to for membership? Did she do anything to any of the members that would cause them to want to murder her?"

"Oh, wow, that's going to be a fun visit," Beth said. "How do you plan to get in?"

"Robbie."

"Of course." Beth nodded. "They've been courting him for years and now that they have him on the hook, they're not going to let go. I think the bigger issue then is how are you going to get anyone to talk to you?"

"I might have to rely on Robbie for that, too," Lindsey

acknowledged. "I'm not exactly known for my extroverted charm."

Beth smiled. "You don't need it. You are the person that people instinctively trust, which is why they confess things to you that all the charm in the world couldn't get them to admit to."

"Maybe." Lindsey shrugged.

"I'm about to open the doors, ladies." Paula popped her head into the room. "To your stations!"

Beth and Lindsey shared a smile at Paula's enthusiasm and left the break room, taking their coffee with them.

Lindsey texted Robbie about her idea and then began her shift at the reference desk. She spent the morning answering the variety of questions that came in, from books about how to live with lung cancer—a tough one—to looking up property disputes in the town charter and code, and of course her favorite question about what to read next.

It was a busy morning, which was helpful because it kept her from brooding about Gwen Capshaw. At midmorning when Ann Marie arrived to take over the desk, Lindsey headed to her office, where she found Robbie sitting in one of the visitor's chairs waiting for her while thumbing through a men's fitness magazine.

"Hello, pet." He stood when she entered. "I got your text."

"What do you think?" she asked.

"I think it's brilliant," he said. "If you come with me, I'm sure you'll get me kicked out before I have to officially join."

A small laugh escaped Lindsey but she shook her head and said, "No drama. If we do this, I don't want a scene. The people at The Club are the sort who could lock down the library for good."

"Like Gideon Trask?" Robbie asked.

"Is he a member?" Lindsey asked in surprise. Why hadn't she thought of that? He was exactly the sort of person who'd belong to The Club.

"Apparently." Robbie frowned. "When he found out I'd been sponsored to join, he made sure to stop by my table at the Blue Anchor last night and tell me that he would be voting against my membership. And now I simply have to be accepted just to spite him."

Lindsey grinned. She'd known Robbie long enough to know that he ran on spite, which was probably why he was so successful. He was not one to take a punch and not punch back.

"What time were you thinking?" Lindsey asked. "I don't get off work until five."

"Perfect," Robbie said. "I've been invited to their annual spring fling tonight, which starts at six o'clock."

"Will Emma be joining us?"

"Sadly, no," he said. "She's tied up with the investigation, although she did give me a list of things to inquire about, so we have our homework cut out for us."

"How will you explain my presence to the other members?" Lindsey asked.

"You're acting as my personal assistant since Katie is out of town," he said.

"Is Katie out of town?"

"No, but she was thrilled to have the evening off," he said. "Meet you at the pier at five-thirty. I've left an outfit for you from Emma's closet." He gestured to the garment bag hanging on the back of her door.

"Another one?" Lindsey asked. "I'm sure I have something—"

Robbie shook his head. "You don't. Trust me."

"Fine. What about Sully?"

"I already talked to him. He'll captain us out there but he'll have to wait at the boathouse with the other captains and crews," Robbie said. "I can't really find a reason for him to be at the party, too."

"He'll probably prefer that," Lindsey agreed.

"Undoubtedly." Robbie squeezed her arm as he walked to the door. "Chin up, Lindsey. This will be fun."

"Right up there with a root canal or a day spent in line at the department of motor vehicles," she mumbled.

"Never say I don't know how to show a gal a good time." Robbie sauntered out of her office with a wave.

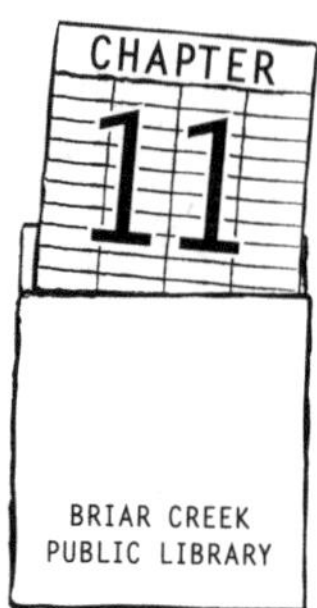

How is a person supposed to walk in these shoes?" Lindsey asked. "They're four inches high on tiny little spindle heels and the only thing holding them on my feet is a tiny strap across the toes and around my ankle."

"As Christian Louboutin says, 'High heels are pleasure with pain.'" Robbie steadied her as she stepped onto Sully's boat.

"Figures a man would say that," Lindsey grumbled.

"Hmm." Sully didn't say anything as he scooped her up about the waist and set her gently into the boat as if she weighed nothing.

Lindsey was trying to get used to Emma's dress, which was a Retrofête floral silk minidress. It was beautiful and short—so very short—Lindsey knew she wouldn't be sitting down all evening, which was a bummer as her feet were already beginning to cramp.

"No wonder Emma doesn't like going to events with you if she has to dress up in outfits like this," Lindsey said to Robbie.

"She doesn't *have* to—it's just that a lot of the parties we attend frown on women showing up in a uniform with a gun on their hip," Robbie said.

"I feel like that dress warrants carrying a gun." Sully dropped his coat around Lindsey's shoulders, for which she was grateful. The thick windbreaker was almost as long as her dress.

"I promise I'll keep a close eye on her." Robbie put his hand on his heart but Sully didn't look convinced.

"I'll be fine," Lindsey said. "I'm certain I could use one of my spiked heels to defend myself if I had to." She was only partly kidding.

The ride to King's Island wasn't long but the breeze was chilly and Lindsey knew her hair was going to be a tangled mess when they arrived. She'd brought a hair tie that matched her dress for just that reason. When the island came into view, Lindsey felt her jaw go slack.

There was wealth and then there was *wealth*. Yachts were anchored around the island, their captains cooling their heels until the owners finished their party and were ready to be taken back to their own islands or potentially to sleep off the effects of the night's debauchery on their yachts.

The island itself was a hidden gem. A large stone mansion was tucked into the island and partially hidden by a thick copse of trees, but the yellow lights illuminating every bit of the building made it glow in the growing darkness.

Sully motored the water taxi right up the private pier. When their boat pulled alongside, a teenage boy in a bright blue windbreaker and khaki pants took the rope Sully tossed to him and secured the vessel.

Sully stepped out first and offered Lindsey his hand. She wobbled on her heels when she stood on the wooden dock and hoped she didn't do a face-plant. She slipped off his windbreaker and handed it to him. The chilly breeze coming off the bay whipped right through her silk dress and she shivered.

"You can hang on to it," Sully said.

"No, she can't," Robbie said. "We need to make an impression and that jacket does nothing to further our cause."

Sully glared but Robbie didn't flinch. Lindsey kissed Sully's cheek and patted his chest.

"Don't worry. I'll be fine," Lindsey assured him.

"It's not you I'm worried about, it's everyone else at this party. Be careful, darling."

"I will." She gestured to the boathouse at the end of the pier where several of the boat captains and crew members were lounging until the party was over. "Go see what you can find out."

"On it." He gave her one more long look. "Call me if you need me. I can be up there in minutes." He gestured to the mansion that loomed above them.

"Oh, for Pete's sake, I'll be with her," Robbie said. "It's not like she doesn't have backup right there with her."

"You have your own agenda," Sully reminded him.

"I can do both," Robbie said. Then he glanced at Lindsey and added, "But keep your phone close just in case."

He held out his arm and Lindsey took it, knowing the walk up to the mansion was going to be hopeless in these heels. She could feel Sully's eyes on her, and when they reached the wrought iron gate manned by a pair of security guards, she turned back to wave at him. For the first time, she felt a prickle of unease creep down her spine as the gate closed, locking Robbie and her on The Club's private grounds.

Stone steps led the way from the pier to the mansion. Landscaped rose bushes lined the walkway and the pungent scent of the blooms filled the humid air as they wound their way up, up, up to the mansion's entrance.

The main doors were oversize ornate wooden doors with brass studs embedded in the wood. Several staff stood by the entrance, wearing black pants and white shirts with *The Club* embroidered in fancy gold thread on the upper-left shirt pocket.

Robbie presented his invitation to a man in a suit, who was clearly in charge. The man looked it over as if he were doubtful that the famous Hollywood actor was standing right in front of him. Lindsey wanted to roll her eyes at the obvious power play, but she didn't.

"Mr. Vine?" the man asked. Lindsey glanced at the breast pocket of his suit and noted that his name tag read *Geoffrey*.

"The one and only." Robbie smiled, but it was more a show of teeth than a grin.

"It'll be just a few moments," Geoffrey said. "We need to authenticate your invitation."

One eyebrow ticked up on Robbie's forehead. Lindsey knew him well enough to know he'd run out of patience. "You do that, mate. Meanwhile my assistant and I will leave as we have better things to do than stand out in the cold." Robbie removed Lindsey's hand from his elbow and turned on his heel, offering her his other arm. Lindsey turned and tucked her hand into the crook of his elbow, hoping that Robbie hadn't just prematurely ended their evening.

"This is not helpful," she muttered under her breath.

"Trust me," he hissed back.

He started to guide her away when he paused and glanced over his shoulder. "By the way, Geoffrey, be a good fellow and be sure to give my regards to George Carraway, my sponsor, and the membership committee ladies, Leslie, Mallory, Harper and Tina. I'm sure they'll be *disappointed* that we missed each other."

He turned back to Lindsey and they took two steps when Geoffrey called out, "Mr. Vine, my mistake. Of course I can see this invitation is authentic."

Robbie winked at Lindsey before he gave Geoffrey his attention. "Can you now? Isn't that . . . convenient?"

"Jasmine will escort you in." Geoffrey pointed to a young woman standing nearby. "Enjoy your evening."

"I'm sure we will." Robbie guided Lindsey past him and

Lindsey concentrated on not faltering or tripping and ruining their entrance.

Jasmine smiled and gestured for them to follow her inside. Together they slipped through the open doors and stepped into a Gatsbyesque party of extravagance and excess that made Lindsey gasp. Jewels glittered under overhead lighting that was undoubtedly crafted for just that purpose. Men wore linen suits in shades of neutral and blue with a few bolder hues thrown into the mix. The women wore shimmering dresses in an explosion of spring colors, most with short skirts like Lindsey's, but some long and flouncy in tufts of tulle.

Taking it all in, Lindsey was suddenly very glad that Robbie had brought her something of Emma's to wear. She owned nothing that would have blended into this crowd unless she chose to dress like one of the staff in black pants and a white shirt. She glanced at the comfortable shoes Jasmine was wearing and felt a twinge of envy.

"I told you so," Robbie whispered as if reading her mind. "And you're welcome."

The aching arches of Lindsey's feet refused to let her thank him, so she huffed out a breath instead—*pfft*—which made Robbie laugh.

A jazz quartet played softly in one corner of the large ballroom. It was circular in shape with marble columns and an ornate terrazzo floor. On the far wall, large French doors opened out onto a veranda that overlooked a golf course and the bay beyond. Tables were piled with food. Everything from crab legs to filet mignon to macarons were arranged on one side of the ballroom while several fully loaded bars—with bartenders at the ready—were interspersed at stations amid the ballroom and the veranda outside.

As Robbie guided them into the thick of it, Lindsey took in the towering floral arrangements of pink and white peonies and cream- and cocoa-colored ranunculus with eucalyptus sprigs tucked in between. They were stunning and probably cost more than she made in a month. Twinkling lights were strung overhead twined with dried grapevines, giving the room an ethereal feeling like something out of one of Lindsey's favorite cozy fantasy novels.

As they moved through the crowd to the far side of the room, Lindsey tried to count how many people were in attendance. It had to be over two hundred. She frowned. How was she going to find out anything about Gwen and her relationship with The Club members in a crowd of this size?

"Robbie, how delightful to see you." Mallory Masterson approached them with a glass of champagne in each hand. "And you, too, Lindsey, although I must say I didn't expect to see you here."

There was a certain unfriendliness in her tone. Lindsey couldn't determine if it was meant for her or Robbie, but she suspected it was her. Mallory handed them each a glass and Lindsey took it just to be polite. She had no intention of drinking anything and losing her wits. She was having a hard enough time maintaining her short hem and spiky shoes.

"Lindsey's doing me a favor and acting as my assistant tonight," Robbie said. "Given that mine is out of town, I needed someone to keep things straight for me. I have a terrible memory—it's too full of scripts and screenplays—so I like to bring someone with me who is good with remembering the details."

"Is that so?" Mallory gave him an assessing stare with one eyebrow raised. Her auburn hair hung loose about her shoulders and her pale green micromini dress with long angel sleeves matched her eyes perfectly. Mallory was intimidatingly beautiful and it was clear that she knew it.

"It is." Robbie snagged a canapé off a tray being proffered and popped it into his mouth. Lindsey politely waved the waiter away. She was so far out of her comfort zone, she couldn't eat a bite without risking it coming back up or giving her a scorching case of heartburn.

"Mallory! Robbie! Lindsey!" A voice chirped and they turned to see Tina Baldwin skipping toward them on the toes of her pink stiletto sandals that matched her clingy pink silk chemise with a sparkling beaded fringe. Tina looked beautiful in the soft lighting with her blond hair styled in a chignon at the nape of her neck with two large ringlets framing her face.

"Where have you been?" Mallory asked as they exchanged air kisses. "And why do you smell like a campfire?"

Tina flushed and stamped her foot. "Shoot, I was afraid of that. Dave insisted on smoking a stinky cigar in the closed cabin on our yacht on the ride over. I told him I was going to have that smell in my hair for days but he wouldn't listen. Men. They're just not civilized." She turned to Robbie and added, "Present company excepted, of course."

"Of course, if it's any consolation, I find the smell of a cigar very attractive." Robbie greeted Tina with a kiss on each cheek, which Mallory observed with narrowed eyes.

Mallory crossed her arms in an impatient gesture and the sleeves of her dress fell back revealing her forearms. Several scratches appeared and Tina cried out. "Mall, your arm!"

Mallory immediately covered up the scratches with her sleeve. She frowned and said, "Damn kitten."

"Is that the new little fur baby your husband brought home?" Tina asked. "He's the cutest little tuxedo cat. Show them a picture."

"I don't have my phone on me." Mallory glowered. "And if it scratches me again it won't be our kitten for much longer."

Tina's eyebrows rose in surprise but she turned to Lindsey and gave her a quick hug. "You look beautiful, Lindsey."

"Thank you. You do, too." Lindsey shifted uncomfortably, whether it was from the compliment or her shoes, she didn't know. She did note that Mallory was right. Tina did smell like smoke. The effusiveness of Tina's greeting caused Mallory to look even more put out. She probably didn't like Tina fraternizing with the help, who would be Lindsey.

"I'm so excited to be attending my first spring fling," Tina gushed. "I've heard about these parties for years."

"What have you heard?" Lindsey asked, hoping she

didn't sound too nosy. She figured now was as good a time as any to get on with their investigation.

"Let's just say that whatever happens at The Club during spring fling stays at The Club." Tina giggled. Mallory looked annoyed, but Tina just took a long sip of her champagne and ignored her.

"That sounds delightfully wicked, Mrs. Baldwin." Robbie turned up his charm to maximum and Lindsey glanced away to keep from rolling her eyes at him.

Tina giggled and took Robbie's arm. "Come along. I have so many people to introduce you to and I know Harper and Leslie will want to say hi."

Lindsey wasn't sure what to do but Robbie reached out and grabbed her hand, tugging her along with him. "Keep up, Lindsey, I'll need you to make a note of who we're sending gifts to tomorrow."

"Right." Lindsey set her untouched champagne down on a passing tray.

Mallory watched them go; her head tipped to the side as if she was displeased by something. Lindsey suspected it was her or maybe it was Robbie. Tina had taken to the British actor immediately, as had Leslie and Harper, but Mallory was a tougher sell. Good thing Leslie was the person in charge because if it was up to Mallory, Lindsey was quite certain she and Robbie would be on a boat headed for shore by now. Lindsey scanned the ballroom for Leslie but there was no sign of her.

"Robbie, Lindsey, I want you to meet my husband," Tina said. She wiggled her way into a group of older men and latched her diamond-loaded fingers on to the arm of a short, portly fellow who had more hair on his chin than on his head. "David, this is the actor I told you about. Robbie Vine and his associate Lindsey."

Lindsey blinked. She was surprised Tina had leveled her up to associate instead of keeping her in her place with the title assistant. She suspected Mallory wouldn't have been so generous.

"Pleasure to meet you, Robbie." David shook his hand and then turned to Lindsey and shook hers as well. "You, too, Lindsey."

"Thank you." Lindsey took his hand. David Baldwin had a dry, firm grip that was reassuring and not punishing. He didn't feel the need to crush her fingers to prove anything.

"I'm off to mingle, lovie." Tina twirled away, the beads on her dress shimmering in the light.

David watched her go with a look of bemusement before he introduced them to the three men he was standing with, and while Lindsey was sure they were all very important in this world of affluence, unless they were library patrons or looking to cut a check for the library, she didn't particularly care. She studied the guests, recognizing several faces from various programs hosted at the library. The cooking and gardening ones, in particular. That was heartening. They might not be book borrowers but they liked the programs. She'd take the win.

"You don't mind, do you?" Robbie asked.

"I'm sorry, what?" Lindsey turned to find the men looking at her as if waiting for her answer.

"David is going to show me the room where the gentlemen retire," Robbie said. He had his back to the men and his eyes bored into Lindsey's as if trying to tell her to go along.

"Ah, a no-ladies-allowed room." She nodded.

"It's just whiskey and stinky cigars," David said. "Nothing that would interest a lady like yourself."

"Your wife said you enjoy a fine cigar." Lindsey wondered if Robbie would come out of the gentlemen's room smelling like a campfire, too.

"I do," David agreed. "And the party's been underway for an hour. I'm overdue."

"Don't let me keep you then." She smiled at the group and then turned to Robbie and said, "I'll be right here when you need me."

"Don't wander off." Robbie squeezed her hand. "I don't want to answer to Sully if I lose you."

Lindsey watched the gentlemen leave, collectively looking relieved that she hadn't made a fuss. Robbie sent her a wink as he left and she sighed and turned to face the room. Now she wished she'd kept the champagne—at least she'd have something to do with her hands.

She decided to stroll the perimeter of the party. Her personality was more of the wallflower type and she was relieved to escape to the outskirts of the crowd. Maybe she'd overhear something that would help with the investigation.

A murder on a neighboring island had to be the talk of The Club, hadn't it?

Lindsey made it halfway around the room, skirting clusters of people talking and laughing, feeling more and more like an outsider, when a white-haired lady, sitting on a padded bench beside one of the French doors, beckoned her with one bony finger.

Beneath the perfectly coiffed white hair was a wizened face, heavy on the eye makeup and lipstick. Lindsey guessed the woman's age to be somewhere in her eighties. She was adorned in a choker of diamonds and amethysts over a lavender suit that had the cut of Chanel. Her shoes were low-heeled Mary Janes in a complimentary purple. From head to toe, she was very timeless and classy.

Lindsey prepared herself for the woman to assume she worked there and give her a drink order. Lindsey knew it had to be obvious to the regulars that she wasn't a member. Instead, the woman's shrewd gray eyes looked her up and down and in a raspy voice, she said, "Sit before you break an ankle in those ridiculous shoes."

Tugging the hem of her skirt as low as it would go, Lindsey sat beside the woman and crossed her legs to keep from inadvertently flashing anyone. "Hi, I'm—"

"Lindsey Sullivan, director of the public library and married to the dashing Captain Mike Sullivan, I know." The woman turned to look at her and Lindsey saw a glint of amusement in her eyes. "Your husband talks about you quite a lot while ferrying me about on his water taxi."

"Oh." Lindsey felt her face grow warm with pleasure. She glanced at the woman out of the corner of her eye. She had a dowager duchess air about her and it occurred to Lindsey that she likely knew everyone and everything that happened on the islands. "I'm sorry to admit, I don't know who you are."

"That's not surprising, I live here at The Club," the

woman said. "I don't leave the island unless it's for an appointment on the mainland."

"You live *here*?" Lindsey echoed in surprise.

"My father, Elias Whitcomb, was one of the founders of The Club," the woman said. "So I have a well-appointed apartment on the upper floor. With three restaurants, room service, a maid, laundry and any other service I could possibly require at my fingertips, why would I live anywhere else?"

"Why indeed." Lindsey couldn't argue with her. The thought of having people available to take care of anything she needed at the snap of her fingers—well, it was hard to find a downside.

"There are only a few of us left, children of the founders, and when we die out I'm sure that will be the end of the residency," the woman said.

"I'm sorry, I didn't catch your name." Lindsey shifted on the bench, trying to mind her skirt while extending her hand.

"Because I didn't give it." She was sharp, Lindsey would give her that. After a pause, the woman said, "Eleanor. Eleanor Whitcomb." She put her hand in Lindsey's, and Lindsey gave the frail fingers and papery skin the barest squeeze before releasing her.

"Won't your residence go to the next generation of Whitcombs?" Lindsey asked. "I thought these sorts of places were all about tradition."

"In my case, I have no heirs. I never married so there's no one to leave it to. But as for the others, tradition gets tossed aside when it comes to profit," Eleanor said. "The board decreed years ago that we would be the last of the founders' heirs to reside in The Club. They are ready to move on from the tradition. Honestly, if there was an iceberg handy, I'm sure the current membership would stick us on one and shove us out to sea just to get our apartments."

Lindsey gasped and Eleanor waved her hand dismissively. "It's the way of things. Everyone wants you when you have value but when you stop bringing in money, they're eager to replace you with someone who does."

Lindsey shook her head. She couldn't believe a social club could be so ruthless. Since Eleanor seemed to be feeling chatty, she decided to ask about Gwen.

"Do you know . . . or have you ever met a woman named Gwen Capshaw?" Lindsey asked.

Eleanor's brows rose. "You got right to it, didn't you?"

Lindsey shrugged. "Small talk is not my gift."

"Clearly." Eleanor gave her a critical glance. "Of course I knew Gwen Capshaw. I was the membership committee chairman before Leslie Stone, so I'm the one who rejected Gwen over and over and over again."

"Why?" Lindsey asked. "Why not let her in?"

"Her husband bungled it," Eleanor said. "He destroyed a real estate deal that the chairman of the board of directors had in play and that was it. The Capshaws were never to be admitted to The Club."

"But he was preserving the habitat of the local ospreys," Lindsey protested.

Eleanor waved her arm, encompassing the room. "Do these people look like the sort who care about a bird's habitat?"

Lindsey didn't have to look at them to answer. "No."

"I happened to agree with Perry Capshaw and was delighted when he tanked the development deal," Eleanor confessed. "But there was no talking David Baldwin out of it."

"David Baldwin?" Lindsey repeated. "Tina's husband?"

"No, he's David Baldwin Jr. It was his father who went head-to-head with Perry and lost," Eleanor said. "You'd think Gwen would have been proud of her husband but instead she was furious. She wanted to belong but it was never going to happen, not after that. Gwen, of course, only made it worse."

"How so?" Lindsey was fascinated by the social inner workings of The Club.

"Because she wanted it so badly," Eleanor said. "We can't have people in here like that. Membership can only be offered to those persons who are indifferent to belonging, like your friend Robbie Vine. He's been invited every year since he moved to Briar Creek and he always declines. Because he doesn't need us and he doesn't care."

"So your standard for membership is to choose people who are independent enough to take or leave belonging and Gwen was rejected because it was too important to her?" Lindsey clarified.

"Exactly." Eleanor nodded.

"It seems like inviting people who value the invitation would be more practical," Lindsey said.

"When has exclusivity ever been practical?" Eleanor countered. "It's the law of scarcity. Why do you think certain things retain their value more than others? Is it because they're of higher quality or because of their perceived scarcity?"

"Never really thought about it," Lindsey said.

"People crave having what no one else can have," Eleanor said. "Whether it's Laphroaig whiskey or a Rolex Daytona or an exclusive membership to a social club."

"Sorry, none of that speaks to me. I'm a librarian and, as you know, we're not really about exclusion," Lindsey said. "We believe there's room for everyone. Inclusivity is our entire purpose."

"Which is probably why Gideon Trask is trying to shut you down." Lindsey started in surprise and Eleanor cast her a side-eye. "Yes, I know about that. He sees no perceived value in the library so he wants to close it."

"You're incredibly blunt." Lindsey knew it was silly to be annoyed with Eleanor when she was speaking the truth, but she was.

"I'm too old not to be," Eleanor said. "No time for niceties when I might not be here in the morning."

"Fair point." Lindsey shrugged. She certainly wasn't going to argue with a woman old enough to be her grandmother. She glanced around the room, studying the brittle smiles and listening to the fake laughter, observing the endless posturing as guests tried to be seen with the right people. It was exhausting and she was just an observer.

"Why do you suppose Gwen wanted to belong to this place so much?" Lindsey asked. She doubted she was doing a good job of keeping the disdain out of her voice. "What would Gwen have had to do to gain acceptance?"

"She wanted to belong for the same reason everyone does. External validation. It's meaningless because it comes from outside yourself, but people still crave it. As for what she'd have to do, she'd have to sacrifice everything she held dear," Eleanor said. She pointed in the direction of a sixty-something man in an ecru linen suit with brown Italian loafers. "See that man?"

Lindsey nodded. He was hard to miss. His thinning gray hair was buzzed short, leaving much of his pink scalp visible. He was built lean but with a decided paunch around the middle. He sported a golfer's tan and had a deep cleft in his chin, although his lips were thin and his eyes a bit squinty. He'd likely been handsome once, but now there was an air of constant dissatisfaction about him.

"That's Malcolm Rutledge," Eleanor said.

He was standing with Harper Winslow and a man Lindsey assumed was her husband as he had his hand on Harper's lower back when Tina Baldwin sauntered up to their group in her sparkly pink dress and shoes.

The group was close enough that Lindsey and Eleanor could hear them.

"Malcolm, could you be a dear and get me another drink?" Tina smiled, biting her lower lip. She leaned close and glanced at him from beneath her lashes in a blatantly flirtatious look.

Malcolm glanced down at her and Lindsey noticed there was a decidedly cruel twist to his lips. He took the empty glass from her fingers and she smiled wide as if he'd acquiesced. Instead, he plopped her martini glass onto a waiter's passing tray and said, "You have two legs attached to that behind—go get it yourself."

Both Harper and her husband snorted with laughter while Tina's face flamed in embarrassment. She gave them a hard smile and tossed her head in an attempt to laugh off his mean refusal. Without saying a word, she hurried away, looking like she might cry. Lindsey felt terrible for Tina and was surprised that Harper had contributed to the humiliation of her friend. With friends like her, who needed enemies?

"If I were her, I'd give up on that one," Eleanor said. "Malcolm Rutledge is about as mean as they come."

"Give up on him?" Lindsey asked in confusion. What did Eleanor mean? "But she's married. I just met her husband, David."

"He won't be her husband for long, according to the current gossip," Eleanor said. "David's financial empire is overextended and he's about to lose everything. Tina has clearly set her sights on a new sugar daddy."

"Hm." Lindsey tried not to sound judgmental. She failed.

"You don't approve?" Eleanor asked.

"It's not my business," Lindsey said, trying to duck the question.

"Isn't it?" Eleanor countered. "After all, your friend Gwen Capshaw was trying to win Malcolm's affection as well. Unsuccessfully, I might add."

"Gwen was not my friend," Lindsey said. "I only met her once and it wasn't what I would call pleasant."

"Interactions with Gwen seldom were," Eleanor said. "She and Malcolm had that in common."

"But Gwen was married," Lindsey protested. Eleanor sent her a pitying look and Lindsey closed her mouth.

"That's how it works out here." Eleanor pointed to a young woman and a middle-aged, debauched-looking man. She was holding him up as he staggered while his hand roamed inappropriately all over her person.

"Is she dating him?" Lindsey asked. "Because she could do much better."

"Oh, no, he's her husband. That's Karl Kilkenny and his wife, Kylie. They've been married about five years now."

"Why?" Lindsey couldn't fathom being shackled to a husband like that.

"Because the Kilkennys are one of the most prominent families in The Club and Kylie's family wanted to move in a higher social circle. Kylie marrying Karl was their way to do it. Don't feel too badly for her. I hear her tennis coach is a great comfort to her."

Lindsey put her hand on her forehead. None of this felt normal or right to her.

"Social climbing is not for the weak," Eleanor said. "Gwen Capshaw tried to worm her way into the Kilkenny family. She threw her daughter, Jordan, at Karl like the girl was a sacrifice being made to a god. Gwen actually took a boat out and deserted her daughter on The Club's swimming raft at night—knowing that her daughter was afraid of deep, dark water—and insisted that Karl go and 'save' her."

Lindsey shivered. She was with Jordan. If there was one thing that scared her silly it was dark water over her head where she couldn't see what was around her. Terrifying.

"What happened? Did he save her?" Lindsey had to know because the drunkard who was groping his wife in public did not strike her as the sort of guy who would go out of his way to save a girl on a raft at night.

"He never got the chance." Eleanor smiled with satisfaction. "Jordan's young fella—"

"Ryan Montgomery," Lindsey supplied.

"He's the one," Eleanor agreed. "He arrived on a Jet Ski that he 'borrowed' from someone at The Club and whisked the girl to safety. It was very romantic."

"I'm guessing Gwen didn't see it that way."

Eleanor snorted. "No, and because he looked like an idiot for not saving Jordan first, it caused Karl to take an unhealthy interest in the young woman."

Lindsey raised her brows in question.

"He stalked her," Eleanor said. "And her mother was delighted."

They sat quietly while Lindsey absorbed this information. She couldn't imagine a mother being so determined to be a member of a social set that she would offer up her daughter as bait. She glanced around the room, wondering how many people had traded a genuine connection with another person for the wealth and privilege they wore like designer accessories. Lindsey knew there wasn't enough money in the world for her to give up Sully.

"Obviously, stalking didn't work," Lindsey said. "So, what happened?"

"From what I heard, there was a fight between Karl and Ryan. Ryan won and Karl's parents threatened to have Ryan arrested."

Suddenly, Ryan and Jordan disappearing on their graduation day made sense.

"But they disappeared," Lindsey said.

"They ran off together," Eleanor confirmed. "Gwen tried to convince everyone that Ryan had kidnapped Jordan but no one believed it. Anyone with two eyes could see that they were mad about each other. I wonder what happened to them."

"They're married," Lindsey said. "They just arrived back in town because of Gwen's passing."

Eleanor nodded. "I suppose Jordan is looking for closure. I hope she can find it. Her mother never gave up on wanting to belong to The Club, even trying to gain access by having a relationship with that odious troll Malcolm Rutledge."

"I have a hard time believing she'd leave her husband for him," Lindsey said.

"From what I heard, she was planning to leave Perry as soon as she had Malcolm on the hook." Eleanor gestured to the cluster of older men standing with Malcolm. "She was hoping to land him because the men her own age were obviously looking for someone much younger."

"Obviously." Lindsey couldn't keep her sarcasm in check.

She studied the older men. Would Gwen really have left Perry for Malcolm or one of these other men? Did Perry know she was planning that? Was that why he'd been drinking when Jordan arrived? Could he have killed Gwen to stop her? Did he purposefully make it look as though it was Ariel who'd murdered Gwen? Was he framing her by banking on their long-running feud to steer the investigation away from himself?

"It's hard to know what someone will do to get what they want, especially when they feel it slipping out of their grasp. Desperation makes people do horrible things." Eleanor met Lindsey's gaze and Lindsey suspected that while living here, Eleanor had seen some stuff.

"I know I shouldn't be surprised by the things that people do," Lindsey said. "And yet, I always am."

"That's because you could never do those sorts of things," Eleanor said.

"You can tell that about me after just a few minutes?" Lindsey asked.

"No," Eleanor admitted. "But I've come to know your husband reasonably well and Sully is not the sort of man to give his heart to a woman who isn't worthy."

"No, he isn't," Lindsey agreed. They shared a smile and Lindsey knew that talking with Eleanor had been the best possible sleuthing she could have done at this event. The woman was the institutional memory of the place.

"Lindsey, there you are. I've been looking all over for you." Robbie panted as he muscled his way through the crowd toward them.

"Sorry," Lindsey said. "I was . . . making a new friend." Robbie glanced between them, and Lindsey said, "Robbie Vine, this is Eleanor Whitcomb. Her father was one of the founders."

"A pleasure, madam." Robbie took Eleanor's hand and gave her a slight bow.

"I'm sure it is." Eleanor took her hand back, looking singularly unimpressed. "How do you find The Club?"

Robbie studied her for a moment and said, "Pretentious, shallow and full of poseurs."

Eleanor's eyes narrowed. "And yet here you are."

"I didn't say I don't like all of those qualities." Robbie grinned. It was his patented Robbie-Vine-the-movie-star smile, which was known to melt the iciest of hearts. Eleanor was no different.

"Humph." Eleanor huffed but a very soft pink blush filled her cheeks. "You aren't like them." Eleanor gestured dismissively to the room.

"What makes you say that?" Robbie asked.

"Because you wouldn't be friends with her." Eleanor pointed to Lindsey. "You wouldn't be dating the chief of police. And you would have joined The Club years ago when I invited you. The pair of you are obviously up to no good."

"I'm just here as his assistant." Lindsey raised her hands in innocence.

Eleanor shook her head and the large amethyst-and-diamond earrings that she wore sparkled in the light. "You have been tied to a shocking number of murder cases, Lindsey the librarian, so I doubt very much that you're here to act as the assistant to Robbie, who has never shown any interest in The Club until after the suspicious death of a woman who was obsessed with joining The Club, so I must deduce that you are here to see if there is a connection with The Club and Gwen Capshaw's death."

Robbie laughed and turned to Lindsey. "I like her despite the fact that she's terrifying."

"I do, too," Lindsey agreed.

Eleanor looked even more put out. "Why exactly does Gwen's death matter to you two? As far as I know, she had no friends, no social life—which was another strike against her, frankly. So, if she wasn't a friend, why are you looking into her death?"

Robbie and Lindsey exchanged a glance. He nodded and Lindsey sighed. She supposed there wasn't much point in keeping the truth from Eleanor. "You know The Club is funding the library's book boat to the islands?"

Eleanor nodded. "It's about time we got some return on our investment in this town."

Lindsey cleared her throat. "Yes, well, the funding has been put in jeopardy because I happened to be the one to find Gwen Capshaw."

Eleanor reared back and stared down her nose at Lindsey, which was quite a feat because even seated Eleanor was shorter than Lindsey. "Says who?" she demanded.

"Leslie Stone," Lindsey said.

Eleanor reached up and fingered the diamond-and-amethyst choker at her throat as if touching it reminded her of her worth and her place here.

"That's ridiculous," Eleanor said. "The money has already been granted. They won't take it away and risk the bad publicity."

"I don't know," Lindsey said. "Leslie seemed to think Gideon Trask would be happy to cut the funding."

"Trask." Eleanor scoffed.

"Did someone mention my name?" A man pushed his way into their group and Lindsey felt her stomach drop. Gideon Trask. The absolute last person she wanted to see.

"Yes, *I* did," Eleanor said. "Did my contempt and disdain summon you?"

"Ouch. That seems harsh even for you, Eleanor." Gideon tugged the cuffs of his shirt out from under his jacket sleeves. It struck Lindsey as a nervous gesture, but why? Was he afraid of Eleanor?

"Not harsh enough, given that you're still here." Eleanor cast a nasty look in his direction before turning away.

"Now, now, you're not still angry about your apartment, are you?" Gideon's tone was mocking. "Times change, Eleanor, and it'll be better for everyone involved if you just sign the ownership over to me before I'm forced to change The Club's bylaws and forcibly take it away from you."

"I'll see you in court," Eleanor said.

"Now why bring attorneys into it?" Gideon asked. "You don't have that kind of money and we both know it. It's time for you to pick out your little retirement apartment in Briar Creek and die quietly there without making a fuss."

"You complete prat!" Robbie spat. "How dare you speak to her like that."

"I'll talk to her any way I like," Gideon snapped. "And don't think for one second that you're going to be allowed in this club. I don't care who sponsors you. I know where all the bodies are and I will happily add yours to them."

Trask's tone was pure malice. Lindsey's gaze moved from Robbie to Eleanor to Gideon. Trask's smile was smarmy as if he was enjoying her discomfort. For her part, Eleanor wasn't giving in to it. She tipped her chin up in defiance and said, "Speaking of bodies, you'll get my apartment when you pry it out of my cold dead hands."

"If you insist." Gideon's chuckle was evil as he gave her a mocking bow. He turned to Lindsey and said, "I'm surprised to see you here. You're way out of your league, you know. Enjoy your little book boat while you have it. I expect to have the entirety of your library shut down by the end of summer."

"That won't happen." Lindsey rose to her feet. The crippling heels had one perk; they gave her a few inches in height, making her over six feet tall. And right now, she wanted every bit of it so she could stare down at this obnoxious man. She crossed her arms over her chest, feigning a calm she didn't feel.

"Oh, yes, it will," Trask hissed as he stared up at her. "The town council is going to eliminate all waste and the library is going to be the first thing to go." He ran his gaze over her in the most insulting manner possible, causing Lindsey to feel completely grossed out. "You should give me a call. I'm sure I can put you to work in some . . . capacity."

The innuendo was disgusting and now Lindsey wanted a glass of champagne to toss right into his smug face.

"Oy, watch yourself!" Robbie protested at the same moment Eleanor snapped, "Trask, apologize at once."

"No way." Gideon smirked. "Enjoy your evening, losers."

Gideon turned and slammed right into Sully, who happened to be holding a fat slice of coconut cream pie on a plate. Sully tried to catch it, but somehow it became airborne and landed smack-dab in Gideon's face with the cream and the crust sliding off his chin and down the front of his bespoke suit as the plate clattered to the floor.

"You!" Gideon shouted, drawing the attention of everyone in the ballroom. "You did that on purpose."

"I'm sorry, but you slammed into me, Trask. You should really watch where you're going." Sully shook his head. "I mean, why would I waste a slice of pie, that I was really looking forward to eating, by dumping it on you?"

Gideon wiped the pie from his face and flung the remnants to the floor. Lindsey knew she shouldn't laugh, she knew it, but when Eleanor let out a bark of laughter, she was powerless not to join in. The tension whooshed out of her as she let the laughter out.

"Sorry, mate," Robbie said. "But the captain has the right of it. Any egg on your face is of your own making."

"I am going to sue you for assault," Gideon fumed.

"You can try, but I'm quite certain the video will show

otherwise." Sully pointed to a security camera mounted on the wall.

Furious, Gideon stormed from the ballroom, leaving a trail of sticky crumbs behind him. The crowd parted with most of the people laughing or jumping out of the way as Gideon plowed through the mass of bodies to leave through the nearest exit.

Eleanor was still laughing. It was a wheezy sound as if she hadn't laughed out loud in a long time. She wiped at her eyes with the back of her hand, trying to keep her mascara from running.

"That's the most entertainment I've had in a very long time," she said. "Thank you, Sully."

"Accidents happen." He shrugged, the picture of innocence, but Lindsey knew better.

"Either way, your timing was spectacular," Robbie said. "Ms. Whitcomb, Eleanor, can I escort you out of this mess?" Robbie gestured to the pie on the ground.

"Yes, please." Eleanor rose and took his proffered arm, allowing him to lead her safely through the detritus that the waitstaff was attempting to clean up.

"Sorry about that," Sully apologized to a man in black pants and a white shirt who arrived with a broom.

"Don't be." The man grinned. "That guy is the worst, and if need be I can bear witness that he walked into the pie."

Sully exchanged a knuckle bump with him before they followed Robbie and Eleanor.

"What brings you to the party?" Lindsey took Sully's

arm, noting that even in his boating attire of an insulated windbreaker and a pair of jeans, he was by far the handsomest man in the room and she was thrilled to be with him.

"I saw Trask anchor his yacht and I didn't like the idea of you being caught off guard if he popped up on you, which of course he did." Sully shook his head in disgust. "Did you learn anything useful?"

Lindsey gestured to Eleanor. "So many things. I need to go home and sift through it all."

"That works for me."

They followed Robbie and Eleanor to an elevator. A man in The Club's uniform was manning the small people carrier. He tipped his head to Eleanor. "Done for the evening, Ms. Whitcomb?"

"Yes." Eleanor let go of Robbie's arm and turned to face them. "I'm going to think about what we talked about, Lindsey. If I have any more . . . insights, I know where to find you." As regal as a queen, she stepped into the elevator and was whisked upstairs.

Lindsey turned to Robbie and noted the pungent scent of cigar smoke coming off his linen jacket. "Ready to go?"

"More than." He started for the exit, not waiting for them to follow.

Lindsey and Sully exchanged a glance. Sully dropped his windbreaker around Lindsey's shoulder and she burrowed into the warmth.

"Come on," he said. "We can talk on the boat."

They departed from the grand mansion and Lindsey

realized she'd never seen Leslie, not once, all evening. She wondered if Robbie had.

"Robbie, did you see Leslie tonight?"

"Leslie?" Robbie paused and they caught up to him. He considered the question and then slowly shook his head. "No, I didn't, which is weird because she was so insistent that I attend tonight."

Robbie was right. Leslie not being in attendance felt off. An ominous sinking feeling hit Lindsey in her gut.

She let go of Sully and approached Geoffrey, the man in the suit, who had been so rude to her and Robbie when they arrived. He didn't look any more thrilled to speak to her now.

"I'm sorry to bother you," Lindsey said.

"And yet, here you are." Geoffrey's face appeared to be frozen in a look of annoyance.

"Do you know if Leslie Stone has arrived yet?" He opened his mouth, looking as if he was about to call her on her impertinence, but Lindsey cut him off. "I'm worried about her."

He frowned. He considered her request and the lines between his brow deepened. He leaned forward as if afraid of being overheard.

"No, she hasn't arrived as yet." He glanced around as if to make certain no one saw him speaking to her. "Which is very odd."

So it wasn't just her who felt that way. Lindsey nodded. "Thank you."

"For what?" Geoffrey asked, and Lindsey knew he would deny speaking to her with his last breath if need be.

Lindsey returned to Sully's side and took his arm. She was certain his support was the only thing keeping her upright on the uneven terrain. They continued their walk to the dock.

"What's the matter, darling?" Sully asked when they reached the boat. Sully helped her aboard while Robbie untied the ropes.

"Maybe nothing," she admitted. "But I think we need to make a stop on our way home."

"Leslie's house?" Sully asked.

Lindsey nodded. "Something feels off."

"Should I call Emma now or wait until after we find the body?" Robbie asked as he tossed the rope and joined them on the boat.

"Was that sarcasm?" Lindsey asked. "Because it sounded like sarcasm."

"I think it's more resignation," Robbie countered.

"Call her and let her know what we're doing," Sully suggested as he fired up the engine. "Then she can decide if she wants to meet us or not."

Robbie took his phone out of his pocket and called Emma. There was silence for a beat and then some yelling, audible over the sound of the boat motor, the wind and the waves. Lindsey glanced at Sully and he reached out and pulled her close, offering her his warmth.

"It'll be okay." He kissed her head and Lindsey felt comforted even though she doubted anything was going to be okay until they discovered who murdered Gwen and Gideon got the library out of his budget-slashing sights.

"Where does Leslie live?" Lindsey asked while Sully maneuvered the boat through the islands with a knowledge and experience born of a lifetime spent navigating the archipelago.

"She's in one of three houses on Pine Top Island," Sully said. "It's one of the farthest islands to the east and gets the brunt of most of the weather, but the thick stand of pine trees on it shelters it from most storms."

Lindsey could see the lights of the mainland growing increasingly smaller. She wondered if she'd made the right call to stop by Leslie's house. Maybe Leslie had taken ill or potentially had never planned to attend. No, that didn't sit right. Given the importance of the spring fling, Lindsey suspected Leslie would be there even if she'd contracted the plague.

"Emma's going to meet us there," Robbie said. "Fair warning, she's very unhappy about this entire case and I don't think a second body is going to help at all."

"That's assuming there is a second body," Lindsey said.

"Does Emma want us to wait for her?" Sully pointed to a large island in the distance. "Pine Top is right there."

"She said for you, Sully, to go ahead and do a wellness check," Robbie said. "We're to call her as soon as we know anything. She's on her way but will turn back if everything is fine."

"I really hope I'm wrong," Lindsey said.

Sully and Robbie shared a look that Lindsey suspected meant that they hoped she was wrong, too, but neither of them said as much. By the time they reached Pine Top Island, it was after nine. If Leslie had intended to go to the party, she would be there by now as this was well past "fashionably late" time for a party that started at six.

Robbie hopped out of the boat and tied it to the dock. There were three slips, which Lindsey took to mean that all three of the homeowners on Pine Top shared this particular dock.

Only one slip had a boat in it, and Sully frowned as he studied it.

"Do you know whose boat that is?" Lindsey asked.

"No, but I do know that the Hodges and the Feinsteins also live here, and I saw both of those couples in the ballroom when I followed Trask." Sully frowned at the houses on the island.

"Does that mean the remaining boat is Leslie's?" Lindsey asked.

"Not necessarily," Robbie said. "If they were all going to The Club, they might have gone together in one boat."

"Except two boats are gone," Lindsey said.

"Possibly, Leslie went with one of them, and we just didn't see her," Sully said. "We won't know until I check the Stones' house."

He started up the dock. Lindsey gave Robbie a side-eye and hurried after Sully. Without a word, Robbie fell in behind her.

Sully glanced over his shoulder. "I thought Emma said I was to do the wellness check." Lindsey and Robbie blinked at him and Sully sighed. "All right, fine. We'll go together."

Relieved, Lindsey took his arm to steady herself. She

was never ever ever wearing shoes like these ever again. She glanced at the houses on the island, searching hopefully for signs of life. She desperately wanted to be wrong and was afraid that she wasn't. But she also knew she couldn't stand to cool her heels down on the dock waiting for news. No matter what they found, it was better to be here.

"The Feinsteins live over there." Sully pointed to the house on the far right. All the lights were off. "And the Hodges live in the one in the center." The lights were off at that home as well. They followed the path to the house on the end of the island. "And this one is Leslie and Arthur Stone's."

Lindsey stumbled and Sully caught her about the waist. She stared at the house in front of them. Every single light was on and the front door was wide-open. There was also the distinct smell of smoke in the air.

"Call Emma!" Sully ordered. He squeezed Lindsey's hand once before letting go and racing toward the house.

Robbie swore and took his phone out of his pocket. Lindsey heard him talking to Emma but her gaze was on the house.

There was no sign of a fire in the house—no smoke pluming out the windows, no flames lighting the night sky. Instead, the smell reminded her of the nights she and Sully spent in the backyard toasting marshmallows over their firepit. Could it be that Leslie had just been enjoying an evening fire? But what about The Club? It made no sense that she would miss the spring fling, which, according to Tina, was the kickoff to the summer social season.

"Sully?" Lindsey approached the house and paused outside. She knocked on the doorframe before entering even though Sully had already gone inside. "Leslie?"

There was no answer.

The house had an open floor plan and she stepped into the great room, which flowed into a kitchen and dining room and out through a set of French doors to a large deck on the back. The glass doors were open so Lindsey crossed through the gray and white rooms with bold red accents sprinkled here and there and out to the back deck.

"Sully?" she cried.

"Down here!" he called.

Lindsey hurried across the deck, making certain she didn't catch her heels in the gaps between the planks. She reached the stairs and leaned over the railing. Sully was standing on a stone veranda next to a firepit that was still smoking.

"Any sign of Leslie?" she asked.

"No." He shook his head. "The fire appears to have burnt out. The last of the embers are still hot and smoking a bit, but it's weird."

"In what way?" Lindsey asked.

"Well, there's a pile of logs here, but this looks to be something else that was burned." Sully stabbed at the smoking ash with a metal poker and lifted a small piece of cloth out of the ashes attached to a narrow piece of wood.

"What do you suppose it is?" Lindsey asked.

"No idea." Sully put the cloth and wood aside. "There's nothing else but ash."

"Why would Leslie leave a fire going in her firepit when she knew she was going out?" Lindsey asked.

"It might have been someone else, a housekeeper maybe," Sully suggested. "If they knew the boss would be out, they might have enjoyed a glass of wine by the fire after Leslie left. And maybe they had something personal to burn."

"*If* Leslie left," Lindsey said. "Because, according to Geoffrey, she never made it to the party. If it was a housekeeper, would it be their boat tied up at the dock?"

"No." Sully pointed across the lawn and Lindsey noted a second smaller dock with a boathouse. "The domestic help would use the smaller private dock. There's no boat there, so they've likely gone home."

"Emma is almost here." Robbie panted as he joined them outside. "Any sign of Leslie?"

"No." Sully shook his head. "We should check the house." He left the firepit and climbed the stairs two at a time to join them. "Let's search inside first and then we can fan out and check the yard if need be. Try not to touch anything."

"I'll take the downstairs," Lindsey volunteered. She was not climbing any more stairs in these heels if she could avoid it. "You two can split the upstairs."

The men hurried up the wide main staircase with Sully going in one direction while Robbie took the other. Lindsey turned and assessed the room she was in. The open floor plan didn't leave much for her to do except check in and around the furniture, the pantry and the laundry room.

There was no sign of a struggle. All the tchotchkes in the house were in place, even the couch cushions appeared to have been artfully arranged. Lindsey could hear the footsteps of the men above as they searched each room, checking closets and under furniture. Lindsey stepped back out onto the veranda in front of the house.

The adrenaline spike of finding the house wide-open and all the lights on had made her heart race and she felt overly warm and a bit queasy. She crossed the veranda to the cushioned wrought iron bench to sit for a minute. As she lowered herself into the seat, her right foot slid out from under her. Lindsey landed with a thump on the bench and she cursed her stupid shoes for the millionth time. She glanced down to see if she'd broken the ankle strap but instead discovered she'd stepped in a puddle . . . of blood.

Lindsey didn't realize she'd jumped and screamed until Emma appeared on the veranda at the same time Sully and Robbie burst out of the house.

"Lindsey, what is it?" Sully raced to her side.

Lindsey pointed to the ground beneath the bench she'd sat on and said, "Blood."

Emma ripped the Maglite off her utility belt and flicked it on, pointing the beam at the stone floor. A small puddle of blood smeared by Lindsey's shoe glistened bright red in the light.

"Nobody move." Emma knelt down beside the bench, shining her light beneath it. In seconds she was on her feet. "Leslie's under there. Help me move this thing."

Robbie and Sully stepped forward, each grabbing an end.

"We're going to lift it straight up, walk it out a few feet and set it down," Emma instructed.

Lindsey scooted out of the way while Sully and Robbie hefted the heavy bench, moving it away from the house and setting it down where Emma indicated. Glancing around the bench, Lindsey saw her then. Leslie Stone was lying on her back, facing up with her eyes closed just as Gwen had been. She was dressed in a sparkling gold dress with a full skirt and a matching wrap, which was draped over her elbow. The bodice of her dress was saturated with blood and jutting out of her chest was the wooden handle of what resembled an artist's palette knife.

Emma checked Leslie's vitals. Lindsey held her breath hoping that her gut feeling was wrong, that somehow Leslie would be all right. Sully took her hand in his and interlaced their fingers in a gesture of comfort and support.

In moments, Emma rocked back on her heels and closed her eyes briefly before pulling out her phone and calling for the crime scene technicians to come out. They were an hour away at another crime scene but would get there as soon as they could. Robbie helped Emma to her feet and Lindsey noticed the weariness in her posture. Emma took crime in her jurisdiction personally, especially when it involved murder.

And there was no doubt that Leslie had been murdered exactly like Gwen had been. Lindsey pulled Sully's jacket more tightly about herself. She felt icy cold on the inside and it had nothing to do with the chilly breeze coming in from the bay. Just like Gwen Capshaw, Leslie Stone had been murdered and her body hidden, which meant both killings had to have been committed by the same person.

"What can we do to help?" Lindsey asked.

Emma met her gaze and said, "Tell me everything. You can start with what made you decide you needed to see Leslie when you're supposed to be at a party."

"It was just a feeling," Lindsey said. "It didn't seem right that Leslie wasn't at the party that is the first big social event of the season for The Club where she is in charge of membership."

"A feeling?" Emma asked. "No one said anything about Leslie while you were at the party that made you worry for her safety or anything like that?"

Lindsey shrugged. "No, sorry. It just felt weird that she hadn't shown up yet."

"It's all right. You have good instincts," Emma said. "Who knows how long she would have been here until someone found her if you hadn't followed your gut. What else did you observe tonight?"

"I had a very long chat with Eleanor Whitcomb," Lindsey said.

"She's terrifying," Robbie chimed in.

Emma frowned. "She's a tiny little bird of a woman—how is she frightening?"

"She has a wit sharp enough to leave a scar," he said. A ghost of a smile moved across Emma's mouth.

"And what about your time with the men?" Lindsey

asked. "Did you learn anything over your stinky cigars and expensive whiskey?"

"Other than the fact that money doesn't buy empathy, charm or intelligence, not really." Robbie frowned. "I will say it was an unsettling encounter. I got the feeling the men were trying to learn something from me, but I couldn't figure out what it was."

"What do you mean?" Lindsey asked.

"They were inordinately fixated on my life as a celebrity—I understand the curiosity about that, you know, what's it like to see yourself on the big screen and such—but they were more interested in my personal life. They assumed I entertain a revolving door of young ladies and they wanted to hear all the naughty bits about it." Robbie looked offended. "Do they really think I'm that shallow?"

Emma glanced at him and said, "They don't appreciate that the love of your life packs heat."

"Clearly," Robbie agreed, and blew her a kiss.

"Question," Emma said. "Did any of you notice if Mr. Stone was at the party?"

Lindsey shrugged. "I've never met him, so I wouldn't know."

"Same." Robbie nodded.

"I've picked Arthur up in the water taxi every now and then, but I haven't seen him in a few weeks, and I didn't notice if he was at the party tonight," Sully said. "I know he travels to the mainland for work quite a bit—he's a defense attorney—but I don't know if that's where he is right now."

"I'm going inside to see if I can find a number to reach him." Emma pulled a pair of blue latex gloves out of her pocket. "Don't touch anything and keep an eye out for Dr. Rogers and Callie."

"Yes, love," Robbie said.

Lindsey shivered and Sully let go of her hand and wrapped his arm around her, pulling her into his side. As if by mutual agreement, the three of them moved away from the bench and the body behind it to the far side of the veranda.

"Is it just me or does the handle of the murder weapon look familiar?" Lindsey asked.

"Palette knife?" Sully asked.

"Looks like it."

"The same as Gwen." Robbie nodded. "Do we know if Ariel and Leslie knew each other?"

"I can't imagine they moved in the same social circle," Sully said. "Ariel and Dane are more like my parents. There's a philosophical division between the old generational islanders and the newer monied residents who've been buying up the islands as luxury vacation homes."

"Aren't the Capshaws like that, too?" Lindsey asked. "Perry grew up on his parents' island and he's never left."

"Yes, but Gwen married into island life. She wanted desperately to belong to the inner circle of wealth and affluence, but they rejected her," Sully said.

"Because she married a man they consider beneath them, a lowly professor?" Robbie's voice was full of scorn for the snobs of The Club.

"As Eleanor explained it to me, it was more Perry's environmental work that put him at odds with the real estate developers who were members. Then it was Gwen's own desperation to belong that caused Eleanor to refuse her time and time again," Lindsey said. "Eleanor said they only want members like you, people who don't actually care if they belong to The Club or not."

Robbie narrowed his eyes as they shifted toward Leslie's body. "Except, they do care if they belong. Very much."

Lindsey and Sully followed his gaze. He was right. Leslie and her membership crew, Tina, Harper and Mallory, wielded their membership power like a cudgel and they did care about The Club, the members, and maintaining their power. Lindsey glanced at her husband and saw his eyes narrow.

"What are you thinking?" Lindsey asked.

"Is it at all possible that someone is trying to frame Ariel for the murders by using her palette knives?" Sully asked.

"That's assuming they're hers," Robbie said. "They might be the killer's weapon of choice or being used to implicate someone like Ariel. We won't know until forensics traces them."

"You're right." Sully nodded. "It just seems like an unlikely choice of murder weapon, especially to be used twice."

They stood quietly in the dark. Lindsey tried not to glance at the body behind the bench but there was a part of her that expected Leslie to pop up and join the conversation. The fact that she was gone just felt wrong, so very wrong.

“Mr. Stone is on his way,” Emma said as she exited the house.

“Did you tell him that his wife was murdered?” Robbie asked.

Emma shook her head. “I didn’t give him any particulars. He was at his office in New Haven, so I let him know that there was an incident at his house and he was needed right away. Officer Kirkland is waiting for him at the pier and will bring him out to the island. Thankfully, it seems to be a quiet night in Briar Creek and Officer Wilcox has it under control. You all should head back to the mainland before Lindsey freezes to death.”

“I’m fine,” Lindsey protested even as her teeth chattered.

“You won’t be. I’m going to need to bag your shoes and take them as evidence,” Emma said.

Lindsey glanced down and noted that one of them had smears of blood on the sole and the heel. Emma handed her a bag and Lindsey carefully slipped the shoes into the bag without touching them. “My shoes? I think you mean your shoes. Sorry about that.”

“No problem. They were not favorites. You all should go. I’ll be all right out here on my own.” Emma patted the gun on her hip and gestured for them to leave.

Robbie shook his head. “Absolutely not, love. We have no idea if the murderer is still here. Who knows when the other residents of Pine Top will return. We’re not leaving you on your own.”

"He's right," Sully said. "Also, if the murderer is still on the island, we should at least search it."

Emma considered his suggestion. "All right. Lindsey, you're of no use without shoes. You stay here."

"What?" Lindsey cried. "No, I can walk." The cold stone beneath her feet made a mockery of her protest.

"She's right, darling," Sully said. "If you encountered the murderer, you wouldn't be able to run barefoot."

Lindsey wanted to stomp her foot but she didn't, knowing it would hurt. She felt utterly useless waiting here. It was galling.

"I'll search the house to the right, Sully, you take the one to the left. Robbie, that leaves you with the area surrounding this house since you already searched the inside for Leslie. Lindsey, go inside where it's warm and wait, but don't touch anything," Emma said.

Lindsey glowered but she went into the house, knowing that arguing with them would just hold up the search, and Emma was right, they needed to move quickly if the killer was still on the island.

Once inside, she was relieved to be out of the night air. June in Connecticut wasn't particularly cold unless you were out on the water, wearing next to nothing and there happened to be a surprise cold snap like tonight. Not exactly spring fling weather. She reached down and rubbed her legs, trying to warm them up.

Emma had told her not to touch anything but that didn't mean Lindsey couldn't have a look around. The art on the walls was contemporary; bold colors in sharp patterns. She wasn't sure what emotion she was supposed to feel while studying the pieces but she admired the way the throw pillows on the couches picked up the accent colors. She peered at the signature in the bottom-right corner and in a very tight and controlled handwriting, she read the name Harper Winslow. So, this was Harper's work. Interesting.

She wandered over to the mantel of the large stone fireplace at the far end of the room. Several photographs in matching silver frames lined the broad wooden shelf. She saw one of Leslie in a wedding gown, standing next to a handsome man in a tux. It looked to be about thirty years old and the way they smiled at each other with such pure happiness made Lindsey smile, too. She assumed this was Mr. Stone.

The poor man was on his way home, having no idea what was waiting for him. Her gaze moved to the next photo. Mr. and Mrs. Stone, but now there was a baby, then a baby and a toddler, and on the photos went until they were at the wedding of one of their own children. The pictures were a testament to the happy life they'd built together and now it was all over.

Lindsey turned away, feeling a hollow ache in her chest for the family that was about to be torn apart.

Robbie was the first to return. "Didn't see a soul out there."

Lindsey wasn't surprised. Leslie should have been at the party hours ago and whoever had killed her likely knew that. They must have waited until the neighbors left and then struck Leslie while she was on her way out the door. That would explain why she was dressed and carrying her wrap.

Footsteps sounded out front and Lindsey glanced through the open front door to see Sully and Emma coming up the walkway. They were alone so she assumed they'd had no luck either.

"Whoever it was might have left hours before we got here," Lindsey said. "The party started at six, Leslie would have left before that to get there on time, a little later to be fashionably late, but definitely a couple of hours ago at the latest. How could someone have stopped by this island and not be seen?"

"By the dock out back, no doubt," Robbie said. "With the spring fling happening, there were so many boats on the water. Probably no one would notice just one more and they certainly wouldn't notice that it stopped here."

"Whoever stabbed Leslie knew about the event and that this was the best time to strike," Lindsey said.

"Seems like it," Emma agreed as she joined them. Sully followed.

"It's not a coincidence that both women were stabbed and shoved behind something to hide their murders for as long as possible, is it?" Lindsey asked.

"No," Emma said. "The similarity of the crime scenes can't be ignored because it was done either to intentionally point the blame in a certain direction or it's the killer's own signature."

There was a commotion outside and Lindsey squinted

into the darkness. Coming up the path from the main dock was a man in a suit being escorted by Officer Kirkland. The man broke into a jog as soon as the path became level. Emma went outside to meet him, likely to keep him from disturbing the crime scene. Sully, Lindsey and Robbie followed.

As soon as the man reached the veranda and was lit by the outside light, Lindsey recognized him from the pictures on the mantel. He glanced at their group and frowned.

"What are you all doing in my house? Is Leslie here?" he asked. "Did she invite you over?"

"No," Emma said. "It's nothing like that."

"Chief Plewicki, what's happened?" Mr. Stone narrowed his eyes at her. "I left a very important strategy session with my client to race out here as soon as I could, but nothing seems to be amiss. I expected my house to have burnt to the ground or something equally dire so kindly explain why you called me out here."

Emma clasped her hands together as she stepped forward. "I'm sorry I couldn't talk about it over the phone." She glanced at the group and strode down the steps. She gestured for Mr. Stone to follow her away from the house.

They were out of range but Lindsey knew the minute Emma told him that his wife was dead. Mr. Stone's face went slack and he clutched his chest. Then he started to shake his head vigorously from side to side. His voice was gruff when he said, "No, no, no."

Emma stood patiently beside him. When he glanced at the house, she shook her head and Lindsey knew she was telling him he couldn't see her until after the crime scene people arrived. He didn't take that very well.

"She's my wife!" he cried.

Emma's voice was a low murmur and Mr. Stone sagged at the knees. Officer Kirkland lifted a wooden Adirondack chair from the side yard and carried it over to Mr. Stone, who promptly collapsed into it.

Dr. Rogers and Callie appeared on the path and strode toward them, carrying their gear. Emma excused herself and went to join them. She pointed to Mr. Stone, and Dr. Rogers nodded and went over to speak with him while Callie continued on to the house.

Callie stepped up onto the veranda and took in Lindsey's outfit. "Fancy. But don't you think you're a bit overdressed for a crime scene?"

"My jeans were in the wash," Lindsey countered.

Callie flashed a smile. Then she frowned. "You're not wearing shoes."

"They've been bagged and tagged since I stepped in . . ." Lindsey waved her hand at the puddle of blood.

Callie reached into her bag and handed Lindsey a pair of disposal shoe covers. "They're not much but better than being barefoot."

"Thanks." Lindsey slipped on the booties.

Callie quickly donned her white Tyvek coveralls and put on some gloves. She set out little yellow cones with numbers on them at various spots around the body and started snapping pictures in a clockwise direction, capturing every angle.

"Was anything moved?" Callie put away her camera and took out a measuring tape. With a pad and pencil she wrote down the measurements beside a rough sketch she had drafted.

"Just the bench," Sully said. "We lifted it up and moved it off her as she was tucked behind it."

"A bit like the rose bushes over Mrs. Capshaw the other day," Callie noted.

"Very much like that," Lindsey agreed.

"Show me how it was when you found her." Callie turned to a fresh page in her sketch pad.

Lindsey explained how she'd gone to sit down and found the body because of the blood. Callie nodded and added the information to her drawing.

Callie crouched down next to the body and examined the handle of the implement embedded in Leslie's sternum. "Huh."

Dr. Rogers joined them on the veranda and began to pull on his coveralls. "Lindsey, Sully, why am I not surprised to find you two here?"

Sully held his hands out and said, "The water taxi never sleeps."

Dr. Rogers snorted and left them to join Callie. He took out his flashlight and illuminated the ground in an oblique direction. Every pebble, leaf, twig and insect was suddenly lit up and he started to take pictures of everything that surrounded Leslie's body that could be seen.

Dr. Rogers pointed to a mark on the ground and told Callie to measure it. "This drag mark is similar to the one we found by Gwen Capshaw's body. Like her, this woman was dragged and dropped behind the bench."

Lindsey blanched, thinking about how both women had been stabbed and then dragged and hidden behind something, slowing down the discovery of their bodies. It had to have been done for a reason, but why? What connection did Gwen and Leslie share that they were both murdered? Or was there no connection? Were they just random victims of the same murderer? And if they were just random victims, did that mean there was a serial killer targeting the Thumb Islands?

The thought made Lindsey woozy. She staggered a bit and Sully took her arm and moved her back into the house, where she was out of the wind blowing in off the water.

"Thanks," she said.

"What's wrong?" Sully asked. "You're awfully pale. Do you want to go home?"

Lindsey shook her head. She didn't want to say what she was thinking but she didn't know how else to explain the deaths of two women, of a similar age, in like environments with no real connection between them other than one belonging to a social club that the other one wanted to join. She took a deep breath.

"What if the only connection Leslie and Gwen share is that they were both alone in their island homes when a killer found them?" she asked.

Sully frowned. "As in, there's a serial killer out there?"

Lindsey nodded and Sully blew out a pent-up breath. "I don't suppose we can rule anything out, but that's . . . I can't really wrap my head around that possibility and I don't think I want to suggest it to Emma."

"Not now at any rate," Lindsey agreed.

They glanced through the open door and watched Emma and Officer Kirkland talking to Mr. Stone. He shook his head quite often and ran his hand over his face as if he just couldn't believe what they were telling him. When his phone rang, he silenced it and rested his head in his hands.

"I think this is the most we can do here," Dr. Rogers said. "Let's get her covered up before we allow the husband near her. Transport is on its way."

Callie nodded and together they gently covered Leslie's body, keeping just her face visible. With the heavy cloth draped over her, she could have been asleep.

Dr. Rogers stood and signaled to Emma to bring Mr. Stone to the veranda. Lindsey, Sully and Robbie moved to the opposite side of the stone patio to let him through.

"You're welcome to take a moment with your wife, Mr. Stone," Dr. Rogers said, his tone gentle. "We'll be transporting her to our facility shortly."

Mr. Stone sank to his knees beside the body of his wife and sobbed. "Oh, my dear." He reached out with shaking fingers and brushed a dark curl off her forehead in a gesture full of tenderness. Lindsey was hit with a sense of déjà vu as she remembered that Perry had responded to seeing

Gwen's body in almost the exact same way . . . almost as if it were a scene that had been scripted.

Lindsey shook her head. She was being ridiculous. How many ways could a husband respond to losing his wife in such a sudden and grisly way? Of course the men had reacted similarly. She was just feeling desperate and looking for some sort of clue or revelation to explain the deaths of two middle-aged women who didn't seem the type to have enemies who'd want to kill them.

"Transport is here," Callie said.

Two burly men with a stretcher appeared, and Emma moved to stand beside Mr. Stone. She placed her hand on his shoulder and whispered in his ear. He lowered his head, wiped his face with the back of his hand and then moved aside so that Leslie could be loaded onto the stretcher.

"Mr. Stone, I'd like you to check your home for any valuables you keep here to ascertain whether they were stolen or not." Emma led him into the house. "I know it's late but the forensics team is going to go over your home just to be certain we don't miss any clues pertaining to what happened here tonight. Given that the door was open and all the lights were on, we believe that whoever murdered your wife went through your house as well. It's going to take a while. Is there anyone you can stay with tonight?"

"I can sleep at our house in New Haven," he said.

Emma considered this for a moment and then nodded. "We'll need you to stay in the area."

Arthur Stone ran a shaky hand over his face and his

voice was soft when he asked, "What am I going to tell our kids?"

Emma's face softened. "I know it's difficult. I can tell them for you if you'd prefer."

"No, I'm their father." His voice was gruff. "They need to hear it from me."

"Before you check on your valuables, I'll take your statement as well as those of the people who found your wife." Emma gestured to Lindsey, Sully and Robbie and for the first time Mr. Stone seemed to be aware of them. "I thought my wife was found by one of the neighbors. No?"

"No." Emma shook her head. "They stopped by the island, looking for your wife, but—"

"They found her body instead," Mr. Stone finished for her. He glanced at the three of them. "Sully?"

"Arthur." Sully stepped forward. "I'm so sorry."

"Were you here to pick up Leslie?" Arthur asked.

"No, we were on our way home from the spring fling at The Club when my wife, Lindsey"—Sully paused to gesture to her—"remembered that she hadn't seen Leslie and she was worried. Since it was on the way, we decided to stop by Pine Top and make sure Leslie was all right."

"But she wasn't," Arthur said.

Sully shook his head.

"She was supposed to be at the party," Arthur said. "She planned to be there right at six o'clock to make her entrance. She was furious with me because I was going to be late—if I made it at all." He glanced at the sky. "If only I'd gone with her like she asked."

There wasn't much anyone could say to that. Emma interviewed Arthur Stone while Kirkland took statements from the rest of them. They didn't have any insightful information to offer and Lindsey felt it was a failure on their part somehow. It seemed she should have seen or heard something more at the party or here at the house when they arrived, but whatever had happened here tonight had happened long before they'd arrived.

Once Leslie's body was taken away and Arthur went with Kirkland to check on his valuables, Lindsey took the opportunity to talk to Emma about her concerns.

"Emma, do you think you should issue a warning to all of the island residents to be extra cautious, especially women who might be alone?" Lindsey asked.

"It did occur to me, yes." Emma turned to Sully. "I'll need your help. You know most of the residents and you can reach more of them more effectively than I can."

"Happy to help," Sully said. "Our office manager, Ronnie, can reach out to them directly and share the warning. Ian, Charlie and I can start patrolling the islands as well."

"Excellent. We can coordinate that in the morning," Emma said. "Meet me at the station then?"

"I'll be there," he promised.

Robbie opted to stay with Emma, and Lindsey suspected it was because of the fear that the killer was on the loose. Never had she ever thought something as monstrous as a serial killer could happen in a village like Briar Creek, and she knew they were all shaken by the possibility.

* * *

Sully and Lindsey arrived home to find a wet nose making snoot prints on the windowpane beside the front door. Heathcliff was pacing back and forth between the two windows on each side of the door, leaving his mark.

"Brace yourself," Sully said as he opened the front door.

Lindsey hunkered down as her boy Heathcliff, a furry black bundle of love, launched himself at her. It was a struggle to keep her balance even without the heels she'd been wearing, but she managed it. Barely.

Sully kept an eye on Heathcliff while he patrolled the yard, giving Lindsey the opportunity to change her clothes. Throwing out the booties Callie had given her, Lindsey changed into sweatpants and a T-shirt, feeling more like herself than she had in hours. She pulled on a pair of soft fluffy socks and joined Sully in the living room, where he was dutifully rubbing Heathcliff's belly and scratching Zelda's ears at the same time.

"I think we were missed," he said.

Lindsey popped into the kitchen to grab treats for their critters. Once the pets had settled in with their snacks, she joined Sully on the couch. He immediately pulled her feet into his lap and started to rub the arches of her feet in broad strokes with his thumb.

"I don't know how you walked in those shoes all night and I don't think the booties Callie gave you were much better," he said. "My feet started to hurt in solidarity."

Lindsey smiled and relaxed into the couch. No, she didn't own her own mansion on an island, or a yacht loaded with servants, but glancing at her husband and their fur babies, she knew she was richer than all the members of The Club combined because she had a life she wouldn't trade for anyone else's.

"What are you thinking about?" Sully asked.

"Other than how lucky I am?" They exchanged an affectionate smile. "I'm wondering why a killer would go after two middle-aged women just because they were alone in their homes. How would the killer know they would be alone at those specific times in those places? Especially in Leslie's case, when she and her neighbors were going to the same party. It doesn't make sense."

"Unless the killer picked the victims in advance and watched them, waiting for the perfect moment to strike."

"I didn't think I could be more alarmed but now I am." She sat up and leaned against him, needing the comfort of his nearness. "What's the plan for patrolling the islands?"

"I'll meet with Ian and Charlie tomorrow morning after I talk to Emma," he said. "We'll have to commandeer the book boat as well to be able to cover as much area as possible. I think we can formulate a route to give the islands maximum coverage but for how long I don't know. The summer tours are kicking into gear and the water taxi is always in demand, so it's going to take a lot of coordination."

"And there's the problem of not knowing who you're looking for," Lindsey said.

"There is that," he agreed. "Without Leslie chairing the membership committee do you think the funding for the book boat is still in peril?"

"I don't know," Lindsey said. "I mean, Leslie was already unhappy that the book boat was on the scene of Gwen's murder. Ironic, that it was us again at the scene of her murder, although we weren't in the book boat. If Mallory, Harper and Tina feel the same way, they'll probably yank the funding right out from under us. Mallory's the least friendly of the three, but she did send Trask into the water when he tried to stop our first outing."

"That was glorious," Sully agreed.

"Almost as good as when he got a pie in the face," Lindsey agreed.

"What about Tina and Harper?" Sully asked.

"Tina's the friendliest of the committee people and has always been supportive. Harper, I can't really get a read on. Maybe they'll all just forget about the book boat in the aftermath of losing their friend."

"Don't get your hopes up," Sully cautioned. "Rich people seldom forget about money spent or their return on investment."

Lindsey sighed, knowing he was right.

Beth was seated in the workroom with Jordan Capshaw when Lindsey arrived at work the next day. The two women were looking at one of Beth's scrapbooks. She finished every year with a scrapbook about her department—

the story times, programs, teen workers and volunteers—and when old friends came to visit, she always pulled the books out to reminisce.

"Lindsey, look at this picture of me and Jordan from when she worked here," Beth said. "It was one of my first dress-up story times."

Lindsey glanced over their shoulders at the open page. Beth was dressed as a bluebird and Jordan was carrying what looked like a nest complete with eggs. They were laughing in the picture, clearly having a wonderful time.

"You both look so young," Lindsey said.

"It feels like a lifetime ago." Jordan shook her head. "I can't believe I've been away for so long."

"Time does have a way of slipping by," Beth said.

"Growing up here, I never thought I'd leave," Jordan said. She glanced out the window at the Thumb Islands visible in the bay. "Ryan and I thought we'd live on Split Island forever."

"It must have been frightening to leave behind everything you'd ever known." Lindsey paused and then said, "I saw Karl Kilkenny last night."

"He still lives here? Of course he does. He's a nepo baby dependent upon his mom and dad for everything." Jordan grimaced. She glanced at Lindsey and said, "You heard about what happened between us then?"

"One of the older members at last night's spring fling told me about it while she was filling me in on who was who at The Club," Lindsey explained.

"Eleanor Whitcomb?" Jordan guessed. "She was the bane of my mother's existence."

"Why?" Beth asked.

"She refused to let my mother into The Club," Jordan said. "I have no idea why it was so important to Mom but it was enough so that she would have sacrificed even me to belong."

"From what I observed, you dodged a bullet in not dating Karl." Lindsey tried to keep her tone even but her disgust came through anyway.

"Wait. He was the guy who started following you when you worked here, right?" Beth asked. Jordan nodded. "It was awful. Jordan couldn't go anywhere without him showing up and harassing her."

"And my mother encouraged his behavior." Jordan shook her head. She was wearing her blond hair in a messy bun at the nape of her neck. "I remember feeling so angry and powerless. Mom hated Ryan. She said she wanted me to do better for myself, which in her mind meant climbing higher on the social ladder, but that never mattered to me."

"How is your dad doing?" Beth asked.

"He's devastated and he's angry with Ryan," Jordan said. "He thinks it was Ryan that kept us from returning all these years but it wasn't. It was me. I couldn't deal with my mom so I just never came home. Now she's gone and we'll never mend the rift between us." A tear slipped down her cheek and she brushed it away with her fingers.

Lindsey felt for her. The finality of death when so much

remained left unsaid between the mother and daughter was going to require a lot of work on Jordan's part to come to terms with. Of course, the sad truth was that Gwen might never have mended the relationship with her daughter, and Jordan would have spent her life trying to have a relationship with a person who was never going to reciprocate.

"And the real dilemma is that I feel like it's causing problems between me and Ryan," Jordan said. "For the past fifteen years, he's been my family and I love him so much but I can't help but feel guilty that we ran away from everything, and now I'm bitter that I'll never get a chance to make things right."

"First, it's not your fault that things didn't get worked out with your mom," Beth said. "Remember she was the adult in the situation and communication goes both ways. Second, all relationships are complicated. The only thing I can recommend is that you talk and talk and talk some more until you and Ryan work it out, and if you can't, get a professional to help you if you need it."

"You're right," Jordan said. "I haven't even seen him since the night you and Sully dropped us off."

Lindsey was surprised but she hoped her expression didn't show it.

"Not at all?" Beth didn't bother to hide her surprise.

Jordan shook her head. "I mean, we've talked on the phone but my dad is just so sad. I couldn't leave him and he's been so weird about Ryan. I'm only here now because my dad had to come into town to meet up with one of his bird rescue people."

Lindsey wondered if she should ask Jordan about her father reaching out to Arthur Stone the defense attorney but there was just no way to work it into the conversation that wasn't awkward.

"Speaking of Ryan." Beth pointed at the front door.

They all turned to see Ryan dash into the library. He looked frantic, spinning about as he searched the library, desperately seeking someone. Jordan popped up from her seat and waved through the workroom window until he noticed her. When he recognized Jordan, he sagged a bit at the knees. He hurried across the library and behind the circulation desk to enter the workroom.

"I've been looking everywhere for you." He panted.

Jordan stepped forward and grabbed his hands, pulling him fully into the room. "What is it? What's wrong? Are you all right? Are your parents okay?"

Lindsey had the horrible thought that there might have been another murder. She felt her chest get tight with fear but she forced it aside to listen to what Ryan had to say.

"The police came out to our island this morning. They've brought my mom in for questioning," he said.

"What?" Lindsey, Beth and Jordan cried in unison.

"They say the palette knife that was used to kill your mother and some other woman I've never heard of—who was apparently murdered last night—belonged to my mom." Ryan ran a hand through his hair. "The whole thing is crazy. You all know my mom—she would never harm anyone ever. She was in her studio last night until really late, working on pieces for her upcoming show."

"Was anyone with her?" Lindsey asked.

Ryan frowned. "No, but she was there. I know she was."

Jordan let go of his hands and grabbed her handbag. "Is Ariel at the police station now?"

"Yes, my dad's there with her, waiting to take her home." Ryan's voice broke.

"Let's go." Jordan hugged him tight. "It's going to be all right. I'm sorry I've been distant. Losing my mom this way just really messed me up."

"It's okay." He tenderly pushed a lock of hair out of her face. "I know you've been dealing with a lot."

"Maybe." Jordan shook her head. "But that was no reason to shut you out. My mother may not have been there for me for the past fifteen years but your mother always has been. She's been the mom I needed when she didn't have to be and I'll be damned if I'll let the police pin something on her that I know she didn't do."

Ryan perked up at Jordan's strong defense of his mother and he took her hand in his. "Thank you."

"Beth, I have to go, but thank you for seeing me today," Jordan said. "It meant a lot."

"Come by anytime," Beth said. "And let us know if there's anything we can do to help."

"We will." Jordan and Ryan hurried out the library's front door.

Lindsey watched them go, wondering what could have happened that the police had tied the two palette knives to Ariel and brought her in this morning. Lindsey wanted to go to the police station and talk to Emma but she knew the police chief wouldn't discuss an ongoing investigation.

"What are you thinking?" Beth asked. "And what did Ryan mean when he said there was another woman murdered who he'd never heard of?"

"There was a second murder last night." Lindsey sat in the chair Jordan had vacated. She stared blankly at the scrapbook in front of her.

"A second murder? Who?" Beth's eyes went wide with shock.

"Leslie Stone." Lindsey felt her chest get tight even as she said it. "She didn't show up at the spring fling at The Club so I had Sully stop by Pine Top Island on the way home. We found her on her front veranda stuffed behind a bench with an artist's palette knife lodged in her chest just like Gwen."

"Oh, my—" Beth covered her mouth with her hand. "That's horrible. Are you okay?"

Lindsey nodded. "I'm fine. I had Sully and Robbie with me."

"It can't be Ariel," Beth said. "She had no connection to Leslie Stone. They don't even move in the same social circles and just because she had a tiff with Gwen doesn't mean she suddenly snapped one day and killed her. They've been at odds for years—why would she do something now?"

"Agreed," Lindsey said. "Particularly when the issue

was on Gwen's side not Ariel's." Lindsey was quiet for a moment and Beth narrowed her eyes as she studied her friend's face. "What aren't you telling me?"

"Sully and I think that there might be a serial killer targeting women alone on the Thumb Islands."

A serial killer?" A voice cried from behind her and Lindsey spun around to see Nancy, Violet and Paula standing behind her with their mouths agape.

Lindsey turned back to Beth. "You might have mentioned we had an audience."

"Didn't know you were going to tell me we had a serial killer in Briar Creek." Beth shrugged.

"That's fair." Lindsey nodded. She turned to face the others. "It's just a hypothesis; we don't have any proof."

"Both Leslie and Gwen were alone on their islands," Nancy Peyton said. "That seems like quite a coincidence."

"Chief Plewicki is making plans to ensure the safety of the island residents," Lindsey said.

"What about the townspeople?" Violet asked. She strode into the room and took a vacant seat at the work table. Nancy and Paula followed her. "Just because the killer has only struck victims on the islands doesn't mean they won't move to the mainland if it gets too complicated out there."

"That's assuming that the two murders aren't tied together in some way we haven't discovered," Lindsey said. "We don't even have the medical examiner's report. Emma is doing the required due diligence and following protocol trying to keep us all safe while we wait for answers."

"A report from the medical examiner can take weeks," Nancy protested. "We need to figure out who is doing this now."

"But how?" Violet asked. "We'd have to be able to predict who the killer's next victim will be."

"We're smart. Surely, it can't be that hard," Nancy said.

"With our advanced degrees in psychology and FBI profiling?" Paula asked, her sarcasm sharp enough to bite.

"We don't need all that." Nancy waved a hand as she stood and approached the whiteboard that they used for staff meetings. "We know the people on the islands, their habits, their personalities and potentially their schedules, you know, if a handsome boat captain doesn't mind sharing intel to fill in the gaps."

Lindsey considered this while Nancy used a black marker to make two columns on the whiteboard. She wrote Gwen's name at the top of one and Leslie's on the other.

"What do we know about our two victims?" she asked. "Starting with what did they have in common?"

"They both lived on an island," Beth said.

"Married with grown children," Violet offered.

"Neither one was a library user." Paula's voice had a tinge of judgment to it.

Lindsey shared a small smile with Beth. Paula had definite feelings about people who didn't utilize their local library.

"What else?" Nancy faced the group with her marker in hand and her blue eyes alight with determination.

"They were both stabbed with a palette knife, the sort an artist uses for mixing paint," Lindsey said. She'd considered not mentioning it but now that Ariel had been brought in for questioning and her son had all but shouted the information in the library, she didn't feel the need to be discreet.

"Ariel Montgomery is an artist and she lives on Split Island beside Gwen Capshaw," Paula said.

"Which is why she was brought in for questioning this morning," Lindsey confirmed. "But she has no connection to Leslie or The Club that we know of, so why would Ariel kill her?"

"Because Leslie found out that Ariel killed Gwen?" Beth suggested. They all gaped at her. "I know. I don't like it either but one of the many reasons for murder is to keep something secret, and if Ariel did murder Gwen that would be an important secret to keep."

"But how would Leslie have found out?" Violet asked. "She'd have to have been on Split Island when the murder occurred, and if she was opposed to Gwen being a member of The Club, why would she ever set foot on her island?"

"She makes a good point," Nancy said. "I can't see Leslie Stone deigning to visit someone she was actively trying to keep out of her precious country club."

"Maybe Leslie was visiting Ariel instead of Gwen," Lindsey said. "Ariel is becoming a renowned local artist. Judging by the paintings in Leslie's house, she had an eye for art and she might have been at Ariel's to purchase some of her work and saw something she shouldn't have."

"Where was Ariel at the time of the deaths?" Paula asked.

"Ariel was alone on her side of the island when Gwen was murdered, and according to her son, Ryan, she was in her studio at the time of Leslie's murder," Lindsey said.

"So, it's not Ariel," Beth concluded definitively.

"Unless Ariel lied to Ryan and she wasn't in her studio," Lindsey said. She hated even suggesting it. Lindsey thought about what Eleanor had told her about Gwen making a play for Malcolm Rutledge. Could it be that Leslie went to the island to warn Gwen away, telling her she'd never be allowed in The Club even if she managed to bag Rutledge and accidentally came upon Ariel murdering Gwen? "It could be that Leslie had a different reason to visit Gwen on her island."

"What sort of reason?" Beth asked. "I mean, they were definitely at odds, so why would Leslie visit Gwen?"

Lindsey held off on sharing the gossip that Gwen was going to leave Perry for Malcolm. It felt spiteful and until she knew if it was true she didn't want to taint Gwen's memory any more than it already was.

"They were both emotionally invested in The Club," Lindsey said, "although in very different ways. Maybe it had something to do with that. Gwen wasn't a member but it was her life's goal to belong and Leslie was the chairman of the membership board who blocked her."

"I believe we need to look more closely at The Club," Violet said. "Robbie has joined, hasn't he?"

"He's considering it—not really—mostly he went along with saying that he would as a favor to me, so we could get The Club to sponsor the book boat."

"But now we have access," Nancy said.

Lindsey waved her hand in a *more or less* gesture. "I went with him last night in the capacity of his assistant."

"How did that go?" Beth asked.

"I was barred from the 'men's lounge' because it was assumed I wouldn't enjoy their stinky cigars and expensive whiskey," she said.

"Barred? As in, you weren't allowed in?" Paula's brows lowered in a fierce frown.

"It's fine. I met Eleanor Whitcomb, who is the institutional memory of The Club, and Sully accidentally collided with Gideon Trask, who ended up with a big slice of coconut cream pie in the face."

"Accidentally?" Beth asked.

"Absolutely." Lindsey tried to sound firm, but Beth still laughed.

"How can we possibly try and determine who might be next on a potential serial killer list if this is all we have to go on?" Nancy paced in front of the board.

"It might not be that difficult if we use The Club as the common denominator," Violet said. "For example, Sully's mother lives on the island but has no affiliation with The Club, either wanting to belong or belonging. If that's the key to the killer, then she'd be fine."

Lindsey adored her mother-in-law and hadn't thought about the ramifications of a serial killer loose on the islands in regard to her in-laws. She knew her father-in-law was not going to let his wife out of his sight until the situation was resolved, but the potential for something to happen to Joan made her anxious.

"We know there are twenty-three islands with homes on them," Lindsey said. "Of those eighty-one homes, we need to determine which residents belong to The Club and who has applied but been denied membership."

Paula slumped against the table. "This feels like a lot of work."

"It is," Lindsey conceded. "But Leslie did give us the money for the book boat, so I feel as if we owe it to her to find out who killed her or at least help as much as we can."

"What about Ariel?" Beth asked. "The fact that her palette knives were used in both murders feels significant—like the person actually committing the murders is framing her. But why?"

"Because they're a very savvy serial killer," Nancy said.

"Serial killer?" Robbie echoed from the doorway. "Who's a serial killer?"

"Hold on." Lindsey held up one finger in a *wait* gesture. She turned back to the group. "Nancy and Violet, can you make a list of all the island residents who belong to The Club?"

They exchanged a thoughtful look and then nodded together. "Yes."

Lindsey turned to Paula. "Can you reach out to our town historian, Milton Duffy, and have him put together a history of The Club, focusing on any feuds or scandals?"

"Absolutely," she said.

"What can I do?" Beth asked.

"Contact Ariel and find out if she has any enemies, anyone who is jealous of her career taking off or some other reason that might cause someone to try and frame her. I feel like it's significant that they used her palette knives."

"I can do that." Beth agreed.

Lindsey watched as the crafternooners set off on their assignments, then she turned to Robbie, who looked like he was about to explode with questions.

"Serial killer? Does Emma know this? This is terrifying!"

"It's not for certain," Lindsey said. "It's just something Sully and I were considering last night, but we didn't want to say anything and start a panic."

Robbie ran a hand through his reddish blond hair, standing it on end. "Instead, you have the library minions actively investigating the possibility."

"Not investigating, just gathering facts," Lindsey protested. "There's a difference."

She turned and led the way to her office, gesturing for him to follow her. Lindsey sat behind her desk, placing her shoulder bag in the bottom drawer while he took the seat across from her desk.

"Not to be an alarmist but if there is a serial killer on the loose, should you really be letting anyone do research on the residents of the island and their connection to The Club?"

"I'm certain the ladies can keep a low profile," Lindsey said. "And it is just one theory. I've been thinking about what you said about your time spent with the men at The Club. In light of Leslie's murder, was there anything else that struck you as odd?"

"I've thought about that quite a bit since last night." Robbie clasped his hands together. "It was weird the way they kept pressing me about younger women and my bachelor lifestyle. They really seemed fixated on the idea of an older man with a younger woman and bellowed quite loudly that their wives were past their prime and all that rubbish."

"Really?" Lindsey asked. "Did that include David Baldwin, Tina's husband?"

Robbie pondered the question then shook his head. "No. He was drinking his whiskey as if he was afraid someone was going to take it away. He was quite snockered by the time I left."

"So, it was the other husbands who were interested in younger women?" Lindsey asked. "And that's definitely not normal?" Robbie gave her a sharp look and she raised her hands. "I wasn't allowed in the room—how would I know if that's what men talk about?"

"For the record, it isn't," Robbie said. "Not like that, at

any rate." He met her gaze and continued, "I know this is going to sound mental, but what if the men of The Club are getting rid of their wives one at a time so that they can go after younger women?"

Lindsey stared at him in horror. Was that possible? No, it couldn't be, could it? "The problem with that theory is that Perry Capshaw is not a member of The Club," Lindsey said.

"Actually, that supports my theory. Because the membership committee hates Gwen but the ladies might be swayed to include Perry—if he did the requisite amends to the real estate mogul he annoyed—because the ratio of available men to women at The Club is about one man for every three women. Mark my words, if Perry got rid of his wife, he'd be welcome," Robbie countered.

Lindsey slumped back in her seat. "And Perry lives close enough to Ariel to steal her palette knives and set her up for the murder."

"But why would he kill Leslie?" Robbie asked. "Because she denied him admittance?"

"Or because her defense attorney husband, Arthur Stone, wanted to be rid of his wife and offered Perry representation in exchange for murdering his wife." Lindsey blinked at Robbie.

Robbie shivered. "I know it sounds far-fetched, but I really can't describe how fixated that room full of middle-aged, paunchy, balding men seemed to be on freeing themselves of their wives and having a second younger, hotter model to take their places."

"It's like something out of a thriller novel," Lindsey said. "But why would they frame Ariel?"

"Because Perry Capshaw has lived the rift between Ariel and Gwen for over a decade," he said. "Perry knew he could capitalize on their public feud and use it to take out his wife."

"But how would they explain Ariel going on a random killing spree of two women who had no connection other than one blocking the other from The Club?" Lindsey asked.

"At a guess, they'll play the misogynist card and blame it on her being an overly emotional perimenopausal woman," he said. Lindsey said nothing and he leveled her with a stare. "Is it really any more out there than a serial killer targeting women who just happen to be alone on their islands when he comes tootling by?"

"You have me there," Lindsey conceded. "Can I tell you something that struck me as strange?"

"Of course." Robbie relaxed back in his seat.

Lindsey rested her elbows on her desk and leaned forward. "I was there when Perry Capshaw saw his wife's body and when Arthur Stone saw Leslie."

"And?"

"And they both said very similar things at the sight of their wives' bodies. I thought at the time that it was almost as if it had been scripted," Lindsey said.

Robbie rocked forward and slapped his hand on her desk, making her jump. "Sorry. But that—that right there is what I'm talking about. There's something off about the men at The Club."

Lindsey frowned. "Assuming you're right, how do we go about trying to prove your theory?"

"I believe another visit to The Club is required," he said.

Lindsey felt her heart sink. She did not want to go to The Club ever again. The place made her uncomfortable and she had no idea how Eleanor Whitcomb had lived there her entire life.

"I don't think there's going to be another spring fling for us to attend," Lindsey said.

"No need," Robbie said. "I've been invited for a round of golf. Whilst I'm playing, you, as my assistant, can do some snooping."

"I don't snoop." Lindsey crossed her arms over her chest.

"You would prefer the term 'sleuthing'?" he asked.

Lindsey tipped her chin up. "Yes."

"All right, lady, let's formulate a plan."

I don't like that idea at all," Sully said for the millionth time. He was navigating the islands as they had stopped by his parents' house on Bell Island and were now visiting Ariel and Dane Montgomery to deliver a package to Dane.

It was Sunday, meaning the library was closed, and Lindsey was enjoying having the morning off. It was supposed to be an entire day off but Mayor Cole had called for an emergency town hall meeting and after that the crafternooners planned to get together to share what they'd discovered about the residents of the Thumb Islands.

"I don't love it either," Lindsey said. "But if Robbie is right and the men of The Club are up to something truly horrible, we need to give Emma something more to go on than a hinky feeling of his."

"I can't believe I'm going to say this but I think I like the serial killer theory better." Sully shook his head. "Having husbands murder their wives so they can have younger women is just a bad horror movie premise to me."

"I would say it's too bizarre to be possible, but I've listened to enough true crime podcasts to know that it's actually within the realm of possibility," Lindsey said.

"Which makes it all the more horrific." Sully steered the boat to the smaller side of Split Island, bringing it right up against the Montgomery dock.

Lindsey hopped out and tied the ropes while Sully gathered up the package for Dane. Together, they made their way up the dock to the stairs that led to the island above.

Dane and Ariel were working in their garden. Wearing gloves and sun hats, with the birds singing and the sun warm on their backs, it could have been an idyllic way to spend the day, but judging by the dark circles under Dane's eyes and the worry in Ariel's, it was clear that recent events were overshadowing their lives.

"I brought the package you requested." Sully held up the cardboard box.

Dane stepped out of the garden and stripped off his gloves. "Excellent. Thank you, Sully."

"What is it?" Ariel asked.

"Video cameras," Dane said. "I'm going to make certain our entire island is under surveillance at all times."

Ariel let out a sad sigh. Dane reached out and caught her hand in his. "I know and I don't like it either, but whoever helped themselves to your palette knives could come back.

For some reason they're trying to set you up as a murderer and we need to prevent that at all costs."

"I know you're right," Ariel said. "I just feel as if I'm living in a nightmare. When Emma was questioning me at the station, I actually started to wonder if it had been me. I mean, I know that sounds ridiculous but I kept thinking, *How else could it be my palette knife that killed her?* But then, I heard that Leslie Stone was killed with one of my knives as well and I know it wasn't me because I didn't even know that woman except in passing. There's absolutely no reason for me to kill her, and when she died, I was here in my studio. But I still feel some icky sort of shame or guilt."

"Perhaps it's survivor's guilt," Lindsey said. "Maybe the fact that Gwen was murdered so close to your home makes you feel bad that you survived and she didn't. If it's any consolation, we know it wasn't you. We've never believed it could be, not for a second."

"Thank you," Ariel said. "That does actually make me feel better."

"Are Jordan and Ryan here?" Sully asked.

"They took the boat out," Dane said. "I think they needed to get away for a little while. Jordan has been taking her mom's death hard and—"

"Where's my daughter?" An angry voice interrupted. They all turned to see Perry Capshaw striding toward them from the upper deck.

"Afternoon, Perry," Sully said. His voice was measured but Lindsey knew him well enough to know that there was also a warning tucked into it. She wondered if Perry could hear it, too.

Perry waved a dismissive hand at Sully, so that was a no. He stomped right up to Dane, leaned in until their faces were just inches apart and snapped, "My daughter. Where is she?"

Dane stood his ground and said, "Jordan's on a boat ride with her husband."

Perry reared back as if Dane had struck him. "Not for long."

"What's that supposed to mean?" Dane snapped.

"My daughter is going to leave your son," Perry stated. "She can't spend the rest of her life with a man whose mother murdered hers."

Ariel gasped and reared back as if he'd struck her.

"You don't believe that." Dane made it a statement with no room for argument.

"Yes, I do. It's the facts," Perry declared. "Her palette knife was in my wife's chest, which seems pretty clear-cut to me."

"No." Dane shook his head. His gaze shifted to Ariel, who looked distraught at being called a murderer by Perry. He took her hand in his and pulled her into his side, wrapping his arm around her shoulders.

Lindsey noticed that Perry never looked at Ariel when he accused her, and she wondered if something else was going on here. When she studied his face, it wasn't anger that she saw—it was fear.

"It must be very difficult to be alone on your side of the island," Lindsey said.

Perry glanced at her and snapped, "It's fine."

It was clear he didn't want to talk about it, but Lindsey wasn't going to be put off that easily. "Have you ever lived alone before?"

Perry turned to her with an impatient grunt. "No, I haven't. How is that your business?"

"Is that why you want your daughter to leave her husband? So she'll come and live with you and you won't be alone?" Lindsey felt as if she was being relentless but sometimes getting to the truth required that.

"That's not . . . no!" Perry's face turned bright red, whether it was from anger or embarrassment Lindsey couldn't tell.

"You know you're welcome to come over here anytime, Perry," Dane said. "Despite our differences over the years, I still consider you my friend. I still care about you."

Perry closed his eyes. "This isn't . . . I don't . . . Just tell my daughter I was looking for her, would you?"

He began to stomp away when Ariel spoke to him for the first time. "I didn't kill Gwen. You have to know that, Perry."

"Do I?" Perry snapped. He whirled around, looking a bit wild as if he had too many emotions rocketing through him and he couldn't control them all. "Maybe you found out about the relationship between your husband and my wife and that's why you did it. That's why you murdered Gwen."

"Excuse me?" Ariel blinked at him. "What did you say?"

"Go ahead," Perry taunted her. "Ask him. Ask Dane about his affair with Gwen."

Lindsey felt as if all the air was just sucked out of her lungs and, judging by the shock on Ariel's face, she felt the same.

"Perry." Dane's voice was a sharp warning. "Don't do this. Digging up the past serves no purpose."

"Easy for you to say—your wife is alive." Perry held his arms out. "Seems to me, you have everything and I have nothing. Nothing to lose, at any rate. It's time, Dane, to let this secret out once and for all."

"What is he talking about, Dane?" Ariel demanded.

"Nothing." Dane's jaw was so tight he barely got the word out. "He's just trying to stir up trouble."

"Am I?" Perry stepped into Dane's space. He jutted out his chin as if inviting Dane to take a swing at him. "Should I share the note you left Gwen, trying to win her away from me? Want me to let Ariel read about how much you loved Gwen and wanted to run away with her?"

"Listen, I get that you're grieving," Dane said. "But don't try to turn this into something it's not—"

"Something it's not?" Perry cried. He clenched his fists. "You were in love with my wife and you tried to get her to leave me!"

Lindsey felt Sully stiffen beside her. She knew he was preparing to jump into the fray if necessary. The two men were squared off, their faces were red and they were breathing heavily as if getting ready to brawl, but neither of them moved. Instead, it was Ariel who broke the weighted silence.

"Dane, is it true?" Ariel's voice was just above a whisper.

Dane dropped his chin to his chest in a defeated posture. "Yes, it's true."

No one spoke. No one moved. Lindsey felt as if she and Sully were intruding on a private matter among Dane and Perry and Ariel but she didn't think they could leave when the potential for violence seemed like a distinct possibility.

"I don't understand," Ariel said. "You were in love with Gwen?"

"Not in love. It was a crush at best and it was a very long time ago." Dane turned to his wife, his expression pained. "I should have told you, I know that, and I'm sorry."

Ariel gave him a side-eye. "When? When did this affair take place, Dane?"

He sighed and tipped his head back, staring at the blue sky above them. "Before I met you, and it was *not* an affair. If you don't believe anything else, you have to believe that. I never slept with Gwen."

"Bullsh—" Perry began but Dane interrupted him.

"I didn't, Perry," Dane interrupted. "I would never have done that to you. If Gwen had told me she returned my feelings, I would have told you. I would never have lied and cheated behind your back."

"If it wasn't an affair, what was it?" Ariel asked.

"It was just an infatuation." Dane shook his head. He

reached out and cupped her face. "You are the love of my life, Ariel. You always have been and you always will be."

Ariel pressed his hand more firmly to her cheek and nodded.

Lindsey's shoulders dropped and she felt Sully relax beside her.

"Was I an idiot to have feelings for my best friend's girl?" Dane asked. "Yes. Did Gwen encourage it? Maybe. Was it because I was twenty years old and lonely and lost because my best friend—my brother—had abandoned me for a woman? Definitely."

"Pfft." Perry scoffed. "I didn't abandon you. You wanted what I had just like you always did."

"You know that's not true," Dane said. "You were my best friend but then you met Gwen and suddenly, I was shoved aside. You never had time for me so I turned to Gwen, who seemed to have plenty of time."

"Don't you dare blame her for your actions," Perry sputtered.

"I'm not," Dane protested. "I was one hundred percent at fault for crushing on your girl but that's all it ever was."

Perry turned away and stared out at the water. "She told me that you slept with her."

"I never did," Dane said. "When she first arrived, I was completely besotted with her. I wrote an over-the-top maudlin love note, which you've obviously seen, and I kissed her once. But Gwen made it clear that she was only interested in acquiring my side of the island, which was never going to happen. When I refused, she showed you the note and our friendship was dusted and done."

"She told me that you never got over her," Perry said. "She held it over my head that she could leave me and have you anytime she wanted, for years."

"I think I might have had something to say about that." Ariel frowned.

"I wish you had told me," Dane said. "We could have talked about it. I'd have given anything to fix what I broke between us."

"Gwen made certain that was never going to happen." Perry gestured to the chasm between the islands where the bridge used to be.

So many years, so much time lost to one person's lies. Lindsey felt her heart ache for what could have been for these two men who clearly still cared about each other.

Dane let go of Ariel and moved to stand in front of Perry. He didn't say a word; he just opened his arms wide. Perry swallowed hard. He pressed his fingers to his eyes as if to push the tears back. Then he stepped into Dane's arms and hugged his lifelong friend.

Lindsey felt her own throat get tight and reached out for Sully, who grabbed her hand in his and gave her fingers a gentle squeeze.

"Dad?" Jordan appeared hand in hand with Ryan at the top of the steps. "What are you doing over here?"

Perry stepped back from Dane and patted his shoulder. Then he turned to Ariel and said, "I'm sorry. Please forgive me."

"Of course." Ariel hesitated for a moment then she stepped forward and gave him a quick hug and then stepped back beside her husband.

"Seriously, what's going on here?" Ryan asked.

Perry took a deep breath and nodded as if coming to terms with something in his own mind. "Dane, Ariel and I were just talking about rebuilding the bridge."

Ariel's eyes went wide with surprise while a small smile tipped Dane's lips. Ryan and Jordan exchanged an incredulous glance and then turned back to their parents.

"I think that would be great," Jordan said. Her voice was shaky as she continued, "Then your grandchild could run back and forth between his or her grandparents' houses."

Ariel was the first to get it. She gasped and clapped her hands to her chest. "A baby? You're having a baby?"

Jordan nodded and Ryan grinned. Ariel let out a happy sob and rushed to the couple to hug them close. Dane and Perry stood frozen as if they couldn't comprehend what was happening. Then they looked at each other with tears in their eyes. Perry threw an arm around Dane's shoulder and gave him a half hug before they joined Ariel, Ryan and Jordan in their family group embrace.

Lindsey felt her throat get tight. This moment was not for her and Sully. In silent mutual agreement, she and Sully backed out of the garden and made their way down the stairs to the dock below. Lindsey untied the boat and gently pushed off while Sully started the engine.

"I have something in my eye," Lindsey said as she dabbed at the tears that welled with the back of her hand.

Sully pulled her close and kissed the top of her head. When she glanced at him, his eyes had a definite sheen as well. "Yeah, that sun is really bright today." Then he grinned and she hugged him tight.

"I think Split Island might need to be renamed," Lindsey said.

"Oh?"

"It should be called Bridge Island now."

"Sounds perfect," Sully said. "We should mention it at the emergency town hall this afternoon."

"Ugh, don't remind me," Lindsey said. "You know Gideon Trask will be there, trying to justify his tax cuts for the wealthy while cutting services to the community."

Sully glanced at his watch. "We have just enough time to grab lunch at the Blue Anchor before we go to the town hall."

"Let's do it," Lindsey said. "We can celebrate Jordan and Ryan's good news with some clam fritters."

"That's my girl," Sully said with approval as he headed for shore.

The auditorium in the town hall was packed. It was standing room only at the back as it appeared all the residents of Briar Creek and the Thumb Islands were in attendance. Lindsey was seated near the front with Sully. On the raised dais sat Mayor Cole with the six members of the town council, flanking her with three on each side.

Sadie, the orange and white tabby that resided in the town hall, meandered through the crowd. She rubbed up against Lindsey's ankles and then Sully's allowing them to pet her but only for a moment before she wandered off, looking for someone else.

Lindsey tried to avoid looking at Gideon Trask, who sat on the edge of the dais, but he was glaring at Sully with an intensity that was hard to ignore. Lindsey was only surprised Sully's hair didn't catch on fire.

"Did you offer to pay for Trask's dry cleaning?" Lindsey whispered to Sully.

"I did and he declined," Sully answered with a shrug.

"Do you get the feeling that he enjoys being angry?" Lindsey asked. "I mean, if you look at it on paper, he has everything a man could want. A lovely wife, a couple of kids, a huge house on an island, generational wealth as he inherited his family's shares in a pharmaceutical company, so why does he want to sit on the board of a small village and try to negatively impact the lives of our villagers by taking away services just so he can pay less in property taxes?"

"You think he just wants to be mad about something and taxes are what he's chosen?" Sully asked.

Lindsey shrugged. "I can't understand why else he'd care. He can certainly afford the low rate someone of his position already receives—why take away the services from the rest of the town unless he just needs to feel powerful?"

"Power." Sully nodded. "You might be onto something

there. When I was in the Navy, I noticed the best commanding officers were the ones who didn't want the job, they didn't want to lead, their ego gained nothing from being in command. The worst ones were the ones who craved the power."

"Who craves power?" Emma took the seat Lindsey had been holding for her and the one beyond that for Robbie.

"Trask." Lindsey rolled her eyes.

"He looks like he's practically salivating," Emma said. "He told me if I didn't solve the murders by the end of today, he was going to fire me."

"What did you say to that?"

"Not repeatable in public." Emma smiled. "And I meant every word."

"Are you going to update the status of the murder cases?" Lindsey asked.

"Yes, Mayor Cole asked me to," Emma said. "There's not much I can say as yet. We're still waiting on forensics."

"Ariel was ruled out though?" Lindsey asked.

"Not yet, although it seems unlikely that she killed Leslie in the narrow window of time she'd have had to get from her island to Leslie's and back without being seen," Emma said.

"But not for Gwen's?" Lindsey told herself not to panic.

"Ariel was home alone and has no alibi, plus they had a well-known acrimonious relationship." Emma glanced at Lindsey's face. "Don't worry. The investigation is ongoing but I don't want to lie to you that Ariel is completely in the clear as yet."

"Understood." Lindsey nodded, thinking Ariel had gotten the best news today. She hoped Ariel would stay on her island and away from town for a while so she could enjoy it.

"Good afternoon, everyone," Mayor Cole spoke into the mic in front of her seat. "As I'm sure you're all aware, this is an emergency meeting to address the current state of the town budget. Some of our new council members would like to make changes to the existing budget and we'll be discussing the ramifications of those changes today. Also, as your mayor, I'd like to take a moment to address our residents' concerns about the horrific events that have happened out on the Thumb Islands. I want to extend my sincerest condolences to the families and friends of Gwen Capshaw and Leslie Stone. We will not rest until we discover what happened to them."

A news photographer was snapping pictures of Mayor Cole and she gave him a look that let him know it was time to move on.

"In that vein, I've asked Chief Plewicki to give us an update on the current investigation." Mayor Cole glanced at Emma, who stood and walked to the front of the room.

Someone in the crowd sneezed in rapid succession and Lindsey glanced over her shoulder to see Mallory Masterson shooing away Sadie, the town hall cat, while holding a tissue to her nose. "Take it away," Mallory said. "I'm terribly allergic."

One of the Parks and Recreation staff scooped the cat

up and removed her from the room with much yowling from Sadie.

"Good afternoon," Emma greeted the townspeople.

Hands shot up in the air right away, but Emma shook her head. She briefed the crowd about the two murders, mentioned that there were no suspects in custody and urged anyone with any information to contact the police. They were standard post-crime talking points but she did add that there would be boat patrols operating around the islands twenty-four/seven.

When she was finished, a few hands remained in the air. Emma glanced at Mayor Cole, who nodded. Reluctantly, Emma pointed to the first person and said, "Yes?"

"Why haven't you arrested Ariel Montgomery?" Harper Winslow asked. Lindsey hadn't seen Harper since the spring fling. She stood in the middle of her row; her dark brown hair was pulled back by a wide white headband and she was decked out in a pink and green Lilly Pulitzer dress with matching shoes. She looked like she belonged poolside at The Club, not at a town hall meeting in the village.

"Generally, you don't arrest people unless you can prove they committed a crime," Emma said.

"But she did it," Harper insisted. "Everyone knows Gwen Capshaw and Ariel Montgomery hated each other."

Lindsey shifted in her seat. Is this what everyone thought about Ariel?

"When the evidence supports an arrest, we'll make one no matter who it is," Emma said. The unwavering stare

Emma leveled on Harper made her flinch, and Harper quickly sat down.

"That's all I'm at liberty to say for now." Emma returned to her seat.

"Thank you, Chief Plewicki." Mayor Cole glanced at the people gathered and continued, "Councilman Trask has called this budgetary meeting so I will turn it over to him."

Mayor Cole switched off her mic and leaned back in her seat. Lindsey admired her poise. Then again, Mayor Cole had worked for the town for decades and had likely seen her fair share of ridiculous policies being made.

"Thank you, Mayor," Trask said. "We're here because the community of Briar Creek and the Thumb Islands needs to reevaluate its priorities. There has been much discussion about raising the taxes on the multimillion-dollar properties on the islands and along the shoreline but this will only cause those property owners to sell, negatively impacting the community when they leave."

"More like don't let the door hit you on the bum on the way out," Robbie muttered. Lindsey snorted, which she immediately tried to mask as a cough. Emma didn't even try. Her shoulders shook as she laughed into her hand.

"This is why I believe it's better to cut the superfluous services in the village and keep the property taxes down," Trask said. Silence met this pronouncement, and Lindsey glanced around the room and noticed there was a definite feeling of hostility coming from the crowd.

"What services did you have in mind?" Geraldine Pucci asked. Geri was one of Lindsey's favorite patrons because she was a genre junkie, reading everything from John Scalzi's science fiction to Abby Jimenez's romances and everything in between. Also, at the end of every summer when she harvested her garden, she baked dozens of pumpkin pies, some of which she brought to the library for the staff to enjoy.

But of course, Trask didn't know any of that. He didn't know that Geri was on a fixed income since her husband died and that the library's collection of books allowed her to escape the loneliness of her house to visit fictional friends and find comfort in stories of all sorts.

Trask met Geri's stare and said without hesitation, "The library, for starters."

Lindsey kept her face blank. It wouldn't do to let Trask think he'd scored a victory.

"You can't!" another person in the crowd shouted. Lindsey turned to see who it was and saw Henry Caldwell, standing up and looking furious. "I can't run my book club without the library's meeting rooms."

Henry was a retired military officer with a love of thrillers and spy stories. He had started an old codgers book club of a dozen thriller readers that met at the library every month to discuss their latest read. Paula used interlibrary loan to get the books for the club as there was no way the library could purchase that many copies of their chosen selections.

"You can find another place to meet," Trask clapped back.

"It's not just the space," Henry argued. "The library borrows the books for us."

"Might I suggest you buy them?" Trask snapped.

"Hey! Not everyone owns multiple houses and a yacht." Peter Fleishman erupted from another corner of the room. "Maybe books aren't luxury items for you but they are for us."

Lindsey knew Pete because when he'd decided to buy a dog, he'd come into the library and checked out every book about dogs they had as he tried to figure out what sort of breed to get. He'd settled on a Labrador–pit bull mix named Gingersnap, who was his constant companion and the sweetest girl with her pink nose, rust-colored coat and amber eyes.

"Your failure to afford something as cheap as a book sounds like a you problem," Trask said, sniffing. "Now, I've been tracking the frivolous spending of the library and I have a PowerPoint to show how much we can save if we close it."

Lindsey knew Trask had been in the library with his little black notebook, scribbling notes while he watched the staff and patrons going about their business. She had no idea what waste he'd thought he'd found but she braced herself to defend the library and her staff no matter what he said.

"The annual library budget is seven hundred thousand dollars." Trask announced this as if it were an egregious amount of money. Lindsey knew for a fact that his yacht was worth several times more than the library's entire budget.

The crowd shifted uncomfortably and Lindsey glanced

at Mayor Cole, who looked supremely bored, which was surprising because as a former librarian, the mayor had always been loyal to the library and its mission.

"If we cut that expense out of the town budget and lowered your taxes accordingly, you would have enough money to buy your own books." Trask stared pointedly at Henry.

"That sounds great!" Mayor Cole said into her mic, and Lindsey felt the sharp stab of betrayal in her chest. How could the mayor be encouraging him?

Trask looked at the mayor in surprise and then grinned as if delighted with his unexpected ally. "I knew you'd see reason once the numbers were presented."

"Do go on." Mayor Cole waved her hand for him to continue.

Trask dove into his subject with gusto. He called out the cost of children's programming, the amount of money spent on books and other materials, the salaries of the staff, the cost of building maintenance, the free computers, the maker space and the popular clubs and activities hosted at the library.

Lindsey glanced around the room. It was subtle but with each item Trask mentioned, she felt the energy change. It was as if Trask was reminding everyone of exactly how amazing their library was. Lindsey met Mayor Cole's gaze and saw a wicked glint in her eye. Mayor Cole had knowingly let Trask have the floor, fully aware that he was going to end up being an advocate for the library and its services.

Lindsey lowered her head and hid her smile.

"Are you okay?" Sully asked.

She turned to him and winked. "I'm just fine."

"And one of the most over-the-top expenses I found in the library"—Trask was speaking rapidly now, excited that he had the crowd's undivided attention—"was a cupboard full of diapers in the family restroom in the children's section. I'm sorry but I am not paying to diaper anyone's child but my own."

There was a sharp intake of breath behind her followed by some muttering, and Lindsey turned to see Beth and her husband, Aidan. Beth looked ready to brawl and only Aidan's gentle hand on her back appeared to be keeping her in her seat.

The crowd was murmuring and Lindsey wasn't sure if Trask had just won them over or not. Surely, they didn't begrudge helping parents out with diapers. She heard Mayor Cole clear her throat, and Lindsey braced herself as she knew what was coming next. She told herself she was ready for it even as her nerves fluttered in her belly like a kaleidoscope of butterflies.

"Thank you for your very detailed and insightful report, Councilman Trask," Mayor Cole said. "In the interest of presenting all the information, I'd like to invite our library director, Lindsey Norris Sullivan, to take us through these expenditures that you find so egregious."

Sully squeezed her hand and Lindsey stood and made her way to the front of the room. She hated public speaking even more than deep dark water but her library was at stake and she wasn't about to go down without a fight. She glanced out at the audience and saw the crafternooners scattered among the crowd.

Nancy raised her fist in the air in solidarity. Violet gave her a nod. Paula clasped her hands under her chin, looking nervous. And Beth was still fuming, judging by the grim set to her mouth and the flare of her nostrils. Mary and Ian were standing at the back of the room and they both sent her a double thumbs-up. Lindsey appreciated their confidence in her and knew that no matter how this went, she had their unflagging support.

"Good afternoon, Mayor, Councilpersons," Lindsey began. Her voice was shaky, which annoyed her so she cleared her throat. "I'd like to start with Councilman Trask's last item, if I may. The diapers he refers to are donated by our new-parents support group. The moms and dads meet once a month at the library to discuss parenting, and as a thank-you for the space, they committed to maintaining the stockpile of diapers in the family restroom as a courtesy for other new parents, so Councilman Trask need not fear that his money is going to diaper someone else's baby."

Trask's face immediately flushed a deep red and he opened his mouth to argue but Mayor Cole reached over and switched off his mic. "It's not your turn. Please continue, Lindsey."

"As the councilman mentioned, our budget is seven hundred thousand," Lindsey said. "A rough breakdown of our expenses is fifty percent on staffing, twenty-five percent on the collection and another twenty-five percent on operation costs. But what does that mean to you, the taxpayer?"

Lindsey had the undivided attention of the entire room. Trask had already highlighted how great the library was with its resources and programs, but this was the most critical part. Helping the community see how little they spent for so much. Lindsey took a deep breath and felt herself grow calm in her purpose. She moved her gaze across the room, meeting the eyes of as many people as she could.

"The library's budget is five percent of the town's total budget. Just five percent." She paused to let that information be absorbed by the crowd. "Now if we ignore all the grants, state funding and other revenue streams that the library utilizes and assume that our entire budget is based on property tax, and if we divide that total budget of seven hundred thousand by the number of property taxpayers in our community, a number that can be verified with the tax assessor's office, then we are left with a cost of ninety-three dollars per year per property tax–paying household. Ninety-three dollars per year. The most popular streaming services cost almost two hundred dollars per year per household so the library is only half of that. And given that the average household size in Connecticut is two-point-five-three, then we're looking at about thirty-six dollars per person per year. I don't think two-point-five-three people can even go to the movies for that price."

The crowd responded with a laugh, which was what Lindsey had been hoping for.

"That's not accurate!" Trask insisted.

"Of course not." Lindsey sent him a dismissive glance. "Because we do have other sources of funding, which are all disclosed to the public in our budget, so it's actually less than thirty-six dollars per person."

Lindsey turned back to the crowd. "How many new books do you think you can buy for thirty-six dollars? Depending upon the format, it could be one to three books at most. Would that be enough for a monthly book club? A small one, for one time only, I suppose. Is it enough to keep your young child who is learning to read engaged with a stack of new books every week? No. And how about our free programs? Would you pay thirty-six dollars for our summer concert series? Our cooking classes? Our painting classes? Our free tax help?"

The room was silent and Lindsey studied the faces of the crowd, wondering if they cared and hoping desperately that they did. And then, someone in the back started chanting, "Save our library! Save our library!" And she knew everything was going to be just fine.

Save our library!" The crowd took up the chant and it quickly became deafening. Trask switched on his mic and tried to shout over them, but the crowd wasn't having it.

Lindsey glanced at Mayor Cole, who nodded at her. She was dismissed. Lindsey returned to her seat, relieved to be out of the spotlight.

"Well done, darling," Sully whispered.

"Thanks."

Eventually, Mayor Cole raised her hands for quiet and because she was Eugenia Cole, the crowd settled down quickly. She glanced at the notes in front of her and said, "Councilman Trask, I think the council can now take a vote on your proposal to cut funding to the library."

"Wait," Trask protested.

"No." Mayor Cole shook her head. "All those in favor of cutting the library budget, raise your hand and say 'Aye.'"

"Aye." Trask's was the lone vote. The crowd booed so loudly he dropped his hand back into his lap.

"Those not in favor say, 'Nay,'" Ms. Cole instructed.

The remaining councilmembers all raised their hands and said, "Nay."

Lindsey felt a surge of relief take her out at the knees. Sully hugged her close and Emma gave her a high five that was so enthusiastic it stung.

"Councilman Trask, did you want to continue with your proposed budget cuts to the police and fire departments or perhaps the school?" Mayor Cole asked.

A hiss of outrage started to froth up from the townspeople, and Trask finally had enough sense to read the room. "No."

"Then we will consider this meeting adjourned and the subject of your proposed budget cuts closed," Mayor Cole announced. The crowd cheered and Lindsey felt a surge of victory sweep through her. So, this was what it felt like when the good guys won. It was glorious!

As the townspeople filed out of the room, many of them stopped to shake Lindsey's hand and declare their support for the library. When Mayor Cole paused beside her, Lindsey gave her an assessing stare.

"You knew, didn't you?" she asked.

"Knew what?" Mayor Cole blinked.

"That Trask's misguided PowerPoint was going to do all

the heavy lifting in outlining why the library is such an asset to the community," Lindsey said.

Mayor Cole shrugged. "Sometimes the best way to handle an adversary is to just let them keep talking."

Lindsey grinned.

"I hope I'm wrong," Mayor Cole said. "But Trask strikes me as the type who doesn't like to lose, so I wouldn't let your guard down quite yet."

"Noted." Lindsey glanced at the dais, where Trask was throwing his notes into his designer messenger bag with unnecessary force. He stomped off the platform and exited out a side door, not bothering to speak to anyone in the room.

"Can't wait to look at my email later," Mayor Cole said. "You know he's going to hit me with every grievance he can possibly manufacture in his angry little mind."

"Sorry about that, but it's time he caught on to the fact that we're a community and everyone needs to contribute. If he doesn't want to then he needs to start his own little kingdom someplace else," Lindsey said.

"I'll be sure to suggest that," Mayor Cole said with a chuckle. "It should be received really well."

"Lindsey, could we have a word?"

Lindsey turned around to find Mallory Masterson, Harper Winslow and Tina Baldwin standing there. Caught by surprise, it took Lindsey a moment to respond.

"Of course," she said. She turned back to the mayor and said, "Excuse me."

Sully was standing nearby, talking to their neighbor. She

met his gaze and tipped her head to indicate she was leaving to talk to Mallory, Harper and Tina. Sully raised his eyebrows slightly in surprise and nodded.

Lindsey led the way to an empty part of the room. "What can I do for you?"

Tina bit her lip and looked uncomfortable while Harper studied her phone, looking bored. Mallory's nose was red and her eyes watery. Lindsey frowned. It was strange that Mallory had recently gotten a kitten, given that she was so allergic to Sadie.

With a final dab of her tissue, Mallory tossed her long red hair over her shoulder and said, "We're not going to fund your little book thing anymore."

"I don't understand," Lindsey said. Although judging by the sinking feeling in her chest, she did understand all too well.

Mallory sighed and waved her tissue at Harper, who rolled her eyes and said, "It's not complicated. We. Are. Not. Funding. Your. Book. Thing. Anymore."

The condescension was thick enough to spread with a knife, but Lindsey chose to ignore it.

"May I ask why?" Lindsey asked. "I mean, the biggest part of your investment was outfitting the boat and that's already done."

"And you're welcome," Mallory said. "But now it's over. Your little book boat was Leslie's project, but she's gone now so things are going to change. Come along, ladies, this place is depressing."

Mallory stalked away, like a model on a catwalk, with

Harper keeping stride beside her while Tina glanced from Lindsey to her friends and back with sad eyes. "I'm really sorry, Lindsey. With Leslie gone, Mallory is in charge now and she's determined to get rid of any trace of Leslie. I tried to talk her out of cutting the book boat funding but she wouldn't listen to me and Harper doesn't seem to care either."

"It's all right," Lindsey said. "As I said, the big investment was already made. There isn't much to the upkeep, so I'm certain I can find another sponsor."

"Of course you can." Tina patted her hand. "Listen, I've got to dash. I have no doubt those two will leave me here if I don't keep up."

Lindsey watched the petite woman with the head of big blond hair hurry from the room after her friends. She supposed she should just be happy with the win the library had gotten at the meeting, but now that they had the book boat, she didn't want to just dry-dock it and call it a day. She was establishing some real connections with the islanders and they deserved to be served as much as anyone.

"Why the frown, darling?" Sully asked as she joined him by the main door.

"The Club will no longer be sponsoring the book boat," she said. "Which is fine, but it just felt off."

"What do you mean?"

"It was Leslie's project, and Mallory just ended it," Lindsey said. "They could have promoted it as Leslie's last contribution to the community, but no. It's just cut loose. It felt as if Mallory was actively trying to get rid of anything that had Leslie's stamp on it. Does that make sense?"

"Do you think Mallory wanted Leslie's position so much that she might have killed Leslie for it?" Sully asked.

"I hate to think it, but I know people have killed for lesser motives than social power," Lindsey said.

"If what you're thinking is true, then would Leslie's murder actually be a copycat killing since there was no reason for Mallory to kill Gwen?"

"Copycat killing?" Emma repeated as she and Robbie joined them.

"It's another theory," Lindsey said. "Mallory is flexing her muscles as the new head of The Club's membership board, which includes community outreach projects, and Tina was just telling me that Mallory is consumed with erasing anything that Leslie did so she can put her own stamp on the committee."

"That feels like a typical response from an insecure person," Emma said. "Which does not make the person a killer . . . unless, it does."

"Is there any news from the crime scene investigators or the medical examiner?" Sully asked.

"Nothing that we didn't already know," Emma said. "Both deaths were caused by an artist's palette knife being shoved into their chests. They were able to extract some paint flakes off the palette knives and they'll try to match them to the paint in Ariel's studio, but that'll take time. Also, the bit of cloth you pulled out of the firepit appears to be the edge of a canvas. Whoever stabbed Leslie also took the time to burn a painting in her firepit."

Lindsey felt her heart thump in her chest. "Do you think it was Ariel?"

"As I mentioned, the timeline is a concern," Emma said. "Getting out to the island, stabbing Leslie, hiding her body, burning a painting in the firepit would take too much time from Split Island to Pine Top Island."

"How about from King's Island?" Lindsey asked.

Emma frowned. "It's much closer, for sure. Why?"

Lindsey glanced at Robbie. "Do you remember when we saw Tina at the spring fling? When we hugged her, she smelled like a campfire but she blamed it on her husband's cigar."

Robbie snapped his fingers. "That's right, but perhaps it was from the firepit at Leslie's."

"Also, Eleanor told me that Tina's husband is about to lose his fortune and she's been positioning herself to find a new man, namely Malcolm Rutledge, who Eleanor said Gwen Capshaw was also making a play for."

"Giving Tina a reason to eliminate her competition," Emma said.

"I don't know. I feel like shoving a knife into a person's chest would take a lot of physical strength," Robbie said. "Plus, the bodies were stuffed into places to delay being found, which would also take a lot of muscle."

"Are you saying you think the killer was a man?" Lindsey asked.

Robbie shrugged. "Not specifically. A woman feeling

duly motivated could likely shove the knife as deep but moving a body would require some serious upper-body strength."

Lindsey wondered how motivated Mallory might have been to be the one in charge of memberships. Enough to stab Leslie and then move her body to replicate Gwen's death? How would she know Gwen's body had been stuffed behind the bushes, unless she'd been there? She felt her phone buzz in her handbag and pulled it out to see who was calling.

"Hi, Nancy." Lindsey scanned the room. The crafternooners had just been in the auditorium but now there was no sign of them.

"Congratulations on shutting down that blowhard Trask," Nancy said.

Lindsey grinned. "Thank you. Where are you?"

"We're going over our suspect list at the Blue Anchor," Nancy said. "Come join us."

"We'll be right there," Lindsey agreed.

It seemed most of the town had the same idea after the town hall meeting. Thankfully, Nancy and Violet had dipped out of the town hall as soon as the meeting ended and snagged an outside table on the deck overlooking the water. Paula, Beth and Aidan were there as well.

Lindsey and Sully had just settled into their seats when Ian arrived at their table with a bottle of champagne and several glasses. "That's on the house for saving our library."

Ian popped the cork and they all cheered. Lindsey raised her glass and said, "To the library."

Everyone echoed the toast and Lindsey took a sip of the sparkling beverage. It tasted like victory. Best champagne ever.

Lindsey's feeling of achievement was short-lived. Harper Winslow entered the outside dining area of the Blue Anchor with her own party, not Tina and Mallory, but an assortment of well-to-do people who definitely looked as if they belonged to The Club. As they walked by, Harper paused to take in the group at Lindsey's table.

"You may have saved your library today, Lindsey, but if you hire that murderer to teach painting classes this summer, I'll make certain the library gets shut down." Harper loomed over her chair and Lindsey felt Sully shift into a defensive posture beside her.

Lindsey set her glass down and stood up, forcing Harper to back up. "I watched you demand that Ariel be arrested in the town hall meeting. What is your obsession with Ariel Montgomery?"

Harper tossed her head, sending her long brown hair over her shoulder. She cast Lindsey a sly glance for an answer. She was about to walk away when Beth stood, blocking her exit.

"Harper took Ariel's private painting class last summer at The Club," Beth said. "Isn't that right, Harper?"

Lindsey glanced between them. "You two know each other?"

"In passing. The local art scene is a small community,"

Beth said. "If I remember right, it was your show that was prematurely ended so that the gallery in New York could expand its showing of Ariel's work. Isn't that right?"

Harper crossed her arms over her chest and thrust out her chin. "I chose to pull my show. I didn't feel the gallery was living up to my expectations."

"Right." Beth snorted. "Why did you take Ariel's class last year, given that you're an artist in your own right?"

"I was curious," Harper said. "Tina was taking it and raved about what a talent Ariel was so I wanted to see if Ariel's work lived up to the hype. Self-taught with no formal art education of any kind, so needless to say, it did not."

"Interesting." Beth mimicked her stance. "Ariel getting arrested for a murder she didn't commit would put you back on top of the local art scene, wouldn't it?"

"There are two things wrong with that statement," Harper said. "First, Ariel did commit murder and she's going to get caught, and second, I'm still on the top of the local art scene, which is where I belong."

Harper went to push past her, but Beth blocked her. "So many ladies at The Club had access to Ariel's tools. Wouldn't it be wild if one of the 'ladies' actually stole Ariel's equipment and used it to commit murder? That's a frame job worthy of an artist, don't you think?"

Harper gasped. "Exactly what are you accusing me of?"

Beth cocked an eyebrow. "You tell me."

"I did not murder Gwen Capshaw," Harper said.

"If you say so." Beth shrugged. "Frustrating to be accused of a crime you didn't commit, isn't it?"

Harper stormed past her, joining her group in the far corner of the restaurant.

Lindsey glanced at Beth. "You put her in her place."

"I did, didn't I?" Beth nodded. "That felt good. We're having a day, aren't we?" She sat back down and Lindsey did as well. She glanced over at Harper's table and watched as the woman tossed back a glass of wine. She looked as if she were trying to douse a demon. Interesting.

"Oh, no." Sully studied her face.

"What?" Lindsey asked.

"I know that look," he said. "You've figured something out, haven't you?"

"Maybe," Lindsey acknowledged. "I need to think about it, but I'll explain later."

"Looking forward to it." Sully kissed her head and turned back to the table.

Why had Harper said only that she hadn't killed Gwen Capshaw? Wouldn't it have been more logical to deny both murders? Lindsey took out her phone and texted Emma. She had a very specific question for Dr. Rogers and Callie and she hoped Emma would facilitate the request.

Are you sure that everyone who is anyone in The Club is going to be at this golf tournament and high tea?" Lindsey asked Robbie as Sully drove them in his water taxi back to The Club.

"That's what I was told," Robbie said. "Don't be getting cold feet now. You're the one who thought up this scheme."

"I know," Lindsey said. She clapped a hand to her head to keep the wide-brimmed navy hat with white piping on the crown and edge of the brim on her head as it was buffeted by the breeze. She'd been to high tea only once when visiting London, and she knew that the hat was a critical component. Mercifully, she was wearing her own clothing for this visit, a long blazer dress, also in navy blue with white piping along the edges, and navy blue, peep-toe slingbacks. She felt very Princess Kate today.

"Be careful, darling," Sully cautioned as he pulled up to the dock at The Club. "Emma has set up surveillance so you'll be protected at all times but I still don't like this."

Lindsey cupped his face and kissed him quick. "Don't worry. With any luck, we'll have our answers before the second pot of tea is served."

He grimaced, clearly worried. A teen dock worker tied up the boat, and Sully helped Lindsey onto the dock. Robbie took her arm and they passed through the gate, leaving Sully to wait at the boathouse with the other crew members. Much like the night of the spring fling, boats and yachts filled the area around the island and Lindsey took comfort in knowing that several of the boats out in the bay were police boats, as Emma had called for backup.

"Eleanor is expecting you," Robbie said. "She's to be your companion for the tea since I'll be out on the links. I managed to get placed in Malcolm Rutledge's foursome so I'll try and get him talking about the women of The Club and see if he knows anything."

Lindsey nodded. As they approached the massive wooden doors, she was oddly relieved to see Geoffrey of the sour expression there. He nodded at them.

"They're expecting you on the course, Mr. Vine," Geoffrey said. He gestured to a young woman in uniform. "Willow will escort you."

"Thank you." Robbie squeezed Lindsey's hand and gave her a meaningful look before he followed Willow down the hallway that led to the course.

"If you'll follow me, Mrs. Sullivan." Geoffrey started to

walk in the opposite direction and Lindsey felt an irrational urge to flee. She didn't.

In daylight, The Club was even more magnificent as planters overflowing with petunias in vibrant shades of pink and purple and gently trickling fountains seemed to be tucked into every available space. They left the main building and followed a stone path across a courtyard that was adjacent to the long building on her right. Whoever had designed the mansion definitely had castle aspirations.

They exited the courtyard via a large stone arch and Geoffrey led Lindsey to a large white lawn tent with open sides that had been set up on the top of a small hill that overlooked the bay. It was a stunning view of the mainland and Lindsey paused to take it in.

Geoffrey stood beside her and cleared his throat, bringing her attention back to him. Lindsey thought he was attempting to remind her to dismiss him, and she hastily said, "Thank you, Geoffrey."

"If I may speak out of turn?" he asked.

"Of course." Lindsey braced herself for a critique of her manners or dress.

"Mrs. Stone was always very good to me and the rest of the staff." His voice was gruff but he continued, "I appreciate what you did in going to look for her and I just wanted to say thank you."

Lindsey could feel his genuine sorrow and she nodded. "I wish I'd arrived sooner and we'd had a different outcome."

Geoffrey nodded and straightened up. "It's gauche to

put your pinky out when holding your teacup. Don't do that."

Without another word he turned and left before Lindsey could protest that she would never.

"I see Geoffrey has taken to you." Eleanor approached, wearing another Chanel-style suit but this one in a jaunty shade of peach. Her hat was a gauzy confection that perched on the side of her head with an air of irreverence that made Lindsey smile.

"Good to see you, Eleanor," she said.

"Of course it is." Eleanor waved her hand at Lindsey. "Come along. I didn't agree to be your companion to be left standing about."

They entered the tent and Lindsey had to fight to keep her jaw from dropping. She'd been told it was a high tea where items were auctioned off to raise money for charity but this was not like any charity auction she'd ever been to.

Circular tables draped in white cloths had enormous ribbon-festooned balloon bouquets in gold and silver as their centerpieces. She was certain she'd never seen so many balloons in one place at one time. Along the far wall, the auction items were on display and she checked to see that number ten was exactly what it was supposed to be, thanks to Eleanor, who had donated it on behalf of Lindsey.

Mallory Masterson, wearing an enormous hat of dove gray with pearl accents that matched her gray dress, stood at the podium. "Ladies, please take your seats so that we can start the bidding."

Eleanor led Lindsey to a table at the front of the room.

Already seated were Tina in her usual vibrant pink, Harper in a bright apple green and several other ladies whom Lindsey didn't know. They each wore matching hats with their ensembles and Lindsey rather wished hats would make a comeback for more than high teas and horse races.

"Oh, Lindsey, hi!" Tina waved enthusiastically. "I didn't know you were coming today. Isn't this just amazing?" Her bubbly personality reminded Lindsey of the champagne she'd had the other day. It was impossible not to smile in return.

"What are you doing here?" Harper asked. She was less pleased to see Lindsey.

"She's bidding for Robbie Vine while he's playing in the tournament," Eleanor said. "And she's *my* guest."

Harper's upper lip curled and she turned her chair away with more force than was necessary.

"Making friends wherever you go?" Eleanor asked.

"It's a gift," Lindsey said.

Eleanor let out a soft chuckle.

As the auctioneer took the podium, Mallory stepped down and joined them at the table. She paused at the sight of Lindsey and then tipped her head to the side. "Here to look for a new sponsor?"

"Something like that." Lindsey smiled.

The auction began and Lindsey turned to the podium and watched as luxury items were bid upon with a dizzying speed. Finally, number ten was up. An assistant held up the piece while the auctioneer read from the information card Eleanor had provided.

"It seems our donor has made a last-minute change," he said. The assistant holding the piece turned it around so that it was no longer a vintage painting of The Club, but rather it was the piece Lindsey had seen in Ariel's studio when she visited it the day of Gwen's murder. "What we have here is an Ariel Montgomery original in oil. For those of you who follow the local news, this artist has recently been tied to a couple of murders, so this piece could increase in value exponentially if it turns out to be her final work before being sent to prison." He gave them a dramatic wink. "I'm just saying."

Gasps and murmurs filled the room and paddles shot into the air as the price went up and up and up. When there was a break in the bidding at seventy-five thousand dollars, Lindsey stood.

"Stop." She held up her hands. The entire tent full of hatted women turned to look at her. She glanced at Eleanor and said, "We can't in good conscience let them bid on this piece, knowing that Ariel is not a murderer."

Eleanor sighed and said, "I suppose you're right. It isn't a sound investment."

Lindsey knew everyone was watching her so she channeled her inner Beth and spread her arms wide and exclaimed dramatically, "Especially when we know the killer is sitting right here."

Mallory jumped to her feet. "What do you think you're doing? Security!"

Harper scoffed. "Somebody clearly needs to be the center of attention. Have her thrown out."

Meanwhile, Tina blinked at all of them as if she couldn't comprehend what was happening.

"What's the matter?" Lindsey asked. "Aren't you happy that I know who murdered Gwen—"

"This is ridiculous," Mallory interrupted. "The only murderer is Ariel Montgomery. She clearly murdered Gwen, was caught by Leslie, and then had to murder Leslie, too. Gwen Capshaw was a nothing, a nobody. Why would anyone else want to murder her?"

"Because she was going to leave her husband, Perry, for Malcolm Rutledge, a man someone else already had their sights on," Lindsey said with a pitying glance at Tina.

"That's the most ridiculous thing I've ever heard," Mallory said. "I demand that someone get her out of here."

No one moved.

"You're right," Lindsey said. "It is ridiculous, and I really thought that might have been the motive." She glanced at Eleanor, who shrugged. "But I was wrong."

"So, Ariel Montgomery *is* the murderer?" a woman at the back of the room called out.

"No," Lindsey said. "And we know this because there is a peculiar eccentricity about most artists. They find their medium and they stick with it. For example, this piece by Ariel is done in oil paint—in fact, all of her work is done in oil paint." Lindsey paused to gesture to Ariel's painting. "But the murder weapons—which, for the record, were palette knives belonging to Ariel—for both Gwen and Leslie, didn't have any oil paint on them. Isn't that interesting?"

"Not particularly. Maybe they were new and unused," Mallory said. "If we could get back to our auction now?"

"Not just yet," Eleanor said. "I'm interested in hearing what Lindsey has to say. Were the knives new?"

"Thank you. I happened to be talking to the crime scene investigators, big library users, this morning and they told me that the paint found on the palette knives used by the killer had acrylic paint on them," Lindsey said. "Imagine my surprise when I remembered that Ariel told me when she taught her students she had them use acrylic paint because it dries faster."

The rumbling of the crowd grew louder and Lindsey stared at Mallory, letting her put it all together. Mallory stumbled toward the exit and Lindsey called after her, "If you're racing home to destroy the piece you did in Ariel's class here at The Club, don't bother. The police already have it."

"That's not possible!" Mallory protested.

"I assure you it is. They had a search warrant and your husband let them in." Lindsey made a show of checking her phone. "Look at that. I have a text right here from the police that they have the painting in question."

"I told you to destroy it!" Harper jumped up from her seat and charged Mallory.

Tina let out a yelp and scurried out from between the two women.

"Oh, like you did? Burning your painting in Leslie's firepit after you murdered her?" Mallory snapped.

"Shut up! That's a lie!" Harper shouted. "Mallory did it! She killed both Gwen and Leslie."

Mallory snatched a knife off the table and waved it at Harper. "This was all your idea. You said no one would suspect me of murdering Gwen—that everyone would think it was Ariel."

"I said no such thing!" Harper insisted. She glanced wildly about the room, looking for an ally. "She's trying to frame me."

Lindsey narrowed her eyes. The two women had just confirmed what she suspected. "Ariel taught classes here at The Club last summer. I know this because I saw pictures of it on social media." She took her phone out of her pocket and opened up the photos where she'd saved two very important pictures. "In fact, here's a picture of Mallory holding her piece of a sunflower with the distinct color canary yellow. Guess what paint residue was found on the palette knife used to kill Gwen Capshaw? Canary yellow."

The occupants of the tent gasped as one.

Lindsey slid the screen to the next picture. "And here's Harper, holding her own piece from the same class, and look at that, the apple she painted was done in crimson. The same paint was found on the palette knife used to kill Leslie Stone. Oh, and there was a teeny tiny bit of residue of that same crimson found on the painting that had been burnt in Leslie's firepit the night she died."

Now the occupants of the tent were murmuring in shocked tones as they stared at the two women.

"So, it appears, given the evidence, that Mallory murdered Gwen for Harper and Harper murdered Leslie for Mallory. Did I get that right?"

Tina let out a gasp and clapped her hand over her mouth. Her eyes were huge and her face pale. "You murdered Leslie? But why?"

"Don't say a word," Mallory ordered.

Harper's eyes darted from side to side as if assessing a getaway route.

"You're not going to get away with it," Lindsey said. "The police are already here."

Mallory's head whipped from side to side. "She's lying. She's trying to get you to incriminate yourself."

Harper spun on Mallory. "You told me you were going to help me. You told me that framing Ariel for Gwen's murder would get rid of her."

"And it will!" Mallory cried. "Ariel is the murderer! She murdered Gwen and when Leslie caught her, she was forced to murder Leslie, too!" She yelled it as if the volume of her statement would make it true.

"No, she isn't." Lindsey shook her head. "In order for Leslie to have seen Ariel murder Gwen, she would have to have been on Split Island, but she wasn't."

Both Harper and Mallory went pale.

"You can't know that," Mallory scoffed.

"Oh, but see, I do," Lindsey said. "It just so happens, I emailed Leslie right before I departed for the second run out to the islands, and she emailed me back. I'd forgotten about it until I happened to go over my correspondence with her because, as you said, you were ending the funding for the book boat and there it was. I reached out to the chief of police and they were able to pinpoint the internet service provider Leslie used when she sent that email to me, proving that there was no way she was on Split Island, meaning she didn't see Ariel murder Gwen, because of course Ariel didn't murder Gwen." Lindsey turned to Mallory. "You did."

"You said there was no way they would figure it out," Harper cried.

"Shut up." Mallory ordered.

"I'm not going down with you." Harper shook her head. She pointed at Mallory. "It was all her idea. She said we could help each other. She said if we murdered Gwen then Ariel would get blamed, then we'd murder Leslie and tell everyone that Leslie knew something about Gwen's murder, setting up Ariel for that murder, too."

"Shut up! Shut up! Shut up!" Mallory yelled.

"It's a little late for that, don't you think?" Eleanor asked.

Mallory let loose a string of curses and bolted for the exit. Officer Kirkland caught her before she set one toe outside the tent, and Officer Wilcox swooped in and snagged Harper.

Emma, who'd been sitting at the back, took off her enormous hat and strode forward, wearing one of the many outfits Robbie had bought her with the requisite killer heels. As she passed Lindsey, she said, "Nicely done."

Lindsey tipped the brim of her hat and said, "Thank you."

Tina scurried to Lindsey's side. "I can't believe this. I was friends with two murderers. I was alone with them. It could have been me that they stabbed." She tottered on her heels and fainted delicately into the nearest chair.

Eleanor shook her head as she took in the pretty picture Tina made. "No spine in this younger generation at all."

Several other ladies in the crowd took off their hats and approached Lindsey's table. Nancy, Violet, Beth, Mary and Paula joined her to watch as Mallory and Harper were handcuffed and led out of the tent.

"How did you know it was the two of them?" Paula asked.

"I didn't," Lindsey said. "I actually thought it was Mallory and someone else, but when I bluffed to draw the killer out, they revealed themselves."

Tina's eyes popped open and she sat up straight. "Me. You thought it was me."

"Eleanor did say Gwen was your competition for Malcolm," Lindsey said.

"Ah! I am happily married," Tina said. "I would never. Everything I've ever done is for David—" Her voice trailed off as her gaze shifted to the opening of the tent where both Malcolm and her husband, David, stood.

"Woman, I've offered him a job and he's accepted," Malcolm said. "Now will you leave me the heck alone?"

Tina let out a squeal and on tiptoes she ran across the room and threw herself into her husband's arms. David let out a whoop and a laugh and asked, "Whatever did I do to deserve you?"

Tina giggled as he spun her out of the tent and into the sunlight. Lindsey shook her head. All this time she'd thought Tina was making a play for Malcolm when she was really just trying to convince him to give her husband a job.

She turned and glanced at Eleanor, who met her gaze and said, "Oops."

Guess who I just saw in the library? Tina Baldwin and her husband, David," Beth said as she stepped out of her star costume and hung it on the rack by the door to the crafternoon room.

Handmade from a large piece of bright yellow organza strung across wire that had been bent into a star shape, it was one of Beth's most creative pieces. Beth had added a string of battery-operated LED lights that lit up along the edges of the star, delighting the kids, but she hadn't factored in the need to sit down, and wire doesn't bend. She put her fist to her back and stretched before she plopped into her seat at the crafternoon table. "She said to say hi and she forgives you for thinking she's capable of murder."

"Oh, yeah," Lindsey agreed. "I really called that one wrong."

"Well, your information was faulty," Eleanor said. She was the newest member of their crafternoon group, and Lindsey admired that she acknowledged her intel had been wrong while at the same time taking no blame for it.

"Harper really killed Leslie so that Mallory could be the head of the membership committee for The Club?" Nancy asked. "That's a hunger for power I will never understand."

"It is a position that comes with a lot of perks and, quite frankly, bribes," Eleanor said. "Now that Tina has been made head of the membership committee, she's doing a little overdue housecleaning of the memberships."

"Gideon Trask is getting booted, isn't he?" Beth asked.

"Right out the front door." Eleanor giggled and Lindsey smiled. Being rejected from The Club couldn't have happened to a more deserving guy. Given that he'd just been removed from the town council, she suspected he'd be putting his island house up for sale any day and moving on to a town that appreciated his privileged elitism more than Briar Creek and the Thumb Islands.

"What did you all think of this week's book, *Little Women*?" Lindsey asked.

"I can't believe it's taken us this long to read it," Nancy said. "I read it when I was a teen, which is over fifty years ago. I have to say it was a totally different experience this time."

"Did you read it or watch the movie?" Paula asked.

"Both." Nancy grinned and bit into a taco.

"Which version?" Mary asked. "I mean, there've been so many."

"George Cukor's, of course, with Katharine Hepburn as Jo. It's the best one," Violet answered for her friend.

"Agreed," Eleanor said.

"I prefer Winona Ryder's Jo," Beth said.

"And I'm here for Saoirse Ronan," Paula said.

"I thought we were discussing *Little Women*," Mayor Cole said as she entered the room.

"We veered over to the movie versions of Alcott's novel," Lindsey said.

Mayor Cole rolled her eyes as she took the plate of tacos Lindsey handed to her. "The book is always better than the movie."

"That's true, but Christian Bale as Laurie is poetry," Beth said, and fanned her face with her hand.

"That's fair," Lindsey said. "Why do you think the story *Little Women* has endured in popularity for one hundred and fifty-eight years?"

"It's a coming-of-age story," Mayor Cole said. "Every woman can see herself in one of the sisters."

The crafternooners all nodded in agreement.

"I read that the original manuscript was four hundred and two pages and it took only ten weeks for Alcott to write it," Lindsey said.

"Which is really impressive considering she didn't want to write a novel for young women," Beth said. "Of course, I've always been partial to Beth."

"Understandable. Which sister does everyone else most identify with?" Paula asked.

The crafternooners shared all different answers, and

Lindsey was about to say which sister she felt the most akin to when she heard her name. She turned to see Sully standing in the doorway.

"Sorry to interrupt you, darling, but I have a special delivery for you," he said.

Lindsey rose from her seat at the table and asked, "What is it?"

Sully stepped aside and Ariel Montgomery entered the room, carrying a brown paper package. "Sorry to interrupt, but Perry, Dane and I are heading up to Boston for a few weeks to help Ryan and Jordan prepare for the baby. I wanted to give you this before I left."

Ariel handed the flat package to Lindsey. The crafternooners grew silent as they watched Lindsey unwrap the canvas. It was the piece that had been on the easel the day Lindsey had toured Ariel's studio, the same one she had used at the auction to reveal Harper and Mallory.

"Oh, this is beautiful," Lindsey said. "But I can't accept it. You need to put this in your show and sell it for a small fortune."

"No, I insist you keep it," Ariel said. "I have my freedom because of you and I can't put a price on that. I can never thank you—all of you—enough."

"All right then," Lindsey agreed. "We'll hang it someplace special in the library so everyone in town can enjoy it."

"Perfect," Ariel approved.

"Going back to our previous discussion about Harper and Mallory, there's something I don't understand," Paula said. "If Harper was jealous of your success and thought that getting rid of you would benefit her career, then why didn't she have Mallory murder you instead of Gwen?"

"Hey now," Ariel protested. She gestured to Sully to come into the room and he picked up a large plastic tub, which he placed on the floor beside her. Lindsey shot him a questioning glance and he shrugged.

"Sorry," Paula said. "I just don't understand."

"Honestly, neither do I," Ariel said. "But I suspect Harper had Mallory murder Gwen because the art world runs on scarcity. So, if an artist is dead, their work becomes much more valuable because there will be no more of it. Harper couldn't risk giving me that sort of posthumous notoriety."

"Oh." Paula nodded. "So, she murdered Gwen, because everyone knew about the bad blood and assumed you'd get blamed, possibly imprisoned, and it would ruin your career."

"Precisely. It's hard to paint when you're in prison. Also they could then pin Leslie's murder on me by spreading the rumor that Leslie had seen me murder Gwen—rather cunning of them, actually." Ariel lifted the lid off the tub. "Now, ladies, are you ready for your craft today?"

Lindsey, who'd prepped the food for this week's meeting, tried to distract her. "How about some tacos before you get started?"

"I never say no to tacos," Ariel said. "But you're still not getting out of the craft. It's a tiny little canvas painting in acrylic and I'll Bob Ross you through it, I promise."

Lindsey glanced at her husband, who was leaning against the wall by the door. Their gazes met and he motioned for her to join him. Lindsey crossed the room and stopped right in front of him.

"Help me," she said.

"Always," he said. Without a word to the crafternoon ladies, he swept Lindsey out of the room, closing the door behind them.

Crafternoon Guide

Are you crafty? Do you enjoy reading and talking about what you've read? How about food? Do you enjoy sharing a meal with friends? Well, a crafternoon is a gathering of friends who make a craft while sharing food and discussing a book that they've all chosen to read. The following pages include some ideas to kick-start your own crafternoon.

Readers Guide for *Little Women*

1. Which of the four sisters—Meg, Jo, Beth or Amy—do you identify with the most and why?

2. Do you think you could live during this time period when women's opportunities were so limited?

3. Why do you think *Little Women* has endured in popularity for so long?

4. How did you feel about Beth's story line? Was it necessary to the story?

5. Do you believe that Jo made the right choice for her

own life? How do you think her life would have been different if she'd made a different choice for a life partner?

6. How does their father's absence shape the March sisters' lives?

7. Can you think of another novel about sisters (for example, Jane Austen's Bennet sisters) and how they are similar to and different from the March sisters?

8. What do you believe is the main theme of *Little Women*?

9. Do you have sisters? Does Alcott portray sisterhood accurately?

Craft
Lavender Sachets

This craft is about as easy as it gets for the noncrafty among us.

Small drawstring bags, cotton or linen
Rubber stamp
Colored ink pad
Dried lavender

Place the bag on a flat surface. Dab the rubber stamp on the ink pad until fully coated. Carefully press the stamp onto the cloth bag. Gently remove. Once the ink has dried, stuff the bag with dried lavender and pull the drawstring tight, tying it off so it doesn't open.

Recipe

STROMBOLI

Dough Ingredients

1⅓ cups warm water
2¼ teaspoons (1 standard packet) instant or active-dry yeast
1 tablespoon granulated sugar
2 tablespoons extra-virgin olive oil
1 teaspoon salt
3½ cups all-purpose flour, plus more for work surface

Whisk the warm water, yeast and sugar in the bowl of your stand mixer using a dough hook. Cover and allow to rest for 5 minutes. (If you don't have a stand mixer, simply use a large mixing bowl and a wooden spoon.) Add the olive oil, salt and flour. Beat on low speed for 2 minutes.

Knead the dough. Keep the dough in the mixer and beat for an additional 5 minutes, or knead by hand on a lightly floured surface for the same amount of time. After kneading, the dough should still feel soft.

Lightly grease a large bowl with oil or nonstick spray. Place the dough in the bowl, turning it to coat all sides in the oil. Cover the bowl with a clean kitchen towel. Allow the dough to rise at room temperature until double in size, about an hour.

Preheat oven to 400°F. Line 2 large baking sheets with parchment paper.

When the dough is ready, punch it down to release the air. Divide in half. On a lightly floured work surface using a lightly floured rolling pin, roll each half of dough into a 10 × 16-inch rectangle. If the dough keeps shrinking as you try to shape it, cover it lightly and let the dough rest for 10 minutes before trying again.

Filling Ingredients

3 tablespoons butter, melted
2 garlic cloves, minced
2 teaspoons chopped fresh parsley
1 pound thinly sliced Italian meats—pepperoni, prosciutto, salami
3 cups shredded mozzarella cheese
Egg wash: 1 large egg beaten with 1 tablespoon water

Mix melted butter and garlic together. Spread all over each rectangle of dough. Sprinkle each with parsley. Leave a 1-inch border on the bottom and sides and a 3-inch border on top as you start layering the meat and cheese. Use half the meat and cheese for each stromboli—about 1/2 pound meat and 1/2 pound cheese. Brush all edges with egg wash, including the 3-inch gap at the top. This helps the stromboli hold its rolled shape. Slowly roll each into a tight 16-inch log, folding in the two ends as you roll. Carefully transfer each roll to the lined baking sheets. Tuck in ends to seal if they became unfolded. Brush the top of each stromboli with egg wash and sprinkled toppings. Cut 3 to 4 slits into the tops of each roll, which helps steam escape.

Bake for about 25 minutes or until crust is golden brown—if you have an instant-read thermometer, the center of the stromboli should be at least 200°F. Remove from the oven and cool on baking sheets for 5 minutes before transferring to a cutting board and slicing. Serve plain or with marinara sauce for dipping.

Top of stromboli (optional): Sprinkle top with chopped fresh parsley, sea salt, course pepper, Italian seasoning and/or Parmesan cheese.

Acknowledgments

First and foremost, I want to acknowledge the readers of the Library Lover's Mysteries. It's amazing to me that you've stuck with me for sixteen mysteries. It's been an absolute delight to write each and every one of these mysteries and watch these characters grow and change in ways I had never envisioned when I wrote the very first story. Thank you from the bottom of my heart.

Many thanks to my team at Berkley: Kate Seaver, Amanda Maurer, Kim-Salina I, Kaila Mundell-Hill and Stacy Edwards. Deepest appreciation to the art department—the best in this business—especially the brilliant cover artist for every cover of this series, Julia Green. Much gratitude to my literary agents, Christina Hogrebe and Jessica Errera, and the entire Rotrosen Agency.

Lastly, I'm so grateful for my family and friends who encourage and support my chosen occupation. The writing life can be lonely, but I never am because I have all of you. Many hugs to Chris Hansen Orf, Beckett Orf and Wyatt Orf. Love you forever.

Keep reading for an excerpt from
Jenn McKinlay's novel . . .

WITCHES OF DUBIOUS ORIGIN

Available from Ace!

Package for you, Zoe." Bill Reed, my coworker at the Wessex Public Library, dropped a thick padded envelope, clearly holding a book, onto my desk. I glanced up at him. I was the reference librarian. He was acquisitions. Generally, book purchases went right to him.

Bill shrugged at the confusion on my face. "I know, but it's addressed to you and stamped *Personal.*"

I glanced at the brown envelope. Sure enough, there was the stamp in an imperative shade of red right above the handwritten name *Zoanne Ziakas*—my name—and the library's address. Weirdly, there was no postmark or stamps or anything to indicate it had been delivered the usual way through the post office.

"Be careful opening it." Bill's eyes narrowed behind his wire-framed glasses. "It could be—"

He paused. Clearly his imagination had run out or he was hesitant to say *bomb* or *poison* or whatever nefarious thing could possibly be stuffed into a nine-by-twelve-inch padded envelope. Bill had the pasty complexion of a man who'd spent his adult life under fluorescent lighting. He was in his fifties, happily married to his wife, Meredith, of thirty years. They had two kids in college and spent most of their time dreaming about retirement. There wasn't much that disturbed Bill, so I was surprised by his unusual caution.

"Could be what?" I prodded.

"I don't know." He ran a hand over his thinning hair in a self-soothing gesture. "I just have a bad feeling about it."

"It's probably a catalog from a publisher or a library supply company that got misdirected to me," I said. Although, when I studied the loopy script of my name written in felt-tip pen, I felt the hair on the back of my neck prickle, and a flutter of alarm tickled my insides. I knew this handwriting. It was my mother's.

No, it couldn't be. My mother had passed away a month ago. There was no way she could have addressed this envelope from beyond the grave. It was just an unfortunate coincidence. Shaking off the unsettling feeling, I grabbed my scissors and sliced the envelope open. It didn't explode. No plume of poisonous smoke was emitted. Instead, out fell a thick black book encircled with a half-inch metal band that was engraved with a series of interlocking lines similar to a Celtic knot. The band latched into a decorative hexagon on the front cover. Fancy.

"Well, that underwhelms," Bill said. He appeared visibly relieved. "Looks like a journal of some sort. You were right. It's probably a promo item from a publisher."

I set the book down and glanced into the envelope. There was no note explaining what the book was, no flyer, nothing. I put the envelope aside and picked up the book. I pressed on the hexagon, thinking that might open the band. It didn't work. I tried turning the hexagon. It didn't budge.

"It's a pretty pricey item for a promo," I said. "Especially since I can't open it."

"Do you want me to try?" he offered.

"Go for it." I handed him the book.

Bill did the same pressing and twisting that I had. He tried to tug on the band but it was secured too tightly to give him any leverage. He handed it back and I returned it to its envelope for safekeeping.

"What we have here is a very decorative paperweight," he concluded.

I laughed. I opened my desk's bottom drawer and dropped the book inside. "I'll look at it later."

Bill headed back to his office, and I returned to my weekly report, forgetting all about the strange black book.

October was my favorite month, when the sticky humidity of summer departed and jeans-and-sweater weather returned. As I walked the half mile from the library to my cottage, I reveled in the chilly temperatures, the scent of wood fires on the air, and the satisfying crunch of leaves under my feet.

The village of Wessex, where I lived and worked, was nestled between the Appalachian Trail and the Housatonic River, in the northwestern corner of Connecticut. It was a small community known for the private boarding school that resided on the west side of the river. I had attended that school before leaving to go to university in New Haven and then doubling back here to the only place that had ever felt like home.

As soon as I stepped inside my cottage, I slipped into my pajamas while I microwaved a big bowl of mac and cheese. I flicked on the television and scrolled through the streaming channels until I found a mystery series I had yet to watch. I preferred the British ones because I loved that the actors and actresses in them looked like real people, as opposed to American television shows, where everyone looks like a supermodel pretending to be a real person.

I was halfway through my bowl of cheesy goodness and a third of the way through the first episode when I heard a thump on my front porch. I paused the show and stopped chewing, listening intently. Living in Wessex, where everyone knew everyone, I wasn't as worried about crime as I was about a neighbor dropping by to chat. It wasn't that bad things didn't happen here—of course they did—it was just that it was very rare, and usually the person who did the crime was known for having a dented moral compass, so it wasn't a big surprise.

Thump!

The noise sounded again, only more forcefully. Putting my bowl down on the coffee table, I shoved my chenille throw aside and crossed the room to the front door, switching on the outside light. I peered out the side window that looked onto the porch before opening the door. If it was a rabid raccoon looking for food, I didn't want to get into it with him. The porch was empty.

Just to be certain everything was all right, I opened the door and poked my head out. I glanced from side to side, seeing only my large potted geranium on one side and my small wicker table and two chairs on the other. Satisfied, I went to close the door and glanced down at the doormat. I gasped. Placed on the center of the mat was the same envelope that Bill had delivered to me at work. But I knew I had left it in my desk drawer. What the hell was it doing here?

I glanced around the porch to see if someone was lurking in the shadows, playing a prank on me. It wasn't really Bill's style—he was more of a dad-joke type of guy—but he was the only person who knew about the book, so logic dictated it had to be him.

"Not funny, Bill!" I called into the darkening evening. There was no answer. No one was there.

I picked up the envelope and pulled the book out, experiencing the same twinge of unease I'd felt before. A flash of green lit the porch as the envelope was immediately engulfed in emerald flames. I yelped and dropped it. In seconds the envelope was gone, leaving no ash or smoke behind. I examined my hand and noted that the weird neon fire hadn't even felt hot.

I glanced out at the street, making certain no one had seen what had just happened. Ever since my childhood, unexpected magic had always made me anxious.

I took another look around the porch and yard before I went back inside, then locked the dead bolt. I studied the aged volume more closely. It was a shade of black so matte it seemed to soak up light. The edges of the pages were jagged and uneven. And the book's hexagonal metal latch was rusted from humidity or lack of use, I couldn't tell which. I brought it to the kitchen, thinking I could open it with a knife.

Not wanting to lose a finger, I chose a butter knife. I slid it under the decorative metal band and tried to pry it loose. The metal didn't budge. I tried to pop the hexagon with the blade as well, but it held fast. I set down the utensil and glanced at the door. If it wasn't Bill who had dropped the book off and made the envelope go *poof* . . . nope. I refused to go there.

The pin pricked my finger and blood beaded up out of the wound. I yelped and dropped the pin. Drops of blood dripped from my middle finger and I pressed my thumb to the tip to stop the flow. Had I just stabbed myself with a pin . . . *on purpose*? I blinked. I glanced down, noting that I was wearing my pajamas.

Relief whooshed inside me. It was okay. It was just a dream. An awful, stupid, painful dream. I shook my head, trying to wake myself up. It didn't work. It couldn't . . . because I was already awake.

I glanced down at my kitchen counter, where small

splats of blood marred the smooth surface. The battered old book that I had tucked into my shoulder bag earlier sat on the granite beneath my pricked finger.

Shit! I had almost bled on the book. I spun away from the counter and rinsed my finger in the sink. What the hell had just happened? Sleepwalking? Night terrors? Had I actually pricked myself with a pin? *Why?*

Grabbing a paper towel, I wiped the blood off the granite. I rinsed off the pin and returned it to the container I kept in the utility drawer at the end of the counter. I threw the towel in the trash and stood, staring at the book in confusion. What was the book doing on the counter when I was certain I had put it in my bag?

Insistent whispers sounded at the edge of my mind. Like shadows that faded as the sun rose, the words weren't quite loud enough for me to make out, but I knew. I knew without a doubt that those whispers had been in my dreams and that they had instructed me to stab myself with the straight pin. I glanced down. Goose bumps raised on my forearms as I gazed at the black book. I ran an uninjured finger over the cover, half expecting it to be absorbed into the black leather, as if it could pull me in just as it seemed to soak in the light. It didn't and I lifted my hand and noted my fingers were trembling.

I'd had a strange feeling about this mysterious volume from the moment I'd first touched it, and I knew of only one person who might be able to help me.